It's One of Ours

It's One of Ours

Joan M. Moules

ROBERT HALE · LONDON

© Joan M. Moules 2007
First published in Great Britain 2007

ISBN 978-0-7090-8362-7

Robert Hale Limited
Clerkenwell House
Clerkenwell Green
London EC1R 0HT

www.halebooks.com

2 4 6 8 10 9 7 5 3 1

Typeset in 11/15 pt Palatino
Printed and bound in Great Britain by
Biddles Limited, King's Lynn, Norfolk

For my darling husband, Leon. Thank you for your love and for your unswerving belief in me. With all my love.

GLOSSARY

Bees and honey – money (usually shortened to bees)
Rub-a-dub-dub – pub (usually shortened to rub-a-
Rosy Lee – tea (usually shortened to rosy)
Horace – one of the imaginary children of music hall and
wireless artiste Harry Hemsley. Horace chatted in
unintelligible baby talk, and Winnie, another of
the imaginary children, interpreted it.

Chapter 1

London 1939

Dason Street was long and curving, crossing several other smaller ones, King Street, Ebdon Street, Church Street, Grey Street, Brown Street, and almost at the end, Tailors Yard, a cobbled alley which housed a ramshackle-looking clothing factory. A few yards beyond this it ran into the High Road, where every Saturday Hope Street Market was held. It was still called Hope Street Market even though it had long since spilled over from that tiny thoroughfare and into the High Road.

The Victorian terraced houses ran the whole length of Dason Street, but the ones on the corners where the smaller streets criss-crossed had a bit of extra garden. There were several corner shops too, which sold a variety of commodities ranging from candles and children's colouring books to cheese and custard powder. These were a boon to many of the residents, saving them the long trek to the High Street where Liptons, Home & Colonial and Maypole jostled for trade, along with Sainsburys and David Greig.

Each section of the street was different. The houses at the top, where Anna and Joe Putt lived at number 5, were two up, two down and although the rooms were small, most of them were clean. You saw women washing their steps every morning, cheerfully calling out to each other about the latest street news.

Further down where Queenie and Fred Parkes were, at number 52, the places were bigger: in that section they had three bedrooms, and some of the tenants, the few who were actually buying their houses, had built a glass lean-to at the back to give even more space. When you got beyond number 100 however, the street deteriorated. It became much narrower and was back to the smaller houses and these were much shabbier than those at the top end. Here the women sat on the doorstep feeding their babies, and most of the children ran about barefoot and runny-nosed. The two newsagents, tobacconists and confectioners were situated one near each end of the long street.

3 September 1939

'I'm off then Anna – no don't get up, have a rest, luv, you had a very disturbed night.'

'So did you, Joe, and you've got to work today too. Don't know what was up – p'raps the baby had indigestion. It certainly gave me some gyp.' She patted her swollen stomach gently. 'Still, it's settled down now.'

'Sure?'

'Yes. Anyway there's only just over another week to go.'

He leant across the double bed and kissed her softly on the mouth. 'Want me to get Queenie to look in later?'

''Course not. It's Sunday, she'll probably have her family there. I'm OK Joe – honest.'

He turned back at the door of the little room. 'I love you, Anna. You know that, don't you?'

''Course I do you daft 'aporth. Go on, or you'll be late.'

'I'm on me way.' He raised his hand and grinned. 'But remember what I've told you and have an easy day, gal.'

As he clattered down the stairs, his shoes making a tap-dance on the hard-wearing lino that covered them, Anna heaved her heavy body into a sitting position. In the middle of the night she had thought the baby might be on its way, judging by the painful twinges, but when they subsided she put it down to the bread and dripping she had eaten several hours earlier. She'd be glad when the child was born. Her once slender body was blown up like the silver barrage balloons in Royal Park behind the Green Man pub and she felt clumsy and awkward and so very tired all the time.

She couldn't stay in bed, she'd get up, dress, and maybe her back would ease a little if she walked about. A sharp pain caught her as she slipped the voluminous maternity dress Queenie had given her over her head. Clinging to the bedpost she bit her lower lip and closed her eyes. The pain seemed to fill her entire being, it was like nothing she had experienced before. Certainly not like the twinges in the night. Maybe she *should* have asked Joe to go for Queenie after all.

When the pain subsided she still clasped the wooden bedpost, not sure if it was sweat or tears running down her cheeks. After a few moments she gingerly moved away, wiping the moisture from her face and neck with the screwed-up handkerchief she was clutching. Better get downstairs, then if it happened again she could ask one of the kids playing in the street to go for Queenie Parkes. Queenie knew about birth and death and had promised to be there to help when the time came. Anna touched her bulge with a trembling hand, 'Hang on in there 'til tonight, little 'un. I don't think I can manage you by myself – I've never had a baby before.'

Twenty minutes later another pain engulfed her and she cried out. She was downstairs in the little kitchen now, and as she leant across the scrubbed table in an effort to ease herself, she knew without any doubt that her baby would be born today – and she was terrified.

Suppose it got tangled in the cord, squashed, got stuck halfway and died. She had heard of these things happening, some people seemed only too keen to tell her about the dangers once they knew she was expecting.

The pain receded and she stumbled into a chair. Joe had left at five to eight and he wouldn't be back until six. Her stupid bravado in not letting him know how bad she felt had done for her now. 'But I didn't really think it was this,' she said aloud, 'I've had bad nights before …' Pushing her long fair hair away from her face she made up her mind. She would time the pains, because first babies seldom came quickly, according to Queenie, and if she could last out until Joe got back he'd nip round for her. Anna didn't want to be a nuisance to anyone. If the worst came to the worst she supposed she could get Rosie Bateson opposite to give a hand, only she was so loud and bossy, and anyway Joe couldn't stand the woman.

The woman in question, Rosie Bateson, who lived in number 6 Dason Road with her husband Jim, had had a late night and they were having a lie-in on Sunday morning. It was gone ten before either of them surfaced, and Rosie spent the first half-hour chasing the time she had missed.

'For pity's sake, Rosie, slow down. You're going it as though all the devils in hell are after you.'

'Don't blaspheme, Jim. Anyway I'm only trying to catch up.'

'What for? There's only us here, we can please ourselves now we're retired, gal.'

'Can't help it, Jim. I don't feel right 'til everything's done. And I want to hear Mr Chamberlain's speech. He'll be on at eleven. What d'you think's going to happen, mate?'

Jim lit his pipe slowly. 'There'll be a war. Can't see how we can avoid it, and this time we'll all be in it. You've only got to read the papers to see that. Reckon our boys'll have to go, Rosie, they're young and healthy …'

'Oh God. Suppose they get killed.'

'Now don't talk like that. I come through the last one, didn't I? We've just got to wait and hope.'

Rosie's bright cheeks grew pinker with emotion. 'I suppose so,' she said, turning away quickly and busying herself with the china on the dresser that was her pride and joy. Young Jimmy, their eldest son, had made it for her birthday a couple of years ago, as she never wearied of telling anyone who would listen. 'Good workman, he is. Never be out of a job if you've got a trade like that.' Now he'd more than likely be going to fight. Oh, it didn't bear thinking about.

She and the house were clean and tidy by five to eleven. She ran her hands over her bright pinafore, smoothing it down with nervous gestures as they waited for the news. She shivered as the sound of Big Ben came over the air, and it was an anticlimax when the announcer said the Prime Minister would speak to them at 11.15.

'I'll make a cup of tea, Jim, I can't just sit here waiting.

'All right, old girl, but whatever you do won't make any difference now. The die's cast and—'

'Well, I can't sit here calm like you. There's got to be something we can do, there's always something everyone can do. Nothing's ever so bad if you can help. Why couldn't he have spoken at eleven like he said – keeping us all on tenterhooks like this, it ain't right.'

Liza and Sid Wentworth ran the newsagent's and tobacconist's on the corner of Church Street, which served all the top half of the long road. The other newsagent was near the end where Dason Street turned off into the High Road. It was a busy little shop, and on this Sunday morning they did something they had never done before in their business lives. Sid wrote out a large notice that read: BACK IN TEN MINUTES, so they could both go upstairs to their sitting room above the shop and hear the Prime Minister, Neville Chamberlain's speech on the wireless. To Liza's relief, Sid, at forty-one, would be too old to be called up, but he had volunteered for the post of street warden. She hadn't wanted him to, but on this occasion he overruled her.

'Apart from the fact I want to do my bit, we'll both be put on to something,' he said. 'After all, we've no children or old people dependent on us.'

'But what about the shop?'

He shrugged. 'We'll carry on while we can. After all, folks are going to want news, but I might get directed, mind. There was a bit in the paper the other day about it. Sent to work in a factory or something—'

Liza gripped his arm, 'You're not fit enough. Anyway, you've the shop to run, I can't see to it all by myself, not the deliveries and everything.'

'You'll have to have a young girl assistant, I reckon. Come on, Liza, don't let's talk about what may never happen. If you don't get a move on we'll miss that speech.'

Queenie Parkes loved Dason Street. She had lived in the area all her life and in her present house for the last thirty years. A born homemaker, she kept her house comfortable and welcoming. Her four children were born there, and although all but one had moved from the district, they still referred to it as 'coming home'. The one who was still close was Jenny, her youngest, who now lived in Ebdon Street.

On that Sunday morning of 3 September Queenie rose early as she did most days. There had been a storm in the night, but now the street was awash with early-morning sunlight. She stood by the window for a few moments after she pulled back the curtains, and marvelled to herself at the beauty it gave to the grimy bricks of the houses opposite. What would happen to them all if war came? It seemed certain it would. Neville Chamberlain had done his best, she supposed. That other war didn't seem so long ago to her. She had lost two of her brothers on the Somme in 1916, and Dave, the youngest, silly little fool that he was, had put his age forward to enlist. He came back wounded, and had been a bitter invalid ever since. It broke Mum's heart, she thought now, losing her sons, because Dave became so withdrawn and touchy that it often seemed he too was lost to them.

She moved into her neat little kitchen and put the kettle on. Fred would be hollering for a cuppa as soon as he woke, and it was easier to comply than defy. She ceased to love Fred within six months of their marriage, but she stayed because ... well, what else could she do? In any case the children came rapidly, the first a year after the wedding, when she was eighteen, the next at nineteen and a half, the third before her twenty-first birthday, and Jenny when she was twenty-three. She almost lost her life with Jenny – the doctor called a halt then; she smiled even now as she remembered how he had put the fear of God into Fred with the image of him left to bring up four kids on his own.

She heard her husband get out of bed. She reached for his giant-size mug and prepared his first 'cuppa' of the day. I might pop up to Anna's after breakfast, she thought, she's getting near her time and yesterday she looked as if she might have it any minute. It looks ready to me, and Joe's away working at that café every Sunday. I can be back in time for the Prime Minister's speech.

She said as much to Fred just before ten, after she had washed up the breakfast things and prepared the dinner. 'But just in case anything's stirring up there and I don't get back, I've done the vegetables and—'

'I won't be here to put them on,' he interrupted. 'I'm going down the pub later. We can eat when you get back.'

It was the sort of answer she expected, but she said nothing as she took her handbag and left the house.

No one had prepared Anna for the pain. 'Push,' Queenie said, 'one last big effort and – that's right. Good girl, you're nearly there.' The sudden wailing note of the siren came with the emergence of the baby's head....

Queenie trembled as she got on with the delivery job, and seconds later the shoulders and tiny body of Anna and Joe Putt's firstborn slithered out. The air-raid warning was still going, the infant's cries mingling with the eerie danger signal. The baby stopped first, when Queenie put her to Anna's breast, 'It's a girl,' she said, 'a beautiful baby girl.'

Anna gazed down at the child fumbling unsuccessfully at her nipple, and gently stroked the soft, blood-smeared cheek.

'I'll clean her up in a moment, luv.' Queenie's voice was matter of fact. 'Just make you comfortable first, then we'll have a cup of tea. I reckon you can do with one. It's not called labour for nothing, eh?'

The long, steady note of the all-clear sounded as she was making the tea. 'That was short and sharp anyhow. Here, get that down you, luv, I'll take the little 'un.'

An hour later Queenie was walking back home along Dason Street, having promised to look in on Anna again during the afternoon. She smiled to herself as she remembered the feel and smell of the new babe. What a day to be born, the day war was declared. She had listened to Prime Minister Neville Chamberlain's speech round at Anna's place after all, because when she got there the poor girl answered the door doubled up with pain. They had both listened in between Anna's contractions.

She returned to number 5 just after 2 p.m., taking the new mother a basin of home-made broth, and letting herself in with the key Anna had given her.

'What time will Joe be in?'

'About six, Queenie. But don't you stop, I'm fine now, and thrilled with little Joanna. And I'm so grateful to you. Joe'll come and settle up later.'

'I don't want nothing, luv. You buy the baby a present instead.'

Wentworths, the newsagent's, stayed open until 4.30 every Sunday and Queenie stopped on her way back to buy some of her favourite strong peppermints.

'Forgot 'em when I was in yesterday,' she said.

Liza tipped some from the jar into the brass scales which stood on the counter. 'Hear the air-raid warning this morning?' she said. 'Reckon we'll have to get used to the sound of it, don't you?'

'Anna's baby was born to its wailing. Uncanny it was, for a few minutes.'

'What she have, Queenie?' Liza deftly swung the white-paper sweet-bag over a few times to twist the corners.

'Girl. Bonny little thing. Mass of dark hair. Mind, that'll probably rub off, usually does. My Ruby was born with a lot of hair and a week later she was nearly bald, but it all came back. Now Jenny had hardly any to start with. What little she had was very fair and fine, so it didn't show much anyway. Everyone took her for a boy 'til she was nearly a year old.'

Liza's booming laugh rang out. 'Anna have a bad time?'

'No, quite good really. Small, shouldn't think it weighs more'n six pounds, if that, but then she's only a slip of a thing herself She was a bit nervous. Well, it is her first '

'What are they going to call the baby?'

'Joanna. Bit of both their names. Joe doesn't know yet, he'd left when she started this morning. Works at Nick's café on Sundays and doesn't get in 'til five or six. The baby wasn't due for another week but as I said to 'er the other day, "It'll come when it's good an' ready, they always do. Nature's a wonderful thing".'

She paid for the peppermints, tucking them into her capacious handbag. 'Must go, Liza, my Jenny said she'd come round. Her kids were evacuated on Friday and I know she'll be in a bit of a state.'

She left the shop and carried on down the street. Queenie could imagine how Jenny would be feeling with Tom and Doris away. She had called in to see her yesterday but there was no one there, and one of the neighbours said Jenny was out shopping. Strange, really, that Jenny hadn't come in home on her way back, but maybe she needed to be by herself for a while to come to terms with life without the children. Queenie could understand that, there was a little bit of her that needed to be absolutely private sometimes. Not always so easy either, when you were surrounded with family as she had been years ago when the kids were small. There's always been babies and children around me really, she thought, except for the first ten years of my life.

The September sun was warm on her face and she looked up into a clear blue sky, finding it hard to believe that Britain was at war. Mr Chamberlain's words echoed in her head as she walked on: '... I have to tell you that no such undertaking has been received and that consequently this country is at war with Germany ...'

For weeks now there had been preparations for this day. Street shelters had been built, sandbags stacked, and some gardens had an Anderson shelter. Queenie had seen one of these in her friend's garden, two doors along. Sunk low into the ground it was made of corrugated iron, covered with earth and sandbagged each side of its narrow entrance. According to Irene it would withstand falling bombs, 'except a direct hit, and if that happens reckon we won't know too much about it either.' Irene's great frame had wobbled with laughter. 'There's room for you and Fred too, y'know. We can have a nice game of cards to pass the time.'

Queenie's grandchildren, Tom and Doris, had also seen a 'dugout' as one paper called them because of the depth they had to dig for the foundations. They described the 'underground house' to her after they had been in one in their friend's garden. 'Hope we get an Anderson too,' Tom, who was nine, said. 'Be fun, like camping out.' Well he wouldn't have his wish there, because the powers that be reckoned the children would be safe in the country and Queenie prayed they were right. She had her doubts – which she hadn't voiced to anyone, but Hitler was hardly going to avoid certain areas, was he? Of course he'd make for military targets whenever and wherever he could, but if he missed them he'd drop his bombs anywhere and get out of the way as quick as he could … you didn't need a posh education to work that out.

Queenie had gone to Church Street school with Jenny and the children to be fitted for their gas masks. Her husband Fred, after much moaning, had gone round later when he came home from work. Fred ran one of Johnny Gambol's fruit stalls in Hope Street market, off the High Road. Queenie had long ago given up trying to talk him into having a stall of his own. 'I'd help,' she used to say, 'and you know the trade so well. Come to that it needn't even be greengrocery, you can turn your hand to at least half a dozen other trades, Fred.'

'Yea, Jack of all trades and master of none,' he'd retorted often enough. 'I'm OK with what I do – I don't keep you short like many of 'em do, so stop moaning. This way Johnny pays me and he has all the worry. All I've got to do is sell the blooming stuff. It suits me, Queenie, so you can forget your highfalutin ideas …'

Her husband might not have kept her short, as he said, but what he earned didn't go far with six mouths to feed, and once the children were at school Queenie had found herself a job. She had worked for old Isaac Solomons in his dress shop in the High Street, which the High Road ran into. She enjoyed working with clothes, loving the feel of the materials, the bustle and camaraderie of a busy shop. And Isaac's shop was usually busy, because he enticed the richer folk into it by going round himself and delivering leaflets about 'the bargains, top quality merchandise, to be bought in luxury and comfortable surroundings …' Queenie admired his approach, his good business sense, and was happy in the knowledge that he spoke the truth, for he did sell good quality stuff. It wasn't all the same either: no, he catered for class right enough, and anyone who bought a dress or blouse in his emporium could be sure they wouldn't see a replica in any other store, nor on any other woman. He had half a dozen girls working in the two rooms over the shop and he designed the clothes himself. He made the girls sign a form stating that they would not copy or divulge future designs for any of the clothes sold in the shop. 'You and yours never get annuver job vith anybody in *any* trade', was his threat, 'old Isaac see to that.' Every garment had his label sewn in, not always at the back of the neck, often into one of the side seams where, he said with a chuckle in his voice, it was less intrusive and more exclusive. The labels were made of delicate material too, which never caused the slightest ripple of a bulge in the flow of the garment.

It was in Isaac's shop that Queenie first met Paul Tranmer, the man she still loved, even all these years on.

She turned in through her gate, closing it behind her with a decisive click, and mentally shutting out thoughts of Paul as she hurried up the short path of the neat terraced house.

'That you, Queenie? What took you so long?' Fred called, and without waiting for an answer: 'Jenny's bin round. I told her you'd gone off to do your midwife act, so she's coming back later. What's for tea, gal?'

'Jenny all right?' she asked as she hung her coat on the hook in the tiny hall.

Fred was in the kitchen, rummaging in the cupboards for food. 'S'pose so,' he said. 'Looked a bit tearful, but I told her she's bound to miss the kids at first. Said she'd pop back later.'

Queenie bit her lip, put her overall on and began to prepare another meal. 'You go in and read the paper,' she said. 'I'll see to this.'

An image of Paul Tranmer seemed to float in front of her eyes as she prepared the meal and she tried to blink it away. It was surprisingly stubborn and she said quite crossly to the emptiness around her, 'Go away, Paul, we both know it can't be.' Then she concentrated on the job in hand with an intensity far beyond its needs.

Chapter 2

Jim Bateson saw Dason Street's unofficial midwife come out of Anna and Joe's that afternoon and called to his wife, 'Queenie Parkes just leaving number five, duck. Reckon Anna's had her little 'un.'

Rosie wiped her hands on her voluminous apron and came in from the kitchen. 'I'll go over then – see if she wants anything.'

Jim laughed. 'Who are you kidding, me old duchess,' he said, patting his wife's ample thighs, 'you're going over so you'll be the first, apart from Queenie, to see the baby.'

Rosie grinned at him. 'All right, what's the harm in that? She might need something, don't forget she'll be by herself 'til Joe gets in, and that ain't usually 'til about six o'clock on Sundays.'

At the front door she paused, then turned back into the room and walked over to the mantelpiece. She lifted the lid of the Bisto tin she kept there for rent and emergency money.

'Got any bees, Joe? They're all two bobs in here. Just a bit of silver to start the nipper off?'

'I got a tanner,' he said.

Firmly she replaced the lid on the tin. 'That'll do. If everyone down the street gave it a tanner it'd be richer than us.'

She paused at the door. 'Won't be long mate, and we'll have tea when I get back.'

Jim smiled, pulled out his cigarette papers and tobacco and rolled himself a whisper-thin cigarette before settling down again in his comfortable old armchair.

Rosie stayed an hour, forcing Anna to keep awake and listen to the tale of the terrible time she'd had with each of her brood, when all the young girl really wanted now was to sleep, to be fresh and bright when Joe returned.

Rosie nursed the infant, rocking her to and fro against her ample bosom, feeling the bliss she always did when she had a newly born baby in her arms. The nostalgia and joy she had known when her own lot were as tiny as this flooded through her, and she very gently kissed the child's forehead.

In spite of her lurid descriptions to anyone who would listen, about the pain and duration of her labours, Rosie sometimes thought the greatest happiness she had ever known was the moment, repeated with each of her seven children, when she had first held them in her arms. That special smell of a newborn baby, that first look at the soft skin, the perfect miniature finger-nails, the tiny, vulnerable, often wrinkled face and limbs that fought blindly in – what, anger, frustration, or discovery of the wonderful amount of room they now had? She wished she could put it into words properly, but that didn't stop the ecstasy she felt. Most of life was ordinary, but these moments were, for her, sheer heaven.

'I'll get off now, Anna,' she said. 'Get my old man's tea. Sure you don't need nuffing?' She laid the baby in the wicker basket on the floor by the side of the bed and the infant started yelling immediately. 'Here, you'd better have her in with you, duck.' Before the girl could say anything she had thrust the baby into her arms.

She met Joe at the door. 'It's a girl,' she said. 'She's beautiful, looks just like ...' but Joe had gone, roughly pushing past her and dashing up the stairs.

Joe was tired and worried as he sat on the bus coming home from Nick's café where he worked every Sunday. He was glad to be a bit earlier, but there was nothing much doing, everyone was indoors now, 'most likely discussing this momentous day's events', Nick said, 'so we'll close early for once and you can get home to that pretty wife of yourn.'

'Thanks, guvnor. She'll be pleased.'

Joe was worried about Anna and their forthcoming child. He knew he would have to go and fight, and dreaded leaving her alone. If she had someone near, someone of her own it wouldn't be so bad, but Anna had no immediate family. She was an only child whose mother died when she was twelve, and who looked after her father for the next year when he died too. 'Of a broken heart,' Anna told Joe. 'He tried to keep going for my sake, but he was never the same after Mum went. If only there had been something I could have done.'

'You were blooming marvellous, I reckon. After all, you were only a kid still, but you looked after him, cooked his meals, did the shopping, and still put in an appearance at school.'

'That was the easy bit,' Anna said, 'I'd never been one to run the streets with the others. Don't know why, just never had. I'd always wanted to get home from school and help Mum. It was no hardship to take over managing the house, but I did used to worry about Dad. I could see him getting sadder each day and I knew, I just knew deep inside here,' she had looked at him with her enormous blue eyes and touched her breast, 'that he was going to die too.'

When he did, after a bad bout of bronchitis, Anna went into a children's home, and it was here that she and Joe met. Joe had left the home several years before, but used to pop back to see them and do odd jobs sometimes. He fell in love with Anna on sight, but bided his time for the next few years until she was sixteen, then asked her to walk out with him. It had been a gentle courtship, for she always seemed so delicate that he was afraid of startling her. They married in 1938, two days before Anna's seventeenth birthday, and he smiled now as he recalled plump, rosy Mrs Cornfield's words to him. 'You look after her now, young Joe. Anna's a very special girl, I'd like to have adopted her myself. So mind you treat her right.'

''Course I will, what d' you think, that I'm going to bash her about every night? I tell you I love Anna, you'll see. I'll remind you what you said when we have our silver wedding ...'

But of course he wouldn't because Corny, as he had always called her, although she was the matron, fell ill and died a few months afterwards. Anna had been inconsolable for a while, and it was all of this that bothered him so much now. With him in the army, Corny dead, Anna would be frighteningly alone. She'd have the child of course, but in a way that seemed to make it worse.

He got off the bus at the Green Man, and crossed the road to Dason Street. They had been lucky to rent that place after they married, he thought. It was a lovely little house, in one of the nicest parts of the street too. Got a bit rough right down the other end, where it narrowed and most of the houses had yards and not gardens and a bit of space. Not that it bothered him, but he wanted everything of the best for Anna.

Joe had started work in the docks when he was fourteen, but after an accident to his arm three years later, which wasn't serious enough to get him compensation, but which neverthe-less kept him in hospital for a fortnight, he decided he didn't want to be a docker – not all his life anyway, and although jobs were hard to get, he'd have a go at anything. One of his pals' fathers worked for Jones & Carter, the builders' merchants on the corner the other end of Dason Street, and he tipped him the wink when there was a job coming up in the stores. Joe began as general dogsbody, and now at twenty-six he was in charge of the stores. The café job he did on Sundays kept his head above water, and even meant he could take Anna up West occasionally to a meal and a show.

Now war had been declared he didn't rightly know what would happen. Of course we couldn't let Hitler get away with taking over countries – it never did to let a bully do that. Next thing you knew he'd be over here, marching his army down Dason Street … Joe shivered at the thought and quickened his steps. The sooner he got home to Anna the better. Only another week or ten days to go and he'd be a father. Funny, he could picture Anna as a mum, but the idea of him as a dad still seemed strange. Hope the little tacker's born with all his fingers and toes and other appendages, he thought, smiling to himself as he reached number 5 and pushed open the gate.

The lights went on in Dason Street that Sunday evening, but behind the blackout curtains. Queenie had bought the material in the market last week, and set to and made them straight away.

'You could have done something in that line, Fred,' she said. 'After all, everyone's got to have it.'

'How many times have I told you I'm not after being a millionaire, Queenie. Anyway you can only sell folk one lot and that's it. Not much future in it, is there?'

Queenie wondered what future there was for them all anyway. A tearful Jenny had been round earlier, convinced she would never see Tom and Doris again. 'I shouldn't have let them go,' she sobbed, 'they're not used to country life. They could be killed by a bull or one of them other animals.'

In vain she tried to tell her daughter she had done what seemed best for the children's safety. 'And I'm sure they won't be anywhere near the dangerous animals, love, they keep them in the fields.'

Fred had taken himself off to the pub again. 'The news is bad enough on the wireless,' he said in disgust, 'without having to listen to you two dreaming up disasters that might never happen.'

When Fred had gone Queenie tried to cheer up her daughter by telling her about Anna and Joe's baby. 'Talk about dramatic,' she said, 'the air raid warning sounded just at the crucial moment. Fair sent shivers down my spine it did, with the baby being born that minute.'

This simply sent Jenny into another spasm of weeping for *her* babies whom she had so recently sent away to the country, so Queenie quickly changed the subject.

Rosie bustled about, twitching at her new blackout curtains, made from the thickest material she could find in the market. 'Don't look very good, but we can have our others inside if you fix up another rail Jim,' she said, 'then we won't have to look on the *black* side every night.' Chuckling loudly at her own wit, she went into the kitchen to make them a pot of tea, while Jim thoughtfully rolled himself another cigarette.

Meanwhile in the Putts' home across the road from the Batesons, Joe was struggling with an assortment of black material given to Anna by various neighbours, and grumbling about Rosie all the while.

'Don't know why she had to be over here poking her nose in at all. It's none of her business.'

'She means well, Joe, and she loves babies.'

'Bloody Nosy Parker, that's what she is. Didn't even wait to let me find out about the baby from you – no. Rosie big mouth had to shout it in me ear as I came through the door. Blast, this damn thing's not wide enough …' He rummaged about on the floor to find a more suitable covering. Later, all the windows having been decently cloaked in black, he made a pot of tea, cut some bread daintily thin and made Anna a couple of cheese sandwiches. Then he cut some more bread, thick doorsteps this time, hacked off a lump of the cheese for himself and carried the lot upstairs on a tray. 'Sorry I blew my top, sweetheart, but that – that woman across the road gets on my wick. Don't you have any truck with her when I'm away, will you. I don't want her coming over here and upsetting you.'

Which set the tears raining down Anna's cheeks. 'Oh Joe, will you have to go? What will happen to Joanna and me?'

Liza and Sid Wentworth from the newsagent's shop had their blackout arrangements taken care of days before it was necessary by law. On the evening of 3 September he dressed to go out, slipped his gas mask case over his shoulder, and called out to Liza, 'I'll be off then. Remember not to pull the curtains now, unless you switch the light off first.'

Liza, who always had some knitting on the go, was in the bedroom sorting through her wool ready to knit comforts for the troop. 'Do you have to go out, Sid?' she said, coming to the top of the stairs. 'I mean, there isn't an air-raid on.'

'Of course I do. It's no use you getting all worried either, because this is only the beginning – you're going to have to get used to it. I shan't be long, but I must check no one is showing a light, and that everything's OK.'

'I don't know why you had to be so quick off the mark with that warden's job. What with winter round the corner an' all, you know how you always get bronchitis. Being out in all weathers isn't going—'

'For Christ's sake, woman, there's a war on now. Until it's over our young men are going to be killed and wounded like they were the last time, and you natter on about bronchitis.' The door slammed behind him as he stumped off down the path, and, her eyes filling with tears, Liza returned to the bedroom.

There were no lights showing the whole length of Dason Street, but as he passed number 5 he heard the new baby trying out its lungs, and for a moment a great longing came over him. Maybe Liza would be less of a nagger if she had been able to have a family. He shouldn't really blame her for fussing him – after all, he was all she'd got to fuss over.

Chapter 3

The phoney war, the newspapers called it, but it didn't seem very phoney to Jenny when she came home from the factory, to a house without her husband and children. She wept uncontrollably when she heard Gracie Fields singing *Goodnight Children, Everywhere*, in a broadcast that December. Were Doris and Tom listening, and weeping too? She wished she hadn't let them go. She longed to visit, but, heeding the leaflets which warned of upsetting them, contented herself as much as she could with writing letters and putting funny drawings on them. They had always laughed at her drawings of cats and dogs, which even she could see looked nothing like the real thing.

Some of the evacuees were returning for Christmas and she felt torn in two between having them home, or leaving them 'safe'. *Leave them where they are* insisted the official government leaflets, although so far there had been none of the mass air attacks on London that were predicted.

She joined the throng of women now working in one of the local munitions factories, and admitted to herself on some of her better days that she enjoyed the independence and the money, but oh how she missed her husband and children. She sent Doris's and Tom's Christmas presents, and a postal order for each of them, longing to make the journey to Wiltshire, but unable to because of curtailed transport over the holiday, and work immediately afterwards.

January was bitterly cold, and the snow became an extra hazard

to cope with. Pipes froze, buses and trams were delayed and sometimes taken off altogether, and although Jenny cleared yesterday's
ashes and laid the fire each morning before leaving for the factory,
it took hours to warm the room. The twists of paper and bits of
wood burned, but the coke and coal-dust usually defied her first
efforts. She had a couple of scares when she knelt in front of the
grate holding a newspaper across it and a sudden great draught
caught the paper and sent it soaring up the chimney. The sparks
fell on to the hearthrug she and Bill had made with the rug kit they
had bought as a joint present for each other the first Christmas they
were married, so she stopped using that method to fan the flames.

As if to outdo the horrendous winter, spring was one of the
loveliest they could recall. In Queenie and Fred's small garden
daffodils bloomed bright and golden, alongside the vegetables
Queenie had planted last summer.

Anna and Joe had little in their patch: a few pallid, straggly
daffodils, and a square of grass. 'I'll make a swing for Joanna
later, when she's older,' Joe said. 'She'll enjoy that, and you'll be
able to see her quite well from the kitchen window.'

In April Hitler overran Denmark, and in Sid and Liza's shop
the customers who called in after work for their evening paper
looked grave.

'Who said it would all be over by Christmas? Which bloody
Christmas?'

'Seems to me, Hitler's having it all his own way.'

'What's our government doing, that's what I want to know?
Chamberlain's no good, too soft by half—'

'Be fair, Alf, he did try for peace …'

Sid listened to them all as they gathered in the shop and
voiced their opinions. Later, when he had locked up for the
night, he read his warden's official notes, and rechecked his lists
so he would be as prepared as possible for any emergency.

*

Eight months after war was declared Joe became a private in the British army. Anna wept when his call-up papers arrived.

'Come on now, luv,' he said, 'we knew it would come. The nineteen- and twenty-year-olds have been in from the beginning, and it might not be for too long.'

'Oh Joe, we were so happy, you settled into your job, and our lovely Joanna getting to the interesting stage. Everyone says men like babies better once they can sit up and take notice.'

He put his arm round her shoulder. 'Rubbish. I loved Joanna from the moment I saw her, same as I did you. Now come on and cheer up. I'm not the only one to have to go.'

''Course you're not. I'm sorry, Joe, and I'll talk to the little 'un about you while you're away, and you'll get leave sometimes, won't you?'

He nodded and kissed her cheek. 'That's better, got to set a good example to our daughter. You know, I still get a thrill when I think about us having a daughter, and such a pretty one. She's so lovely, aren't you, little Jo-Jo?' The child crawled towards him and he bent down and lifted her into his arms. Joanna laughed. 'That's the spirit,' Joe said, rubbing his nose against hers, 'you and Mummy keep each other company until I get back.'

Anna met Rosie the following day when she walked down the road with Joanna in her pram. 'Joe got his papers then?' she said. It was more of a statement than a question. Trust Rosie to know before anyone else, Anna thought. Nothing happens in this street without her knowing about it within minutes. Joe swore she spent all day watching from behind her net curtains.

'If you and Joe want to go up West one evening before he goes, I'll mind the baby for you,' Rosie was saying. 'Do a show or something – all the theatres are open again now …'

'That's kind of you. I'll let you know later when I've talked to Joe.' But when Joe came in from work that evening he said, 'Put your glad rags on, Anna, we're eating out tonight and Queenie's coming in to sit with Joanna. I saw her on the way to work this morning.'

'Oh Joe, I saw Rosie this morning too and she offered to baby sit so we could go out.'

'Don't want that nosy woman over here. Anyway I've arranged it with Queenie Parkes now.'

Later, as they walked up Dason Street to the bus stop he said, 'Why did you tell that old bitch opposite I'd had me papers?'

'I didn't, she already knew. Anyway what does it matter, she's a friendly sort and was only trying—'

'She's an interfering old witch and I'd rather you didn't have much to do with her. Pokes her nose into everything.'

Anna felt tears tingling at the back of her eyes and didn't answer him. The last thing she wanted tonight was a row. There wasn't a lot she and Joe didn't agree on, but Rosie Bateson had been a bone of contention with him ever since they'd moved in. She had come over within the first few minutes with tea and slabs of home-made fruitcake, 'to keep you going until you sort yourselves out.' She sat in one of their second-hand armchairs, and stayed for over an hour. Joe swore afterwards that she'd assessed everything they had in the room and costed it, but Anna warmed immediately to the plump, motherly Rosie. She reminded her vaguely of 'Corny', her beloved matron from the children's home.

Now was not the time to think of things like that, Anna told herself silently, not when they were out together for the first time since the birth of their baby. Resolutely she pushed away the thought that it was probably the last time for some months too.

They went to Lyons Corner House at Marble Arch and carefully studied the menu while the band played the latest songs from the shows. It was a lovely meal, 'no preparing and no washing up afterwards,' Anna said, laughing and reaching across the table to hold her husband's hand. She was determined to make this last night happy for him, to push her terror out of sight, at least until after he left tomorrow. Time for fears and tears then, and anyway she had Joanna to think about now. She needed to be strong for her.

Sitting on the bus going back she snuggled against Joe. 'Tonight's been like it was when we were courting,' she murmured. He kissed her ear then his lips gently brushed her cheek.

They alighted at the Green Man and walked down Dason Street to number 5 with their arms around each other. Their love-making that night was sweet and strong, and more impassioned than at any time since Joanna was conceived.

'Don't come out,' Joe said, the following morning. 'Make yourself a cuppa, and I'll write to you tonight.' He kissed them both, then quietly opened the front door and walked up the road without once looking back.

A few days later headlines screamed from the papers: NAZIS INVADE HOLLAND, BELGIUM, LUXEMBOURG ...

It was the start of the Whitsun weekend, a glorious sunny day when Anna had taken Joanna to the park, and watched her lean forward, straining on the pram harness, to clap her hands at the ducks on the pond. The flower-beds, glorious with colour, and the wonderful scent of the wallflowers strong around her brought tears to her eyes. She silently prayed that Joe would come home to her again. He had written from a camp in the north, saying he was fine and training hard, and sending love and kisses to them both.

He was sure to have to go to the fighting zones, she thought, a young, strong man – that was what he was being trained for. She added another trembling 'please God' to her prayer.

Anna was back home, the baby in her highchair having tea, when she learned from the six o'clock news on the wireless that Neville Chamberlain was out of office and Winston Churchill, First Lord of the Admiralty, was now Prime Minister.

*

Across the road at number 6 Rosie and Jim were also listening to the news. Already two of their three sons were in the army, the third having failed his medical on account of flat feet. He was extremely cross about it, especially when one of his sisters fell about laughing on hearing the news. Another one, however, told him to be thankful. 'I only wish my Charlie had flat feet and could get out of going, that I do.'

Rosie, on hearing the rumpus, said indignantly, 'He was a weak baby, had a spot on his lung when he was four as well. I bet that scar—'

'Give over, Mum,' he interrupted irritably. 'That was years ago. I'm as healthy as anyone now, and I'll try again.'

'Always been touchy about that TB,' Rosie said to Jim when the family had gone home, 'but I'm glad one of them at least won't be in the thick of it, and I make no bones about saying so.'

Jim slipped his arm round her ample waist as he went past, 'Can't say I'm displeased neither, duck, but I know how he feels. It won't be easy for him.'

'I'm worried,' Rosie said now. 'Holland and Belgium gone, they're coming closer. It don't bear thinking about that they'd get here. What d'you reckon, Jim?'

"Course not. We got that lovely stretch of water. Kept our enemies out for hundreds of years.'

Rosie handed him a cup of tea, 'I hope you're right, mate, I hope you're right.'

Most of the family came over on Whit Sunday and, in between listening to every news bulletin on the wireless, the house was a buzz of chatter and children. Margery came into the kitchen to help her mum wash up. 'It's a woman's world now, Mum, with most of the men in the forces. The times I've wished Bill miles away, but I'd give almost anything in the world to have him home. It's funny, but since he's been gone none of them things that used to annoy me matter very much.' Rosie put her arms out and hugged her daughter hard.

*

Queenie didn't discuss the change of premier, nor the capitulation of the Low Countries with Fred. Sometimes she wondered if he talked much when he was down the pub. She thought he probably did, yet the only things he said to her were, 'Tea ready?' or dinner, or whatever meal it might be time for, and either, 'You're late,' when she came in and he was there first, or 'going out again, are you?' when she appeared in her outdoor garments. Years ago she had longed to be able to discuss things with him, anything from the price of potatoes to the political situation, but he never listened, and she knew he thought women shouldn't have ideas about anything beyond cooking, cleaning and looking after their man.

Queenie's mind was usually seething with ideas. Ideas for improved housing, education, hospitals ...

She wondered if she could work in a hospital now, but quickly dismissed the thought. She had no training, and certainly didn't want to be a ward maid, and spend her time mopping floors and emptying bedpans. So she went to work in a factory that used to make clothes and now made parachutes. Fred had something to say about that. 'Never here when you're needed, fancy volunteering for the work, you must be mad.' Queenie smiled to herself, knowing his main concern was the fear that his meals and comfort might be disturbed. At forty-three he knew there was little chance of being called up himself. 'I did my stint in the last war,' he said to her, 'and at your age you wouldn't have to go anyway.'

Queenie wasn't so sure about that, but she ignored his remarks anyway. It was easier.

'What does your Fred think about your job?' Liza asked when she called into the shop not long afterwards.

Queenie grimaced. 'Not much if the truth be told. He thinks I'm mad. I've done some things in my time, but I've never worked in a factory before.'

She broke off while Liza served a group of children. 'Scruffy lot, aren't they? Especially that youngest one. Half-inch a chocolate bar in as long as it takes to blink your eye, honest he will.'

Queenie laughed at the use of the word honest. 'They're the Johnson kids, aren't they?'

'Some of them. Getting pregnant is Riva Johnson's full-time job, I reckon.' Queenie heard the bitterness in her voice, saw the almost imperceptible tightening of her eyes and lips, and nodded her agreement. Years ago Liza had let slip to her how much she yearned for a family.

Like I used to tell my kids though, nothing in the world's fair, Queenie thought when she left the shop. Yet it seems so one-sided that Liza and Sid can't have children when they want them so, and Riva Johnson can't stop falling for them.

'And they're all gorgeous when they're babies, even if the latest one looks more like the milkman than her old man,' Rosie had commented to Queenie recently, after she had seen the newest arrival being trundled along in a battered old pram, by one of his older sisters. Queenie had smiled but kept silent. Trust Rosie Bateson to come out with a remark like that.

The subject of her thoughts, Riva Johnson, lived the bottom end of Dason Street. She had not allowed her older children to be evacuated with the school, because, 'who's going to help with the younger tribe if they're away?'

She was at that moment shouting and lashing out at any of her family who were within earshot or arm's reach. Her husband had just told her he was off that afternoon.

'Joined the army? You could've got out of it if you'd tried. How am I going to manage with all these kids and you away, tell me that.' And she threw herself at him, pummelling hard at his chest and shrieking abuse. Pushing her from him he grinned. 'You'll manage, you will. You'll have me army pay. Now leave off, woman, I got to get me things together.'

'You've known about this for days,' she shouted after him,

'haven't you? Springing it on me like this.' Her beautiful olive eyes were black with fury, and even the toddler who had been clinging to her skirt stumbled away when she began a wail that would have done justice to the most wronged operatic prima donna.

'What if I have? You'd only have kicked up a fuss sooner.' He grabbed her skirt and swung her round and into his arms.

The news from France was grim – thousands of troops on the beaches at Dunkirk being dive-bombed while waiting for a ship to bring them back across the channel – the town itself ablaze. The people of Dason Street gathered in the pubs, in the streets, and in each others' homes to listen to the news. The BBC announcers had to give their names now, so the public would know there had been no take-over by the Germans, *Here is the news, and this is John Snagge reading it.* It wasn't long before they all had their favourite, 'Alvar Liddell,' Rosie said to her friend Liza in the shop one morning. 'His voice makes me shiver with pleasure. If I were only a few years younger, ah ...'

Liza laughed. 'You are a caution Rosie, that's a fact.'

Most of the inhabitants of Dason Street owned a wireless set; the few who didn't went to a neighbour to hear at least one news bulletin during the day. Liza was especially taken with the writer J.B. Priestley when he broadcast a Postscript after the nine o'clock news, and talked about the little boats which went to the rescue of our boys in France, *and the pride of our ferry service to the Isle of Wight, the* Gracie Fields, *went down doing her duty ... she will go on sailing proudly down the years.* His homely everyday voice, with the warmth of his Yorkshire accent, reminded her of her very first boyfriend, and a long-ago holiday at Southend when she had met him. The romance lasted only for the week they were there, yet she had never forgotten it, or him. And the paddle steamer he talked about, the *Gracie Fields*, was one she had travelled on in the July before war broke out, when she had visited a friend in Ryde for two days while Sid looked after the shop. She would never forget that trip either, because there had been an accident with a flying boat, and although no one was hurt, it had been scary.

The evacuation of the British Expeditionary Force from the beaches at Dunkirk in the first week of June, so closely followed by the fall of France on the 17th, brought the fear of invasion closer. Liza said to Sid when they listened to announcer Frank Phillips on the one o'clock news that day, 'For the first time in my life I'm *glad* we've no children. I wouldn't want them brought up as Nazis and there's only a few miles of water between them and us now.'

'Aw, come on, Liza,' Sid chided, 'Hitler isn't here yet – we're not done for. Every German isn't a Nazi anyway; I don't suppose the ordinary people want this war any more than we do. But we can't let Adolph take over the world, an' the way I see it that's what he's set on doing. Listen, every war has its setbacks, and when this one's over and we've won, we'll have the biggest party ever for all the kids in the street. How about that?'

As if to justify his optimism a few days later Winston Churchill stirred the nation when he ended a speech with:

Let us therefore brace ourselves to our duties; and so bear ourselves that, if the British Empire and its Commonwealth last for a thousand years, men will still say, 'This was their finest hour'.

In the heat of the moment Liza had truly meant what she'd said to her husband about being glad they were childless in the present situation, but still buried deep within her was a powerful yearning for a family. An only child of fairly elderly parents – her mother was forty-one when Liza was born – she had envied those of her school pals who had brothers and sisters. There were no aunts and uncles on her side of the family either, to provide companionship in the way of cousins, because her mother too had been a lone child.

Sid did have an older brother, David, who had emigrated to Australia soon after his marriage, and never returned. He had two children, and sent a card every Christmas and an occasional photograph of the children, but never having been close as boys, the ten years between them, and the distance now, made him and his family seem more like strangers than relatives.

Sid thought about his wife's remark too when he walked down Dason Street that evening after they had closed the shop and had their tea. He only cycled when the warning had gone because he said he needed the exercise of walking after a day standing behind a counter. He caught one of the Johnson children banging on the doorknockers then running away, while sometimes irate, and sometimes nervous folk extinguished hall lights and opened their doors to find no one there.

The boy couldn't have been more than five, a huge-eyed, scraggy, barefoot child who thumbed his nose at Sid and slithered easily from his grasp with the movements and grace of a snake.

'That you, Warden?' Old Mr Worth's wavering voice nevertheless pierced the darkness. He had recently come from Bethnal Green to live with his son and daughter-in-law in Dason Street, and didn't yet know Sid very well.

'Yes, but it's only kids banging the knockers,' Sid told him. 'You all right in there?'

'Yus. Bob an' Pat have gone to visit friends tonight.'

'Well, if he knocks again don't answer it. I'll catch the little devil in a minute.'

'We used to do it when we wus kids. And worse.' The old man chuckled. 'All sorts of tricks our gang got up to, but there wus no harm in it really, jest devilment and high spirits. Don't be too hard on him.'

Sid grinned, remembering his own boyhood pranks. 'I won't.

Good-night.' He went on, turning into all the streets which ran off the long line of Dason, and checking, not only that no lights were showing, but that nothing untoward was happening in his patch. Now and then he met someone and exchanged greetings, 'Evening, Sid. Not going to let Adolph spoil our evening entertainment. We're off to the Palace.'

'Evening Billy, hullo Ruth. Enjoy yourselves.'

What a blessing the ban on cinemas and theatres opening didn't last long, he thought. It had come into operation as soon as war was declared, 'to minimize the chances of a large crowd being killed by a single bomb' the official notice said, but within weeks the entertainment scene was as lively as it had ever been. And a good job too, was Sid's opinion, we all need something to keep our spirits up, and you could just as easily be killed shopping in Sainsburys or Woolworths as you could at a theatre or cinema. They were always packed out.

The eerie notes of the air-raid warning sounded when he was almost home, and he turned round and walked smartly back to the warden's post halfway down Dason Street.

The warden's post was a posh name for the sandbagged hut containing an old table and chair and second clipboard with details of all the families on his patch. He kept the first list at home. 'Though I know most of them anyway,' he said to Liza, when compiling it.

It was a clear, calm night. Over the rooftops of the houses, looking towards the park, he could see the silver glint of a barrage balloon swaying gently like a boat on the ocean of the sky, and he felt a security in the knowledge that they were there. Two were anchored in Royal Park, they were soon nicknamed Ben and Tess.

There was a street shelter at each end of Dason Street, and one in most of the side streets that led from it too. Another warden covered Dason Street from the High Road, while Sid's responsibility began the other end with number 1.

He didn't blame people who said they would prefer to stay home and take their chance, for there was no comfort in the street shelters: a wooden bench round the walls, no lighting and no lavatories. But the worst thing about them to his way of thinking was that they were at street level. 'Might just as well stay indoors,' he said to Liza, 'though I wouldn't say that to anyone but you, of course.' In any case there had been few incidents so far, and almost everyone with a garden down the street either had an Anderson shelter, or the use of a neighbour's and these at least were sunk three feet and sometimes more below ground.

He heard the planes before he saw them, forming an intricate pattern in the moonlight, and a shiver of fear ran through his body. Theory was fine, but how would it be when he was called to use his training. He hoped he would not be found wanting. That evening was not to be a testing time however. The planes flew on until the sound of their engines had died away. Minutes later he heard the distant rumble of gunfire, and within a short time the all-clear sounded.

His thoughts returned to his wife as he walked home, and he remembered their courting days, and the disappointments in the early years of their marriage when each month she said to him, 'No, not this time.' It was many years before she accepted that they would probably not have a family. If war hadn't been looming he was going to suggest adoption. The only time they had discussed it slightly was several years ago, and Liza wasn't in favour, she still felt there was a chance of a baby of her own then, but time was against her. Only thing was, if they left it too long the adoption societies might think they were too old.

So engrossed in his thoughts was he that he walked into the unlit lamppost, giving himself such a bang on his face that he literally saw stars instead of the crescent moon that was riding the heavens. He leant against the offending post for several minutes, holding a large handkerchief to his face; eventually he pulled it away covered with blood. He staggered home, trying to stem his bleeding nose, fumbled with his key, and met Liza as she came from the room behind the shop. 'I've got the kettle – what on earth's happened,' she cried, 'Sid, are you all right? Here, sit down and let me look.'

As she gently bathed his face she said, 'Was it a bomb, was anyone else hurt?' and he shamefacedly told her: 'You won't believe this, I know, but I was thinking about *you* and I bumped into a lamppost. Honest Liza, it's the truth I'm telling you.'

As she dabbed at his face now with a towel he saw the sudden quirk of her lips and in her eyes the laughter that she was trying to stem, and although it hurt both his mouth and his pride, he simply had to laugh with her.

Anna had another letter from Joe a few days later.

Pretty spartan up here, but I'm fine apart from missing you and little Joanna. Haven't had much spare time so far; if the army think you're likely to sit down for a few minutes they find you something to do. Often something blooming stupid too. We've been on exercises in the hills round here – did find my arm gave me a bit of gyp after, but I never let on. It often plays up a bit when I do anything specially strenuous. I'll get used to it. It's a pretty barren place where I am, but after six weeks I'll be posted and the real fun starts then. Write to me often and tell me how you both are. I miss you, but I'm so glad we can read and write. (God bless dear old Corny). There are two blokes here who can't, and when the mail comes they're so sad. It's a funny thing, Anna, out of all the blokes in my hut, those two are the ones who fight each other. You'd think they'd be friends, wouldn't you? Nothing else to say. Write to me soon,
All my love for ever ...

She tried to picture him in his hut with all the other men – her quiet, rather shy Joe. For a few moments she wondered if his old arm injury could have kept him out, but quickly realized that he would not have played on that. Looking across to Joanna in her highchair, her fingers and face sticky with marmite, she smiled. 'You've made a right mess with that, but you enjoyed it, didn't you, luv, and Mummy will soon clean you up. Look,' she waved the sheet of paper at her daughter, 'we've had another letter from Daddy today.' Joanna picked up her spoon and banged it vigorously on her highchair.

Chapter 4

1940

'**M**um, fancy a day in the country?' Jenny said when she popped in straight from work one Monday evening.

'You mean go and see Tom and Doris?' Queenie turned from the stove where she was cooking Fred's tea.

'Mmm. I've found out about trains and things, and we can do it in a day. How about this Sunday?'

Queenie did a silent and quick run-through of her commitments, then she beamed at her daughter. 'Suits me. I'm dying to see them. Doris has written a couple of times and Tom wrote *love from Tom*, on the bottom of the last letter, but I miss them kids, Jenny. They were always round here before.'

'*You* miss 'em. What do you think I do, then? Only thing is – will they want to come home with us? I know I'll want to bring them, but I shan't. I'd rather they were safe down there, and now I'm at work all day it wouldn't be easy. But I don't want to upset them too much.'

'Kids are adaptable Jenny. They'll probably be sad for a while, but they'll soon settle again, you'll see. What time do we go? Then I can plan and leave something for your father for each meal.'

'You wait on him too much you do, Mum. Now when Mike was home he'd always turn his hand to getting a meal, if I was busy like. You know, right from a little girl I was determined I'd not be at someone's beck and call like you've been with Dad all these years.' Queenie looked at her daughter, surprise in her face. She had never realized her children even noticed.

'Well, he wouldn't bother on his own, and I am out working most of the day.'

Jenny shrugged her shoulders. 'Up to you of course. I know none of us girls would ever do it. Anyway, I've sorted it all out for Sunday. I wrote to Mrs Fellowes last week, sent it with my letter to the kids, and it's all fixed. I've written the train times down here for you. OK?'

'Wonderful,' Queenie said, excitement bubbling inside her already with the thought of seeing two of her beloved grand-children again.

She set the alarm for six o'clock on Sunday morning.

'Gawd, wot d'you want to do that for, it's the middle of the bloody night' was Fred's reaction.

'You'll sleep through it, you always do. Don't forget to put your dinner in the oven. It's all there in the enamel dish, I've put the meat and veg together so you won't have any saucepans to mess about with.'

'Leave off, anyone hear you they'd think I needed looking after like a child.'

Queenie bit back the retort: 'you do', took her best coat from the wardrobe and laid it on the chair ready for the morning.

'Make sure you leave some beer money, Queen. I'm skint.'

She sighed. 'It's on the mantelpiece. I'm going up now, I'm dead beat.' She had been in bed less than five minutes when she thought about something else, and slipped out again. Her feet touched the cold lino as she wiggled them about trying to find her slippers in the darkened room. Then she fumbled for her handbag which was on the back of the chair with her clothes, ready for the morning. Clasping it to her pale-blue nightie, she stood for a moment trying to think of a safe place to leave it. It would be putting temptation under Fred's nose if it was hanging where he could see it, and he always put the light on when he came to bed, so he'd be sure to notice. Queenie had long since given up quarrelling with him over money. Time was when she used to blow her top when he went to her purse, but she hated arguments, they left her feeling drained of energy and self-esteem. She always ended up feeling worse than he did, and the money was gone anyway. The only thing to do was not to let him know she had any. Often she hid her handbag, tucking it under the mattress, or beneath the cushions on the old bedchairs in the sitting room. Only trouble was he knew most of the hiding-places now, and if he was really desperate he could pull the place apart looking for it.

'Can't think why you married that no-good waster,' her mother used to say in the early days. 'Be a drain on you all your life he will. I'd tell him a home truth or two if he was mine, I would.'

Queenie smiled to herself in the darkness. Dear Mum, she still missed her and her forthrightness. They had got on so well together even though they were such different temperaments. Mum thrived on fireworks. 'I feel better now,' she used to say after a barney, rubbing her hands together in exultation. It never seemed to matter to her whether she won or lost the argument. 'At least I told them, got it off me chest. It won't curdle now.'

Queenie often wished she could do this, but it simply wasn't in her nature, and she had long ago realized it.

The sun shone for Queenie and Jenny's trip to Wiltshire. 'It's a little village near Westbury,' Jenny said. 'Get the train from Paddington to Westbury, then I hope there'll be a bus there. Mrs Fellowes says in her letter there's two a day, one in the morning and one in the afternoon. If not, she says it's only just over two miles to walk. Don't fancy that, do you, Mum?'

'Blimey, no. Not in these shoes. I've got a bit of "ready" Jenny, we'll have a taxi if there's nothing else. I thought they had donkeys and carts in the country.'

Jenny laughed. 'Not outside the station I shouldn't think. And they probably wouldn't allow taxis now, what with petrol needed for the fighting vehicles and everything. They're even limited in London. Don't worry, we'll get there somehow.' She patted her mother's arm. 'The kids seem to be enjoying it anyway. The first two letters I had were full of wanting to come back, but not now. They've made friends, and Doris even wrote something about a chance to go horse-riding. I must say I don't like the idea of her on a horse, but maybe it's only a little pony and not too high off the ground.'

Queenie had prepared jam sandwiches for them both, using her last jar of home-made strawberry and, with a flask of tea, and some apples she had bought in the Saturday market, nestled in her shopping bag, she was looking forward to seeing her grandchildren again.

'I got them something in the market yesterday,' she said when they were comfortably seated on the train. 'Look.' She pulled from her bag two boxes. One was a child's nursing outfit, the other a bus conductor's set. 'Think they'll like them?'

Jenny wasn't sure. From Mrs Fellowes's regular letters she thought perhaps her two were more into outdoor adventure pursuits than dressing-up now. She had talked of sheep and cows and helping on the farm. Apart from missing them badly, one of the reasons Jenny had been keen to visit now was to see for herself. To make sure her children weren't being exploited and used as 'slave labour'.

They had a surprise when they walked out of Westbury station. A pretty girl wearing khaki breeches, a dun-coloured top, wellington boots and a large felt hat approached them. 'I'm Morag,' she said, rolling her r's in a way Queenie found most attractive. 'You must be Doris and Tom's mum and granny.'

'That's right.'

'I had to come in this morning so we timed it for your train. Might not be the most comfortable journey you've ever had, but it'll get you there.'

She led them towards a tractor and trailer, the only vehicle within sight. Queenie gasped aloud, and Morag grinned at her. 'Ye'll be just fine in the trailer,' she said, 'and ye'll have a grand view of the countryside as we go along.'

Jenny said, 'Are the children all right?'

'They're grand. I didna bring them with me because they were busy, and Mrs Fellowes thought it best you have your reunion indoors in private. Very understanding woman she is, I can tell ye that from first-hand experience.'

She helped them both on to the trailer and closed the tailboard. 'Got one stop to make at a farm on the way back. It won't take long. Ye must be longing to see the bairns.'

When the tractor set off they both held tightly to the side of the trailer, but after a few minutes first Jenny then Queenie relaxed a little. 'Thought tractors were only used on farmland, not on the road,' Jenny said. Queenie nodded. 'Still, she said it won't take long. Big thing though, isn't it, Jen?'

They had been travelling for about ten minutes when Queenie began to laugh. 'What is it, Mum, what's funny?'

'Us Jen. Who ever thought we'd be sitting in a thing like this out here in the country. I only ever seen the countryside from a train window before.'

Jenny grinned back at her mother, 'And us all in our town clothes too.' She gazed at the golden fields, 'I hope Tom and Doris haven't changed too much. Their letters don't sound a bit homesick any more.'

'That's a good sign, Jen. I mean, you wouldn't want them to be unhappy, would you?'

'No, no, 'course not, but – well suppose they want to stay here when it's all over?'

Queenie looked at the vast expanse of growing crops which they were slowly passing. 'Wait and see, eh Jen?' Reaching over she touched her daughter's hand. 'Kids are pretty adaptable, and it won't be like going to something new and different when

48

they come back, will it? I mean, when the war's over they'll be coming home. Back to the things they've always known, their school and friends – why, I bet all the evacuees stick together down here anyway.'

'Some of them are home already, mum—'

'Their mothers haven't got no sense of responsibility then. They should have refused to have them back. It's for their own good.'

Morag turned into a farm entrance, and both women straightened their backs and took deep breaths. On either side of them were fields of cows, most of them black-and-white. The drive finished in a circular yard with a house to the right and a huge barn stacked with hay on the left. Morag came round to the trailer, 'Won't be long, got to collect a scythe – the handle's broken on ours.' She disappeared in the direction of the farmhouse.

'I'll be glad when we're there, Mum, I'm getting jittery now. It's been eight months since we've seen the kids. I shouldn't have listened to everyone who said don't go, you'll only upset them if you visit ...' She opened her handbag and took out a handkerchief.

'Now Jen, buck up. It'll be all right once we're there, and if you start the waterworks you'll have me at it too. Tom and Doris will want to see us cheerful any—' she stopped abruptly as she saw the size of the tool Morag and a plump, rosy-cheeked woman were bringing across.

Jenny quickly dabbed her eyes. 'Blimey,' she said, a bit unsteadily, 'where they going to put *that*?'

They knew within minutes, as they had to shift around on the trailer to accommodate the scythe. The farmer's wife had a few words with them, then they were off again.

'Morag handles this thing well, doesn't she?' Jenny said, her voice filled with admiration. 'Look how she turned it round by the barn there.'

Queenie, who was eyeing the blade on the weird-looking implement now sharing their transport, nodded distractedly. 'Evil-looking thing, isn't it?' She pointed to the scythe.

They reached Green Farm fifteen minutes later. The driveway leading to it wasn't as long as the previous one, in fact they could see the farmhouse from the road, a stone-built, very solid-looking two-storey house.

A grey-haired man dressed in an open-necked check shirt and incredibly stained trousers fastened with thick string, came up. 'Got it then, you,' he said to Morag. 'I'll give thee hand.' He nodded to Queenie and Jenny. ''Owdo.' They had to wait for the scythe to be offloaded before they could jump from the trailer.

Mrs Fellowes appeared in the farmhouse doorway, a child standing each side of her.

'Doris – Tom ...' A few steps and they were in Jenny's arms. Mrs Fellowes, tall and lean to the point of scragginess, smiled at Queenie. 'Come along in then, kettle's on the hob.'

After the initial hugs and kisses, the children seemed shy, almost ill at ease, Queenie thought. They sat round a big wooden table which was obviously scrubbed at least once a day, and drank tea from brightly coloured mugs. Mrs Fellowes did most of the talking, asking them about their journey and the state of things in London.

'More tea?' she asked.

Queenie and Jenny shook their head. 'No thanks.'

'Well then, why don't you show your mum and gran round before dinner? Expect they'd like to see your bedrooms and have a look at some of the animals. Go on, away with you both, but be back in time to wash your hands before dinner.' Turning to the two women she added, 'Bathroom's upstairs. Make yourselves at home now, Doris and Tom will take care of you.'

They returned to the station in Dan Fellowes's ancient Ford in the late afternoon. 'I've got a couple of calls to make,' he said, 'so I can drop you.' Saying goodbye to the children hadn't been as hard as Jenny thought it would be. During the time they were at the farm she had seen how content they were with their new lives, and after her emotional first greeting she had listened and looked at everything. 'Then I can picture it all when I read the letters', she said to Queenie when they were once again on a train back to Paddington.

'Isn't she thin?' Queenie said. 'Somehow you imagine farmers' wives to be rounded and pink – like the one at the first farm where we collected the scythe, don't you?'

Jenny laughed. 'You've been reading too many country books since the kids went.' Her smile crumpled. 'Was – odd to hear them calling those strangers auntie and uncle, though, and looking to them for instructions. Know what I mean? Seemed like I'd lost the right to tell them anything.'

Queenie leant across and squeezed her daughter's hand. 'Yes, I do. But it's only for the duration, luv. I'm glad we've seen them though. I've wondered so often if they really were happy, but we've no worries on that score, and you'll see, once the war's over and they're home again they'll settle down and treat these months on the farm as a holiday.'

'They at least looked rosy-cheeked and healthy,' Jenny said. 'And aren't they knowledgeable about all the animals? Why, neither of them knew one end of a cow from the other not so long ago, now they know all the breeds, and all about the crops that are growing in the area. I felt quite proud when they were telling us.'

Queenie reached for her shoes as the train slowed down just before Paddington Station. 'Shouldn't have worn these. I'll know another time,' she said.

'Hope you can get them on again, Mum,' Jenny said, laughing at her. 'Think I'll come back with you for half an hour if that's OK. Be worse than ever going into an empty house now I've seen them again.'

''Course, luv. Stay the night if you like.'

'No – got to be up early for work tomorrow – I'll just stop half-hour.'

The tube was crowded and they had to stand, and the queue for a bus stretched almost from one stop to the next.

'Come on,' Jenny said, impatient now to be back, 'let's walk, it's only a few stops. Will your feet make it, d'you think?'

Queenie grinned at her. 'Reckon so. But I'll be more sensible next time. You live and learn, even at my age.'

The siren went as they turned into Dason Street.

'You can tell we're back,' Queenie said, 'old Hitler's been waiting for us. Aren't you glad now the kids are down there and relatively safe?'

''Course I am. Come on, let's get home before he starts dropping his bombs or his parachutists. They do reckon he's using men dressed as nuns to spy on us.'

'Jen, surely you don't believe that? Sid Wentworth from the newsagent's says that's a load of rubbish. Anyway, he reckons he'll never get here. And so do I. After all, it's much easier to march into Holland and Belgium and France, but we've got the English Channel to stop him.'

Fred was still at the pub when they reached home and Queenie eased her feet out of her smart shoes. The dirty crockery from his meals was piled into the sink, and she sighed softly to herself as she filled the kettle and lit the gas.

'I'll make us a cup of 'rosy' and bring it in', she said, urging Jenny towards the front room. She didn't want her to see the state of the kitchen and start again about her father's laziness and her own lack of control.

Chapter 5

Joe got a thirty-six-hour pass in August. He was now stationed in Scotland, had only been at the original camp a few weeks before being transferred. Wish I could have seen you first he wrote at the time, I'm so far away now there's no chance. Talk about the back of beyond!

They arranged to meet at King's Cross station. Because he wouldn't know until the last minute whether his application had been successful, Anna tried not to get too excited, so she wouldn't be disappointed if it didn't come off. When she received the expected telegram saying simply: 'Thirty-six hours' she rushed over the road to tell Rosie and Jim. 'It's on.'

'Thirty-six or forty-eight?' Jim asked.

'Thirty-six.'

'It ain't long, not with all the journey down,' Rosie said, 'but you make the most of it gal, and don't you worry about this little mite. You just enjoy yourselves.'

It was Rosie who had suggested looking after Joanna. 'It'll be good for you to be together without anyone else,' she said. 'I've already spoken to Queenie and she thinks it's a great idea to share looking after her. She's not at the factory on Sunday so she's having her then and bringing her back to me in the afternoon.'

Anna was surprised when Joe agreed to the weekend together without their baby. She told him in a letter, only saying that she could easily have Joanna taken care of while she was away.

Nevertheless she worried as she travelled to meet his train. It was the first time she had left the little girl, and although Joanna was used to both Rosie and Queenie, what if she fretted for her? Or was naughty and played them up? Or suddenly became ill ... Stop it, she told herself sternly, you've done it now and it isn't for long.

The time flew by. They stayed in a little hotel near Paddington Station, loved each other, talked, danced round the carpeted bedroom floor in their bare feet. 'I want to hold you in my arms even when we aren't, you know ...' Joe said, shyly, 'but here with just the two of us, not in a crowded dance hall.'

She gave him the latest snapshot of his daughter to take back with him. 'Rosie took it in her back garden; it was the last one on her film.' Too late she saw his expression harden, and realized how tactless she had been. Nevertheless he took the photograph from her and studied it.

'She's quite a little girl, doesn't look like a baby any more. But she's very pretty,' he added. 'I wish I could have seen her too, but the time's so short. Who's looking after her now?'

'Queenie's got her.'

'That's good. She's a tower of strength in Dason Street, is Queenie Parkes.'

Anna hoped he wouldn't pursue the subject, so she'd have to tell him that Rosie was also looking after their daughter while Queenie was at the factory on Saturday. He didn't. After three months away he really only wanted Anna.

They went up West for a meal. It was buzzing with activity, pleasurable activity. No lights were flashing the latest theatre news in Piccadilly, as she remembered from a long-ago childhood trip, but hundreds of people, it seemed to her, milling around, some dressed up to the nines, and others in uniform, sauntering, hurrying, singly, in groups, and in pairs, clinging together even as she and Joe were, as they jostled each other along the crowded pavements.

All too soon it was time to leave. She insisted on going to the station with him. 'I can get the tube or a bus home,' she said, 'and I do want to see you off properly.'

'Come on then, and next time I might get a forty-eight, or even more.' The bus to the station was crowded but someone stood up to give Anna a seat. Joe, strap-hanging and letting others move on down the bus, so he could stay near, watched her tenderly. She was so delicate, like a gentle flower, it made you want to protect her. This blooming war, separating them just as they were getting on their feet with a little house and a baby. Several people got off at the next stop, and Joe sat quickly into the vacated seat next to Anna. He slipped his arm into hers, and their fingers entwined. Gently he rubbed her wedding ring, and she laid her cheek against his and tried not to think that their little holiday was all but over.

The bus stopped with a terrific jerk, sending all the passengers, friends, lovers and strangers, into each others' arms.

'What the – you all right, Anna?'

'Yes.' Her voice sounded shaky. 'What is it – what's happened?'

They found out a few moments later, as they tumbled untidily from the bus, smelt the burning, saw the crater in the road, and the bodies strewn about.

'Oh, God.' Suddenly the place seemed full of people, wardens and rescue workers. An elderly policeman appeared, tape in his hands, to cordon off the road. He ushered them back the way they had just come. 'You'll have to walk or catch another, bus can't move now,' he said. Joe put his arm round Anna's shoulders. 'Come on luv, let's go.'

Stumbling over the debris and closing her mouth tightly against the dust that seemed to be all around them, she moved with him.

'Don't come up here while I'm away,' Joe said suddenly, 'and risk getting caught in a raid.'

'Of course I shan't. What would I come up for on me own?' she said sharply, the shock of the sudden devastation and the still, bloodstained figure she had almost stumbled over beginning to register and make her tremble.

They quarrelled over the hypothetical situation as they walked quickly the rest of the way. He held her hand, but there was no intimacy in it, no squeezing or stroking, no crooking little fingers together in a sudden ecstasy of delight. It was just the practicality of keeping together in the blackout.

When at last they reached King's Cross Joe took her in his arms and she sobbed, 'Joe, oh Joe, don't let's fight. I can't bear it.'

He turned her towards him and tenderly kissed her. 'I'm sorry, Anna my darling. It shook me too, but I shouldn't have taken it out on you. I suddenly realized that if the bus had been a few seconds earlier we would have been bang in the middle of that carnage and Joanna might have been an orphan.'

As the train carried him away back to Scotland he wanted to cry too. If only he could get her and Joanna up there with him, yet even as he thought it he knew it was an impossibility, for he obviously would be moved on eventually, and then what would happen to them?

The train rattled and puffed its way through the night. His travelling companions, two soldiers, an elderly woman with a man he presumed to be her husband, and a young Wren, settled themselves as comfortably as they could. The soldiers who were sitting the furthest from him, in the opposite corner, made brief conversation. 'Been on leave, mate?'

He nodded. 'Thirty-six hours. Not long enough.'

'Too right. Still, better than none at all.'

The woman and her husband huddled close together, and within minutes the man was asleep, while his wife looked round the carriage as though she were assessing everybody there. As her gaze rested on Joe she smiled, and he could suddenly see how she must have been as a young girl. The smile altered her features completely, seemed to take away the weariness in the wrinkles beneath her eyes and turn them into laughter lines. He smiled back. The Wren crossed her shapely legs, and gave him a definite 'come hither' look, and Joe was glad he was sitting opposite rather than next to her. He closed his eyes and thought about Anna, and gradually the rhythmic swaying of the train sent him to sleep.

When Anna reached home both Rosie and Queenie were in the house. 'Sorry I'm so late, there was a raid, a bomb, and it had only just happened when our bus came along, and – and we couldn't go any further, we had to walk.' She shivered at the memory of the scene.

'You all right?' Queenie said.

'Yes. We weren't involved, just caught in the aftermath. Joanna – she's not played you up?'

'Good as gold.' Rosie smiled at her. 'Joe all right?'

'Fine. And we're both very grateful to you—'

'Nonsense.' Rosie interrupted her. 'You need some time together while you can. We remember what it was like to be young, eh, don't we, Queenie?'

Queenie, whose marriage to Fred was so different from Rosie's to Jim, nevertheless quietly agreed. When they left Anna went upstairs and gazed at her daughter, who was fast asleep in her cot. They had made no plans for having her looked after should she be orphaned, and the night's terrifying experience had brought this possibility sharply home to her. Joe's brother in New Zealand was the only relative they had between them. If he and his wife didn't take her it would mean a children's home, and she didn't want that for Joanna. The child stirred and shifted a little, and Anna stood silently by the cot, tears streaming down her cheeks, as she faced the knowledge that sudden death was almost as likely for the civilian as it was for the military.

She slept very little that night, her mind darting between the joys of her wonderful weekend with Joe, and pictures of the scene when they left the bus. That body she had almost tripped over – she didn't even know whether it was a man or woman – only that one moment it had been like herself and Joe, alive, breathing and planning, and the next a lifeless heap amid the bricks and glass strewn over the road. When she did doze off for a while she woke with a sudden jerk and the smoke and smell of the bomb in her nostrils.

Joe's next trip home was a few weeks later. Embarkation leave. Joanna was now toddling and climbing everywhere, 'a right little pickle,' Anna said, and Joe was enchanted with her. Especially when she climbed on his knee and rubbed her soft little face against his. 'Daddy play,' she said. 'Daddy play Jo-Jo.' For the first few days they relaxed, and hardly emerged from the house, completely happy to simply be a family again.

Joe was to be home for two weeks. 'Two whole weeks, darling,' he said, 'with you and Joanna.' They returned from a walk in the park on the Monday of the second week to find a message through the door to the effect that Joe had to return to his unit immediately.

It was a tearful Anna who answered the door to Queenie that evening when she called by on her way to night shift at the factory.

'Gone back?' she echoed. 'Oh Anna, I am sorry.' She had actually come in to offer her services as baby-sitter on her changeover from nights to days on Wednesday, but tactfully didn't mention it when she learned Joe's leave had been cut in half.

All through August the Battle of Britain raged in the southern skies. One of Queenie's sons-in-law was in the Air Force, 'Thank God he hasn't had the sort of education needed to be a pilot,' her daughter, Ruby said. 'At least he stands a better chance at ground level. That's what I tell myself anyway, Mum, but we all know they're after the aerodromes, and I just pray every night that he'll come through. My nerves are getting so bad, I'm not sleeping, I'm shouting at the kids, and just lately I've been terrified I'll make a mistake at work and some of our boys will be killed or maimed as a result.'

'No, luv, that couldn't happen. It would be picked up by the inspector.' Queenie drew on her own factory experience to relieve her daughter over at least one of her worries. Ruby lived near Plymouth in Devon, her husband's county, and had come for the weekend with her two children, who were both older than Doris and Tom. Queenie tried to reassure her and give her a boost, while Fred, spearing a succulent piece of Yorkshire pudding on his fork, and full of beer from his lunchtime session at the Green Man said loudly, 'You women are all the same, worrying about things before they happen. He's having the time of his life I bet.' Which ruined the rest of the meal for everyone as Ruby pushed her chair back and ran sobbing from the room. Queenie, usually so placid, went for him then. 'You go right up and tell her you didn't mean that. Poor girl came here to find some sort of peace and comfort and you add to her worries with your stupid and untrue remarks. Go on then, go and apologize, and hope to God your daughter'll find it in her heart to forgive you.' Then she set about comforting her two granddaughters.

The weekend wasn't a great success, although Fred did mumble an apology and a retraction when Ruby came downstairs ten minutes later. 'It was the beer talking,' he said, trying not to look at his daughter's red-rimmed eyes. 'Of course he's not enjoying himself.' Then he sprawled out on the settee and went to sleep until opening time.

Queenie and Ruby went round to Jenny in Ebdon Street in the afternoon, but the sight of her sister's two girls brought such a stab of envy to Jenny, because her own children were miles away, that much of the old camaraderie they usually enjoyed, was missing.

'You're so lucky having the kids home with you,' she said.

'Well, you didn't have to send yours away, no one forced you.

In the end it was your own decision,' Ruby replied, and the tears that had been hovering perilously close all afternoon broke through and poured down Jenny's cheeks. The sisters made up before Ruby and Queenie left, and hugged each other emotionally.

'It's the war,' Ruby said, walking back with Queenie. 'We're all on edge and it doesn't take much to get us going. And to be fair I reckon if I was still living in London I'd have sent mine to the country for safety too.'

That night Queenie knelt by her bed for ages, saying a prayer for each one of her children and their families, and for everyone else she knew with someone in danger. At the end she added very quietly: 'and Paul, please God, look after Paul.' She was still on her knees when she heard the clatter downstairs. Fred was home from the pub.

Rosie set off early for market on Saturday 7 September. The lovely blue sky belied the fact that autumn was approaching, and she said to Jim: 'It feels like spring today, wonder if I'll need a coat?'

'Shouldn't think so.' He lifted the net curtain to look through the window, 'take your thick cardi instead; you can dump that in the basket if it's too much.'

The High Road was crowded, and she made for Blinking Billy's fish stall first. He'd been known as Blinking Billy since an eye operation in his teens had left him with a persistent blink. 'The girls used to think I was winking at 'em,' he often joked. 'Of course I let 'em go on thinking it. By the time they'd cottoned on that I couldn't help it they were hooked on me anyway ...'

'Hullo Rosie. Not much today.'

'Come on, don't give me that, Billy. I bet you've got a nice little titbit hidden away for your favourites, eh? And I do like a taste of fish at the weekend. Never been anywhere else but you for it, neither ...'

He tore a sheet of newspaper from a string hanging on a hook by his side, and ignoring the sad-looking specimens on the slab his hand dived into a bucket under the counter and deftly wrapped up a couple of small plaice.

'You're a pal, Billy. I'll bring you one of my bread-and-butter puddings next time I'm baking. Even if the butter is very thin marg.'

She went on round the stalls, laughing and joking with everyone she knew, and elated with the thought that there was fish for tea tonight, whatever sort it was, because she hadn't seen what Billy had wrapped up and smuggled to her. Bit of cod or plaice I shouldn't wonder at that price – Jim'll enjoy that.

She stopped to have a word with Fred Parkes at Johnny Gambol's greengrocery stall, more because he was Queenie's old man than out of any great liking for him. 'Don't need any veg just now, got some stuff in the garden,' she said, 'how's things?'

'Not too bad. We keep going.'

'That's the way.'

Rosie loved the bustle of the market, and in spite of the war it was as busy as ever. Fewer stalls, but those that were left were doing well when they could get the stuff to sell. By eleven o'clock her basket was satisfyingly full, she had chatted to all her pals and turned for home. At the bottom of Dason Street she met Anna and Joanna.

'Hullo, darling.' Bending her ample body to the level of the pushchair she stroked the little girl's soft cheek. 'How's my favourite sweetheart today, then?'

'Had a letter from her daddy today,' Anna said.

'He OK?'

'Yes. How are your boys?'

'Heard from Peter a few days ago, but nothing from Ricky. Mind, he's not much at writing, never was.' She leaned closer, 'Listen, if you want a bit of fish, gal, go and see Blinking Billy now. He's got some special stuff stowed away. Hold Joanna up in your arms so he can see her, never resist a kid, can Billy, and she's got the loveliest smile – charm the monkeys off the trees when she's older, I bet ...'

They parted, Anna making for the market, still smiling to herself at Rosie's words, and the older woman plodding on up the street. She was within half a dozen houses from her own when she saw the bike leaning against her gate – a telegraph boy's bike. She felt the colour drain from her face, felt dizzy as she almost ran the rest of the way. She saw the boy leap on his bike and pedal off away from her to the top of the road, and she found herself saying aloud, 'No, no, not the boys, oh God, please not my sons.'

Jim still had the telegram in his hand when she went indoors. Suddenly he looked small and old to her, and she braced herself to be strong for his sake.

'He's all right – a prisoner but all right.' His voice sounded hoarse, scarcely above a whisper, but great waves of joy swept through her and tears gushed into her eyes. 'Peter or Ricky?'

'Ricky. Here,' he handed her the telegram, 'it doesn't say much, but he's alive, Rosie, our boy's alive.' His arm came round her, and through the haze of her own brimming eyes Rosie saw that Jim was crying too.

'If that Hitler hurts our Ricky I'll murder him meself, I will,' she said against his chest, and Jim looked at his lovely, easygoing Rosie and burst out laughing.

Just before five o'clock that afternoon the siren went. The first reaction of most of the Dason Street folk was to step outside to see what was happening. Anna opened her front door to see Rosie and Jim opposite gazing into the sky. Within minutes she heard, and then saw the planes, it seemed like hundreds of them, coming towards them: a deadly flock of black ravens in the sky. She grabbed Joanna and whisked the child through the house and into the Anderson in the garden. There had been so much talk of invasion lately – was this it? Were they going to parachute the German army into London, or were these planes bombers? She had snatched her handbag from the chair as she went through, more by instinct than reasoning, and with the thought that at least she would have her ration book with her if the house was bombed.

The planes didn't drop their bombs on them, neither did they disgorge any parachutists. They droned on, and when, not long after six o'clock the all-clear sounded, Anna and a very frustrated Joanna emerged from the shelter, to find half of Dason Street once more outside their homes, and the evening sky lit with a curious red glow. Rosie came over to her. 'It's the docks, Anna, the blighters were after the docks, and they got 'em too, by the look of it.'

The siren sent Anna scuttling down the Anderson again that night, but well prepared, with drinks for both herself and Joanna, a tin of biscuits, and some blankets and pillows. The planes were coming all night, but they passed over Dason Street, and she emerged on the Sunday morning to listen to the devastating news on the wireless, that fires were still raging in dockland.

'Hundreds of incendiaries,' Rosie said, coming over to her later, 'and all that flammable stuff there. Hundreds dead too, poor devils, and those that have survived have lost their homes. Dozens of houses reduced to rubble ...' Tears filled her eyes and her huge body shook with emotion. 'And only yesterday I was feeling sorry for myself because of my Ricky, but at least he's alive, and I read somewhere that the Germans treat their prisoners OK, like we do. Well, they're all someone's sons, aren't they? Wherever they come from, they didn't start this bloody war.'

Chapter 6

1941

Paul Tranmer patted his pocket which held his letter to Queenie. Hardly a letter, he thought. Just a note. He wanted to post it in London, because he couldn't tell her he had been in England for the last two months. His training in Hampshire complete, he was starting a week's leave before his war began in earnest. He didn't know where he would be sent, nor what he would be doing. The thought had even crossed his mind that he might be followed and monitored. Not that he could have told anyone anything because his actual knowledge about what was happening and where was nil. He was hoping he could see Queenie during that week's leave. He wanted to take the memory of her with him wherever he was, and it was all of four years since they had met. He recalled the last occasion clearly as the train grumbled its way towards the capital. They had gone for a meal and he asked her yet again to leave her husband and come to Canada with him. All her children were married, most had children of their own now, and he really thought that this time she would say yes. His grief over her refusal kept him roaming Canada for a considerable time, seeking new scenes in the hope of blocking the chasm….

As the train rattled onwards his thoughts went back to the first time they met. There had been other girls before, but none that had wowed him as she did. He knew he had to see her again, and again, and again. Every week he went back to the shop where she worked and bought something. His mother must have thought it was her birthday when he visited each week and took her scarves, gloves, blouses ... mind, she soon cottoned on, he thought. 'When you going to bring her home, son?' she asked him one day.

Deciding to be frank and avoid a lot of awkwardness he'd replied, 'I'm not sure. You see she's a married woman.'

He was totally unprepared for her reaction. Her face seemed to alter physically, the skin tightening drastically as though she had stretched it as far as it would go.

'I see. In the whole of London can't you find an unattached female to take up with?'

'Of course I can, but you don't arrange who you fall in love with, it just happens.'

'Never heard such rubbish in all my born days. To think a son of mine could break up a marriage, and be so calm and matter of fact about it too. Do you think it doesn't matter, eh? Because I'm telling you it does, Paul.'

'Hey, steady on, Ma, what's got into you? I haven't broken up her marriage, it was already on the rocks—'

'And you believe that? You honestly believe that?' She had stood watching him, her floral wrapover pinafore hiding the smart navy skirt she was wearing; the collar of her clean white blouse showing at her neckline.

'Well of course I do, because it's true.'

A dark angry flush was showing on her cheeks when she turned away. 'Make sure you *don't* bring her home then, because she wouldn't be welcome in this house.'

She had walked quickly out of the room and into the kitchen. He went to follow her, then thought better of it. Never had he seen his mother in such a tizz. She simply did not have displays of temper like this. He would wait until she had calmed down a bit.

But Mrs Tranmer didn't calm down. Two days later when he called in she was tight-lipped and bright-cheeked, answering when he spoke, but not making conversation. On his next visit he gave her a large picture-box of chocolates.

'You won't win me round that way,' she said, returning them to the table.

'Good heavens, Ma, I'm not trying to win you round. They're by way of an apology for upsetting you.'

For a moment she turned eagerly towards him, then the anger returned to her face. 'An apology for upsetting me, Paul? Not an apology for the thing you're doing? Well, you can take them back, because I don't want them.' She marched off into the kitchen.

This time Paul followed her and, placing his hands on her shoulders, from his superior height he easily spun her round to face him. 'Now what is all this? I'm sorry I told you now, but how on earth was I to know you'd react in this way. We do no harm to anyone, nothing's happened and it won't until she's free to come to me. Her husband doesn't care and she and the children would have a better life with me – at least I'd never knock her ab—'

'*Children*? She has a family and still you're pursuing her? I'm ashamed of you Paul, ashamed and disgusted. How do you know that if it wasn't for you she and her husband would make a go of their lives. Who do you think you are to set yourself up as such a paragon. Have a better life with you, indeed; you make me sick. My own son a marriage wrecker ...' To his amazement tears welled in her eyes, and she ran from the kitchen and up the stairs to her bedroom.

To Paul, sitting on the train taking him nearer to London and Queenie every minute, that scene with his mother didn't seem so long ago. He found out the reason for her anger from his sister. It seemed he had been reared on a lie. He had believed his mother was a widow, that his father died when he was still a babe in arms and his sister a schoolgirl. The truth was that his father had left her for another woman. Ruth, of course, ten years older than he, remembered their father, although she had not seen him from the day he left.

'Don't for heaven's sake let on that you know,' Ruth had begged. 'She's so proud, she'd hate for you to catch her out in a lie.' He never had, he loved her too much for that, and she went to her grave three years later believing he still thought his father had died when he was a baby. Neither of them ever mentioned Queenie again.

He looked through the windows as the miles flashed by. Rows of terraced houses, washing hanging on lines in the back gardens, allotments lush with sturdily growing vegetables, here and there a child's swing, a cat stretched out on a path in total relaxation, and he said a silent prayer for his country that he loved so much, closely followed by an even more fervent one for the woman he loved.

He had every one of her letters back home in Canada. All of them in answer to his – she never wrote to him on her own initiative. Perhaps she wouldn't even see him this time, after all four years had passed. He hadn't intended returning: with Ma dead, Queenie not willing to leave the life she knew, there seemed little point. Although fond enough of his sister, she had grown up and married while he was still a schoolboy so the pull wasn't there.

Yet the pull of London was. He discovered this when he thought about joining up in Canada, and realized that he wanted to come home and belong to a British regiment. Suddenly it became tremendously important to get back to England, to be in the fray, to be part of the community again. Strange how things worked out though, he thought, because if he hadn't gone to Mary and John's party that night he wouldn't have seen Albert Duplock who suggested, not in so many words of course, that he was exactly what the SOE were looking for. Because of his French great-grandmother on his mother's side, who had taught him the language when he was very young, and his thirst for knowledge which caused him to pursue it at night school later when he was older and she long since in her grave, here he was, his training finished, and raring to go.

He had left his affairs in order back there in Canada, just in case, and there was only one thing more - to see his beloved Queenie again. And who knows, he thought, as the train spat and billowed its way into Waterloo Station, she may decide enough is enough regarding her marriage, and come to me at last. And if she doesn't want to live in Canada, then I'll move back home after the war. I've done well enough and can afford to stop chasing work so much, I reckon. Grinning to himself he stood up and gathered his luggage together. I can always have a stall in the market again, just for a bit of pocket money and to keep me out of her hair. It all hinges on Queenie, and the One Above, he thought, as he stepped on to the platform at Waterloo.

Queenie was always downstairs before Fred in the mornings. There were three letters on the mat that particular day. Scanning the writing and postmarks quickly she saw one was from Edna, her eldest daughter, who had married a miner before the war and lived in South Wales. The bright-orange envelope was from an old school-friend she sometimes met in the West End for a meal and a show, but it was the third letter that made her heart seem to turn somersaults. Paul Tranmer was an old love who still came into her life from time to time, and never left her heart. Usually he wrote to her care of her friend Marie's address, he must have wanted her to get this without any delay for him to send it here. She took them all into the kitchen with her and after tucking Paul's letter inside her handbag she made a cup of tea and opened the other two.

Her daughter said she would be coming to London for a quick visit next week. Her friend had written a chatty letter about life in the factory where she worked, and the funny situations she got into. Queenie laughed as she read the four and a half pages of comical near disasters. Marie had been forever in scrapes during their schooldays, but there was no better person to have behind you when you were up against it. Strange she should have heard from her today, when there was also a letter from Paul. As she prepared breakfast she recalled the time she had almost left Fred for Paul; Marie had been involved in that episode in her life too.

It was several hours later before she had a chance to open her letter in relative privacy. Although she was alone in the house she took it to the bathroom and locked the door. You never knew when Fred would come roaring in, and if she was downstairs and he was in a mood, he'd likely snatch it from her hand. 'And then God help us,' she said aloud.

Queenie loved her bathroom – it represented luxury. In her childhood home in Ebdon Street they had never had one – none of the houses did – and the lavatory was at the end of the yard. Many was the time she had almost left it too late on dark nights because she was scared of what she called 'the night things', and sitting on the scrubbed wooden seat she would be holding her breath against eerie sounds and feathery wisps brushing her face. Her greatest fear had been spiders. She could still remember how frightened she had been of them. Strange how when you had children of your own you faced your fears so you wouldn't pass them on and make them afraid too; in doing that for the kids she had conquered them for herself.

To this day one of the favourite rooms in her house was the bathroom. Even on a cold winter night it soon warmed through and the smell of the steam as she wallowed in hot water in a bath with plenty of room made her feel like a film star. Not that the tin bath in front of the fire in the kitchen in Ebdon Street had been anything but warm and cosy. Too cosy for her long legs once she'd passed six or seven years old, and much too public for her liking. She had been in and out as quickly as possible in those days, but here, in a proper bathroom, she really enjoyed that half-hour. She always took her bath when Fred was out of the house so she wouldn't have to rush because he needed to come in, yet in spite of this she still locked the door. The wonderful feeling of privacy it gave her never failed to thrill. For thirty minutes or so she could be alone. Now, however, she hadn't gone to that lovely private place for a bath, simply for the security of being able to lock the door and read her letter quietly and in secret. As she pushed the bolt on the door the safety of her haven enveloped her, and she lowered the lid of the lavatory seat, sat down and opened her letter.

The sight of Paul's strong handwriting made her quiver with love. He had come into her life only a few years after her marriage to Fred: a chance meeting when she had been working for Isaac in the dress shop. He'd seen a frock in the window which 'looked exactly right for my dear old mum', he'd later confided to her. Without preamble he had asked the size and price. 'I'll take it. Make sure there's no price tags left on and wrap it up nice, will you?' She saw him studying her as she complied and was embarrassed. Old Isaac kept a tear-off roll of gift paper and another of pretty ribbon attached to the side of the counter, and in reaching for it she knocked a large pair of scissors on to the floor. They clashed as they both bent to retrieve them. With their lips only a kiss away from each other strange physical feelings raced through her body. Paul recovered first, and held out his hand to help her up. 'My fault,' he said. 'You aren't hurt, are you?'

Dearest, the letter began, *when can we meet? I have to go away next weekend and I desperately want to see you before then. Drop me a line and I'll fit in with whatever time and place you say....*

She stood up, her face flushed with emotion.

*

It had been four years since she'd seen him, just before the coronation of the king and queen in 1937. 'You're *my* queen, darling,' he'd said, 'you always will be.' He asked her again to leave Fred – she allowed the scene to fill her mind now. 'Canada, sweetheart – I've got contacts there and you could have a nice house, a car, a different sort of life ...' But the thought of leaving Britain was too much. She would miss seeing the grandchildren grow up, and although they no longer needed her as they had when they were young, she knew she would miss all her daughters too much.

Paul had made money. He began with a stall in Portobello Road Market, 'dabbling in antiques', and had gone on to a crowded little shop near Victoria Station.

After that first encounter when they had literally bumped into each other, he returned to Isaac's shop once a week and bought something from her. They fell in love. It happened instantly for him, he told her much later in their affair, but for her it had been a gradual blossoming. The seed was sown in that first impact – no man had made her skin tingle in that way before, or set her pulses burning with desire, but, realistic as always, she recognized that this was equivalent to a crush on Clark Gable or Ronald Coleman, both screen heroes to her. After all, she told herself, she had never been as close to either of them as she had to Paul when she dropped the scissors. They, and he, were the unattainables.

The unfolding of her love was gentle. Each week she wondered what day he would come and what he would say.

It was a month before he asked her to have lunch with him. 'I bring sandwiches,' she said, and because she couldn't bear to be less than honest, 'and I'm married.'

He smiled and glanced towards her hands. 'Yes, I noticed that, but I'm only asking you to spend half an hour or so with me in public. I'd like to talk to you and I can't do that while you're on duty, now can I?'

They'd threaded their way through the market stalls set up in the street outside the shops, stopping to buy a couple of sandwiches for himself from Deaf Bert, then on to the park and a seat in an alcove sheltered by a plane tree.

That's when the dye was cast, she thought. After that there never has been a going-back point in my feelings.

Now, with his brief note in her hand, her mind was back in the exciting love-flooded days that followed. Because in spite of everything, his love had given her the ecstasy that was missing before they met.

On that first occasion, after eating their food, they talked, and she discovered that Paul was a man with an erudite mind and an ambition. 'To be the best, after all what's the point in learning anything if you aren't going to do well with it. I didn't know much about antiques when I started, but I've learnt as I've gone along, and I've prospered.' In spite of the economic climate before the war, Paul made a very good living. 'There's always someone wanting and someone clearing,' he told her, 'and I'm the boy to bring the two together. They all know I'll play fair with them and they trust me.'

Her fingers trembled now as she held the letter within reading distance once more. It gave his sister's address in Paddington as a place for her to get in touch. She had been there with him once, many years ago. Where could he be going next weekend? Not to war, surely, he was as old as Fred. Perhaps he was returning to Canada and wanted to give her the chance to get away from the dangers here, but she knew she would never go with him now. She wouldn't desert everything and everybody.

Carefully she folded the sheet of paper and replaced it in the envelope. She laid it on the seat while she splashed her face with cold water, and remembered the time when she had considered leaving Fred and her life here behind and throwing in her lot with Paul Tranmer.

The youngest of her four daughters had been nine years old, and Fred, returning drunk from the pub, had hit her when she refused his advances. 'Denying me my conjugal rights,' he slurred, slumping over the bed.

'You're not in a fit state for any rights. Come on, I'll give you a hand to get to bed.' She began to unbutton his shirt. The blow he aimed wildly caught her just below her left eye. She reeled backwards, stunned for several seconds, before staggering into the bathroom where she was violently sick.

Fred had often been drunk before, but had never struck her. She knew a lot of the men round about here did knock their wives about, and she always maintained to herself that it was something she would not tolerate. Drunkenness, meanness, even stealing money from her purse – 'borrowing' he called it, she took in her stride and coped with, but physical violence was the bottom line ...

Paul had come into the shop two days afterwards, when one side of her face was a hotchpotch of purple and yellow bruising.

'What the hell—'

'I walked into a door,' she said, too quickly. 'Nice mess, isn't it?'

'It bloody well is.' It was the first time she'd heard Paul swear. 'I'll get him for this, by God I will. Here, let me look.'

'Paul,' she said, embarrassed as he moved round the counter and gently began examining her face with caressing hands, 'don't. Someone might come in.'

'You don't deny that your – your husband,' he almost spat the word out, 'did this then?'

'I – no, all right, I won't deny it to you, but to everyone else I walked into the front door.'

A customer put paid to any further discussion, but she agreed to meet him in the park at lunchtime. He had calmed down by then, but he had also worked out a plan.

'Leave him, Queenie, I'll look after you and the kids, that's a promise. You'd never have to be parted from them, I give you my word.'

Her first reaction was a definite no. 'I've made my bed,' she said, thinking even then what an apt description that was. But Paul persisted. Gently, nicely, just letting her know all the while that he was there, loving her, and offering her and the children a home.

'Just come and look,' he said one day. 'It's not posh, but it's clean and there's three bedrooms, a decent kitchen, a bathroom and a bit of garden. And it's mine; it could be ours.'

She had gone to look and fallen in love with the house in Leytonstone.

'Well?' His eyes were full of love.

'I don't know, Paul. Fred is my husband, and—'

'And he knocks you about.'

'He's never done anything like that before, he was drunk that night.'

Paul had held her hand in his. 'And what if he gets drunk again?'

'He'll get drunk' she replied, 'but he won't have the chance to take it out on me again. I'll see to that.'

'Queenie, you know I love you.' His face was close to hers, his breathing coming rapidly in short bursts of power. 'Darling, I need you, there'll never be another woman for me.'

As their lips met she had given herself up to the thrill of his kiss, and when his fingers felt the contour of her breasts beneath the thin blouse she shivered with delight.

She went to him the next weekend, and Marie had the children. It was the only time she lied to Fred over anything that mattered. She told him she was spending the weekend with her friend Marie and she banked on his usual lack of interest for him not to ask the children if they had all stayed together. It had been a wonderful two days: the loving, the sharing, the companionship, the sheer joy in being together. He had walked to the tram with her when she was leaving to collect the children from Marie's. 'I love you so much Queenie,' he said. 'That will never change, whatever you decide. I'll do anything and everything in my power to make you happy. You know that though, don't you?'

Fred came home from the pub that night and lashed out at her again, but she dodged out of the way in time. When he'd sobered up next morning he said, 'I hit you again last night, didn't I, Queen?'

'You missed.'

'I'm glad. I bin trying those fancy fags Artie Alec's bin selling. They're drugged, Queen. I didn't know that at first. It's the last time though. I know I'm a bit of a bounder, but I wouldn't 'urt yer Queen. You're me missus and you're a good 'un.'

In the end it was a lot of small things that stopped her going to Paul. She knew Fred would still get drunk most nights, would spend all her money if he could find it, and would continue to lead his own selfish life. But he had drawn the line at drugs – she knew a lot of the Chinese population down in Soho smoked opium and most vices could be bought for a price in some of the pubs Fred frequented. Yet, in his own way, he had not meant to strike her, had even been sorry for doing so. Crikey, she thought, to a lot of the women round here a beating's a fact of life. She had seen so much of it as she did her unofficial rounds. The children were all right. If he laid a finger on any of them she'd be off like a shot.

She told Paul as they sat on their favourite secluded seat in the park at lunchtime the following day: 'I do love you Paul, but I'm not coming. I'd have to live with my conscious for the rest of my life, and I can't do it.'

'So it's goodbye, then?'

She lowered her head. 'Yes. Find someone else, Paul. Someone who's free to love you.'

'Don't talk bloody daft,' he said, reverting to his roots, 'there'll never be anyone but you.' Standing up abruptly he went on, 'You know where to find me should you need to – any time.' She heard the catch in his voice and looked up. For a few seconds their eyes seemed to talk to each other, then he bent down and covered her lips with his. Drowning in his kiss, she closed her eyes, and as suddenly as he had started, he stopped. Then he walked away.

She sat on for a while, trying to compose herself before returning to the shop, trying not to think about how much she loved him. She had sent him away. For a brief time she had glimpsed what it could be like; another life, a life of loving and being loved completely, physically and mentally. But it was too late for her, one husband and four children too late ...

For many months life had been bleak, then a letter arrived from Canada. It wasn't a love letter, but it contained an address, his sister's address in London. 'I've let the house in Leytonstone,' he said, 'but if you are in trouble any time you can go here, to my sister Ruth, and she'll help.' He went on to describe his life in Canada, where he had found work in a store. 'The antiques are a bit different here from the ones in the Portobello Road,' he wrote, 'but I'm enjoying the job and the country.' A few months afterwards another letter arrived. 'I've moved on,' he wrote, 'want to see as much as I can. It's a great country and a wonderful antidote to my heart problems.' She smiled at the implication, guessing he had put it that way in case Fred saw the letter.

She wrote back, care of his sister, and giving Marie's address as a safe one to write to. He did this when he returned to England the following year, and they met under the clock at Victoria Station. Although they didn't fall into each other's arms immediately, she knew nothing had changed. His presence was magic, and his eyes told her it was the same for him. He stayed for a couple of months, during which time they met most lunchtimes, and once at his sister's house. 'So you two will know each other,' he said as he introduced them.

There were no traumatic goodbyes when he went back because Jenny had measles, and she had written, care of his sister, cancelling their last meeting.

Marie said later, 'Why didn't you tell me? I'd have come over and sat with her,' but she shook her head sadly. 'It's wrong, see, Marie – and I'm being stopped.'

'Stopped?'

'When a thing's not meant—'

'Piffle.'

She laughed then for the first time since he had gone. 'Maybe, but I can't help it. It's the way I'm made. What about the kids if things didn't work out? I haven't enough money to get a house. On my own I'd be off like a shot, Marie.'

He wrote from Canada, this time giving her an address there.

I've had enough wandering, it's time I settled down, so I've got me a little house and I'm back to square one by being in business on my own again, dabbling in antiques, and brushing up my French that I learnt from Gran Dupont, Mum's grandmother. Did I ever tell you I had French connections? (That's meant to be a joke, sweetheart!) Mind, I was proud of my other language, because she said I spoke it well, and I was fond of the old girl. She lived with us for a bit when I was a kid.

I'm making money too, Queenie. I'll send you the fare any time you say the word....

The letters hadn't been so frequent since the war had begun. She always answered them, telling him about London, the markets, and as much of what she was doing as she thought it wise for him to know.

77

*

Four years was a long time to be away and it was strange for him to be over here now when he could be safe in Canada. She smiled to herself. When had Paul ever thought about safety? Early in their relationship he had wanted to come to Dason Street himself and talk to Fred, 'man to man'. 'I'm not ashamed of my love for you, these things happen. If you were happily married I'd have to go away and try to forget, but you're not and we love each other.' He listened to her pleading not to rock the boat. Smiling he had snatched a kiss. 'I'm not making any promises, mind, but I won't come tonight.'

Guiltily Queenie dragged her thoughts back to the present, and, tucking the letter into her overall pocket she wondered if it would be wise to see him again. With grandchildren evacuated, and everyone else so busy on war work she only had Fred to consider, and he hadn't really considered her since the day they married.

Queenie answered Paul's letter care of his sister's address. 'Dear Paul, I'm free Saturday afternoon. Half past two under the clock at Victoria Station. Don't write if this arrangement suits you, and I'll be there. My love, Queenie.' She dropped the letter into the pillar box on the corner of Grey Street later that morning, and after re-reading his note she put that in her handbag.

She had known in her heart that she would go, yet she had put off writing over the weekend, telling herself to leave things alone, to let sleeping dogs lie. Today was Tuesday – only four days to go and what was four days compared to four years. That was a long time to be apart. Would he have changed? Had *she* changed? There had been moments when she wished with all her heart that she had said yes and gone to Canada with him on that last occasion: moments of longing and yearning for his arms about her, for his lips on hers. Queenie had long ago given up thinking of this as wicked. She had tried to do the right thing when her family were young, yet when she had been as free to go as she would ever be she jibbed. Made excuses to herself, cowardly excuses; it would be a strange environment, a cold country – she had always felt the cold so, but what had influenced her decision most of all was being apart from her beloved daughters and grandchildren.

Yet the ache in her heart had not abated. Perhaps it had grown less, yes, surely it had. Certainly she hadn't been pining away during these empty years, and there had been letters. Not many, usually one around Easter time, one at the end of summer, another at Christmas and always one near her birthday in February.

Not love letters. Well, only just, some of them. Friendly letters, but with love in them. Letters that told her about his life, what he'd been doing, the places he'd visited and what he thought of them. She often took them out when she was alone and visualized his house in Canada, his friends whom he described so vividly. She pictured him there, going about his business, sitting at the table by the window to write to her, and looking out now and then at the maple trees, the lawn, and the flowers. *Bet you never thought I'd turn into a gardener,* he wrote, *not a very good one, but I haven't killed too many plants off yet. I wish you could see it my darling ...* She cherished the endearments, they seemed to bring him close. He always finished, *My love as ever ...*

Perhaps now he was going to tell her he was married, or getting married. Well, she had tried to persuade him along these lines for years; she stifled the pain that suddenly filled her being. She had had her chance and opted to stay with her husband and family. If now it was too late, so be it.

Queenie's letter arrived at Paul's sister on Wednesday morning. Half past two on Saturday, under the clock at Victoria Station. He breathed happily again. At the back of his mind had been the nasty thought that she might have decided not to disturb things. He knew how she liked a peaceful life.

He went to Bond Street to look at jewellery, and was shocked by the prices. He didn't begrudge the money he would spend on Queenie, but there wasn't anything that took his fancy to such a degree as to warrant the prices asked. So he went to Hatton Garden, where in the old days he had known so many of the dealers.

He knew what he wanted, something good and classy looking. A watch or bracelet or necklace – not a ring though. Something she could wear without questions being asked. A ring, he hoped, would come later and they could choose it together.

He found something very quickly: a sapphire teardrop pendant on a gold chain. It would enhance the blue of her eyes, he'd noticed how brilliant they became when she wore that shade. He had never bought her anything expensive before. Once, when he wanted to, they had quarrelled about it. She said it was wrong and she wouldn't accept anything. He felt a stab of happiness inside him then when he realized that in spite of her beliefs, which he knew to be so strong, she hadn't cut him out of her life when she decided to stay with her husband. It had given him hope then that one day ...

Fred was down in the market, he had taken on more stalls for Johnny Gambol at various other markets during the week, but still did the High Road on a Saturday. Queenie was pleased and surprised when he told her about the extra work, one evening before going round to the pub.

'Well, his sons and daughters 'ave gone off and joined up, better do my bit an' keep the business going for 'im', he mumbled. Not that she saw much of the extra money, *that* kept his two locals in business, as well as Johnny Gambol, she thought wryly. She set off now for the bus stop by the Green Man.

Anna was scrubbing her front step. 'Hullo, Queenie. You're about early for a Saturday?'

'Yes, going up town today. How's little 'un?'

'Fine. Think she's going to be an athlete when she grows up, she's pretty fast, and climb, you wouldn't believe?'

Queenie laughed. 'With three brothers and four girls of my own I would, y'know. She not "helping" you with the step today I see?'

'No, she's in the garden playing with her dolls. We're so lucky having this place with a garden. I'd hate to live down the other end, it's not that I'm stuck up, well I don't think I am – but it's so dowdy, and the houses are smaller and no gardens, just a tiny backyard. I love this little house, Queenie. Joe and I always thought we would try and buy it one day, make it really ours.'

'That's what I – we did. Gives you a secure feeling, Anna. Then later Fred built the conservatory on. I moan about him sometimes but he's a good workman. Never get the weather in, he reinforced it and it's real nice.' She was going to say he'd give Joe a hand after the war if all their plans came off, but she thought better of it. God forbid that anything should happen to Joe, but he was out there in the front line and a lot of them weren't going to come home. Anyway, you never knew with Fred either, he could be an awkward cuss when he wanted to, probably wouldn't agree because she'd suggested it. She became aware of Anna's voice. 'Sorry love, I was thinking. What did you say?'

'I asked if you'd like a cuppa.'

'No thanks, I must be off. I'll see you tomorrow.'

She looked back before she turned the corner at the top of Dason Street, and saw Rosie hurrying across to number 5. Smiling to herself she pictured her having that cup of tea she herself had refused, and asking Anna where Queenie was going, all dressed up. Not much that went on this end of the street missed Rosie's eyes. She always knew who had anything from a new sofa to a new baby, who had callers, men or women, who owed money to the tallyman and who had a bit tucked away. Yet in spite of her nosiness, Queenie liked the woman. She had a big heart, and she made no secret of the fact that she wanted to know what was going on. Dason Street was her world and she kept tabs on her little area of it.

Victoria Station was buzzing with people. Service men and women and civilians, some rushing about and some standing and waiting. She took a deep breath, held her stomach in and pushed her shoulders back as she made her way to the centre, under the clock.

Paul was there. She saw him before he saw her and she marvelled at how little he had changed. She would have known him anywhere. His eyes looked in her direction just before she reached him, and he rushed forward and clasped her hands firmly in his. 'Queenie, my dear.'

Outside the station he bought a tiny bunch of violets to nestle against her breast, gently pinning them on to her floral dress.

'Good luck to you.' The cheerful flower-seller gave them a beaming smile as she gathered more bunches from her basket to wave at likely-looking customers. 'Vi'lets, loverly vi'lets, sixpence a bunch ...'

Sitting in Lyons Corner House half an hour later, with a cup of tea and a bun each, he said quietly, 'Thank you for coming, Queenie. How are the family?'

'They're all OK. Jenny's two are evacuated to Wiltshire. They love it. Jenny and I have been down to see them.' She shook her head at him. 'I couldn't live there, Paul, nothing but fields and cows.'

His laugh made several other diners look over and she flushed, feeling embarrassed. 'Sorry, love, but it sounded so funny. Years ago I daresay I'd have thought the same, but I've seen both town and country now, here and abroad, and they've each their own appeal.'

'D'you reckon you'll ever come back to England to live, Paul?'

'Someday I guess. I've made friends in Canada, Queenie, more especially since I've bought the house and stayed in one place, but there are times I hanker for home. Which is why I'm here now really.'

'How come?'

'I couldn't be safe over there when my country was at war. It didn't feel right, know what I mean? I've done my fair share of moaning about the old place in my time, but I reckon I didn't know how much London meant to me 'til I went away. Anyway I wanted to see you again.'

She felt a warm glow inside her. He did still care. She had never stopped caring. Although she sent him away all those years ago when the children were young, and refused to leave Fred and take a chance with him in Canada later, the caring had gone on. It went against all her principles, all she believed in, all she had tried to teach her children about loyalty and truth. Always there had been this part of her life, the part that loved Paul. The one occasion when they had consummated their love had stayed in her heart as fresh as the morning after. She did everything she could for Fred to ensure his life ran smoothly, she cooked and cleaned, washed and ironed, did everything except love him. And that was something you couldn't force. It was something that came as a bonus to living, she thought now, this wonderful rainbow called love.

'You haven't got to rush back, have you?' Paul was saying.

'No, I suppose not. I don't go back to the factory until Monday, and I told Fred I wouldn't be back until tonight.' She knew he would be down the pub by then anyway.

'Let's walk, shall we? Go to all the old places, have dinner somewhere nice, how about the Savoy ...' She raised her eyebrows and laughed. 'You won the pools or something, Paul?'

He reached across the table and enclosed her hand within his, 'I'm not short of a bob, Queenie. You know I've always worked hard, and I've not wasted my money, gal. If you'd like dinner at the Savoy, or tea at the Ritz it's OK by me.'

She shook her head. 'Not really. Just somewhere we can talk and catch up on the years.'

They left Lyons and caught a bus to Trafalgar Square. The sun was shining, and Queenie thought if it wasn't for so many different service uniforms around London you wouldn't know there was a war on right now.

The same thoughts hadn't occurred to Paul. 'Seems strange to see women manning the buses,' he said, tucking her arm into his as they sat down and a cheerful cockney clippy came for their fare.

Nelson was still at the top of his column, and Paul began to sing softly, 'I live in Trafalgar Square, With four lions to guard me,' and very quietly she joined in the old music hall song, her arm tucked into his, and her body warm with his nearness ... 'If it's good enough for Nelson, Then it's quite good enough for me.' As they turned to each other, laughing, his lips sought hers, and there among the hurrying crowds and noisy pigeons it was as though they were on a deserted island.

They sauntered down the Mall and into St James's Park. 'Let's sit awhile,' he said. 'I want to look at you.'

They found a secluded spot beneath the trees and she sat hugging her knees to her chin, while he sprawled beside her. 'You are so beautiful, Queenie, and I love you very much.'

Pressing her chin further into her knees she said, 'Nonsense, Paul. I may have been once, but now – well I'm not young any more, I'm a grandmother, I've grey hairs and wrinkles ...'

Suddenly he sat up, his gaze still steadfast on her face. 'Not so many, and what do they matter anyway? It's what you are that counts, and what you are shines from your eyes. If we live to be a hundred you'll still be beautiful to me.'

She punched him playfully. 'What's brought all this on, then? You been seeing too many of them Hollywood films?'

He sat up and put his arms round her, and her responses were as passionate as his. 'Queenie, I'm staying with my sister this week. She'll be out this afternoon and she's given me a key ...'

She answered his question without words, and when he released her she said breathlessly, 'When are you going back to Canada, Paul?'

'I don't know. I've a job to do here first. I can't tell you about it, Queenie. Let's just say I'm joining up. I may not even go back after the war. That could depend on you.'

Her earlier thoughts that he had come to tell her he was married wavered, 'Is there no one in Canada Paul? No one you – you care for?'

'No, my darling. Oh, there've been one or two dalliances. I've not been celibate these past years, but they all fall short of you and me Queenie. I love you, I have done ever since that day in old Isaac Solomon's shop, remember?'

They left the park and walked down to Buckingham Palace. 'Canada,' she said softly. 'You know there was talk of the princesses going to Canada, Paul, but the Queen said she wouldn't let them go without her, and she wouldn't go without the King, and "The King won't leave his people." It gives you a thrill to hear things like that, Paul. I've thought, since this little lot began, how glad we should be that his brother abdicated. He wasn't a patch on the man and woman there now, God bless 'em.'

Ignoring her diversion he said, 'I think you'd like Canada, it's very clean. But if you didn't, or if you missed your kids or England too much, we'd come back. Don't forget I'm a Londoner too, even if I have lived so far away.'

They went by taxi to Paddington where Ruth, Paul's sister, had a flat in an elegant eighteenth-century house in one of the squares. Queenie was silent as he unlocked the door and stood aside for her to enter. The last time she had been here was when he introduced her to Ruth in case she needed a refuge all those years ago. Ruth had shown her round the place on that occasion. There was a neat hallway, two bedrooms, a kitchen, bathroom, and very pleasant sitting room which looked down into the tree-lined square. She knew his sister's husband had died very young. They'd had no children and she had not remarried.

'Are you sure your sister won't mind, Paul?'

His hands were on her shoulders, his lips tantalizingly close. 'Quite sure. She offered me the key when she knew I was meeting you.'

'Oh.'

'Darling, it's been so long ...' His arms encircled her, and she knew her need was as great as his as he gently led her to his bedroom.

He gave her the pendant just before they went for a meal in the evening.

'Paul, I can't take this.'

'Why not? In all these years I've never given you a present. I'd like to think of you wearing it sometimes, darling. Please. Here, let me fasten it.'

His lips brushed her hair as he fumbled with the clasp of the chain, then slowly turning her to face him he looked at the deep blue stone lying against the creaminess of her neck. His fingers touched the hollow between her breasts and her warm hand came up to cover his. 'Paul.'

'Yes.' He felt the swift rise and fall of her breathing and they were in each other's arms again.

They went to a restaurant in Edgware Road for a meal afterwards.

'Used to be a nice Italian one on the right down here,' he said.

'Be gone now, Paul. They rounded the Ities up in June 1940 when Mussolini went in with Hitler. Most of them hadn't taken out British nationality and they were all lumped together as "undesirable aliens". A lot of them are on the Isle of Man for the duration, I think.'

'Of course. I did read something about that. Guess I'm a bit out of touch, luv. Seems stupid though; I mean, some of them were born here, and so were their parents. I remember the lovely ice cream from Luigi's down the High Road when we were kids. Gosh, I can almost taste it now. It was scrumptious. He made the best ice cream for miles around.'

'We used to go there too, whenever we had a halfpenny to spend. Used to try to get the old man to serve us, he always piled the cornet high for us kids. Had to lick it quick before it melted and ran down the sides.' Suddenly she was serious. 'People are so easily swayed, Paul. The things they did when Italy sided with the Germans. Smashing the windows in and shouting abuse, in some places even knocking the poor devils about. Yet these were the people we'd all dealt with for years, the kids went to school together, my children brought the younger Luigi's nippers home to play – my grandchildren brought the next generation home. It doesn't make sense. These people weren't our enemies, they were our friends. They hadn't lived in Italy for years, some of them never.'

They stopped to look at a menu in the window of an English restaurant. 'You'd think the authorities would have had some method of discrimination,' Paul said, 'instead of herding them all away, good and bad alike.'

'People thought they were *all* spies, but they weren't, least the ones round our way weren't. But they took them away ...' her voice and eyes suddenly filled with tears.

'Hey,' he said, 'we're celebrating, remember.' He took out his handkerchief and tenderly dabbed her eyes. 'Even without tears you can't see this menu very well, can you? Let's go inside and look at it properly.'

'That wasn't a bad meal,' Paul said, when they had satisfied their hunger and were once more outside on the pavement.

'The steak-and-kidney pie was out of this world,' she

answered, 'like I used to make, but I wouldn't dare put as much meat as that in one now. Crikey, I reckon there was nearly a week's ration in it.'

Paul insisted on taking her home, in spite of her protestations that there was no need. He told her he didn't know when he'd be in London again, 'but I'll be in touch darling, the moment I've some free time. That all right with you?'

'Yes Paul, but I still think I'm not good for you. You need someone who'll be with you every day, not once every three or four years, you need—'

'I need you,' he interrupted, 'and in view of the circumstances now, the war and everything, it's best like this. Afterwards, well, we'll see, shall we? There'll be time to talk again then if we both come through.'

'Paul, are you – I know you said you couldn't tell me anything, but will you be in danger with what you'll be doing?'

'Of course. But from what I can see of it we're all in danger all the time. Up here, anyway. No one's immune, Queenie luv. I guess I'll be in no more danger, if as much, as you are every time the warning goes. Now come on, let's have some happy talk 'til I see you again. Tell me again you love me, like you did this afternoon.'

'I love you, Paul.' They were on the back seat, upstairs, in the bus taking them back to Dason Street.

He leaned close and kissed her ear. 'I love you too. This afternoon was marvellous.' His eyes searched her face. 'Don't go home. Come back with me, we'll find a hotel …'

She shook her head. 'They'd all be worried, back home.'

There were men and women crowded into the doorway of the Green Man when they alighted from the bus, and she said a silent thank you that Fred usually frequented that pub at lunchtimes and the King's Head in the evenings.

'Don't come down, just let me go on my own like we said,' she whispered, 'and take care, Paul.' He squeezed her hand hard, and she walked to the corner and turned into Dason Street.

'Gawd, you're late,' Fred said. 'I'm just off to meet the boys. Tom's 'ad an accident. Fell off a horse, Jenny said. She was round 'ere this afternoon. She's gone down to Wiltshire to see 'im.'

Queenie felt her breath tremble, 'Oh no. Is he badly injured? Where—'

'I don't know. You should've been 'ere if you wanted to know about it. They think 'e's broke 'is leg, Jenny said. They fetched 'er from the factory.'

Queenie didn't sleep much that night. All she could think of was that while she was loving Paul, her grandson had been injured and she hadn't been here to help when her daughter needed her.

Chapter 7

Jenny stayed one night in Wiltshire, and came round to her mother's place the evening of her return. She had wanted Tom to come home, but both he and Doris, and Mr and Mrs Fellowes had pleaded for him to stay. 'He's under the hospital here now and they'll look after him.' Mrs Fellowes's thin lips looked as though they might disappear completely when she spoke.

'I'm sorry I was out and couldn't come with you, Jen,' Queenie said. 'You're sure he's all right now? I thought you'd probably stay down there for a bit.'

'How can I, Mum? I've got to go to work. Anyway what could I do? Mrs Fellowes looks after them both well enough.' She bit her lip. 'They're happy and we've got to face it sometime, they don't *want* to come back.'

'It's not natural,' Queenie murmured, half to herself and half to her daughter. 'Still, at least they're away from the bombing. He's OK except for his broken leg, isn't he, Jen?'

"Course. I told you. He'll be in hospital a while, but they said he can go home, back to the Fellowes that is, soon, and just go to the hospital to check up like.'

'How did it happen?'

'I told you,' Jenny snapped, 'he fell off a horse.' She relented when her mother's eyes filled with tears. 'Sorry Mum. Reckon I'm a bit edgy too. You know, seeing the kids enjoying the farm so much and calling the Fellowes auntie and uncle, well it gets to you, even though I'm glad they've settled so well.'

Queenie gave her a quick, brief hug. 'Course you are. It's strange times we're living in now, everything's topsy turvy, but when the war's over and the kids come home, because they *will*, you know, Jen, and they'll settle back here as if they've never been away, you'll see.'

'I hope you're right. You send them away for safety, but he could have been killed instead of simply having a broken leg. God only knows what's best. Anyway she said – Mrs Fellowes, the farmer's wife – that if you wanted to go down, just let her know the day before and she'd make sure they had something to take to the station so one of them could meet you.'

Queenie looked at her in surprise.

'Because of the petrol, Mum. People can't go gallivanting about between farms and railway stations without a legitimate reason. Don't you know there's a war on?'

Queenie went down to Wiltshire one Saturday. Morag met her as she came from the station. 'I'm parked over there,' she said, 'got the ancient motor today.' Laughing merrily she added, 'That's what we call it, and it's only when I saw the expression on your face that I realized how funny it probably sounds to ye. Anyway it's a mite more comfortable than the tractor.'

The children were thrilled to see her. Tom, proud of his plaster, which was covered with names and messages, thrust his leg forward for her to write something on it too. He told her that when he grew up he wanted to be a farmer 'like Uncle Dan.'

'I shan't,' Doris said, holding her grandmother's hand tightly. 'I shall be a film star and wear beautiful clothes.'

'I'm not being much help now though,' Tom said, 'but once I get this plaster off and can walk about prop'ly ...'

Although Mrs Fellowes seemed spartanly strict to Queenie, the children seemed fond of her. During the meal the talk was at first about the animals, particularly a cow who had had difficulty calving. Tom especially was very articulate when they were discussing it. 'We had problems with her, Gran,' he said. 'Uncle Dan thought he'd have to get the vet in, but we coped.'

Mrs Fellowes said, 'You were a great help to Uncle Dan, Tom, but I'm sure your gran doesn't want to hear about all that. She'll probably be more interested in what you're doing at school.'

Queenie protested that she was interested in the farm and the animals, because she could see that that was where all Tom's thoughts were. Even so he smiled at Mrs Fellowes, then proceeded to talk about school and lessons, something he had never been over fond of. Queenie felt torn between gladness that he was so settled and had obviously found a niche down here in the country, and sadness because each time she saw him there were fewer interests they had in common. She remembered the little boy she had taken down Petticoat Lane, to the Tower of London, Madame Tussaud's, and Buckingham Palace, and she knew those days were over for ever. Even if this passion for farming was a passing thing it would still leave its mark, and take her grandson further from her. She made a mental note to find out as much as she could about cows and horses before she next visited. That way she could still be part of his life, a part he welcomed as before.

Doris hadn't absorbed the farming atmosphere as much as her brother. She looked rosy-cheeked and healthy, and had put on weight, which suited her. Nicely proportioned was how Queenie would describe it, whereas before she really had been rather a pale, skinny child. As the time drew near for Queenie to leave, Doris became more clinging, and she cried when they said goodbye. Close to tears herself, Queenie clambered into the car and was grateful that Dan Fellowes set off with such a jerk that she fell forward and was out of sight of the farmhouse by the time she had regained her balance.

She missed Jenny's children. They had always lived just a few streets away and because of that she had seen more of them than her other grandchildren. It still seemed strange to pop into her daughter's house and not find them there. She called in at Ebden Street before going home. Her daughter was washing up and Queenie reached for the tea towel as she told Jenny about her day. The only thing she omitted from her tale was Doris's tears when it was time for her grandmother to leave. Nevertheless it was this image of the child, rather than the happier ones during the day, that stayed with her long after she was in bed that night.

Another letter from Paul arrived a week after her visit to Wiltshire. 'I can be at Victoria by midday on Saturday. No time to let me know, but I shall understand if you can't make it. My fingers and toes are crossed that you can ...'

The letter arrived on a Friday morning and she had promised to have Joanna on Saturday morning because Anna had an appointment with the dentist for an extraction. She had endured toothache for over a week before consulting him anyway. Damn.

She called in to Rosie's place on her way home from the factory that evening. 'Poor girl's had a raging toothache, and Joanna's not old enough yet to sit in the waiting room on her own, and you know what Dodgy Dan's like – won't have kids in the surgery unless he's treating them.'

''Course I'll look after Jo-Jo. She's like my family now, an extra honorary granddaughter.'

'Ta, Rosie. I wouldn't like to let Anna down. It's an old friend, you see,' Queenie explained, 'and it's our only chance of a meeting.'

'She's such a darling child. No trouble at all. She can come shopping with me, and if the weather holds I'll take her to the park too. You go off and don't worry about it.'

She put her hand on Queenie's arm as she was going, 'Your friend on leave again, luv?'

'Yes.'

'Same one you met a few months ago, is it? Saw you going up the road then, looked real smart you did, Queenie. Like one of them models.'

Queenie had been careful not to mention the sex of the friend she was meeting, but she knew that wouldn't fool Rosie. She'd wheedle it out of her if she could. She was nosy, yet she wasn't a troublemaker, and if she did find out who it was, Queenie was pretty sure she'd keep it to herself.

'Thanks Rosie,' she said, 'I must get off, or Fred'll be in for his tea before I get home. It's, well, it's all above board,' she added, 'I'm simply having a meal with a friend I knew years an' years ago.'

'Of course. You enjoy it, gal. I'll look after Joanna.'

Paul was there first again, and they melted into each other's arms. There was no pretence this time. 'How long have we got?' she whispered.

'I have to be back by two tomorrow afternoon. Ruth's away and I've the key to the flat.'

As their bodies parted from each other he took her hand. 'But it's OK with me if we're just here together, darling. I'll go along with anything you want as long as I can be with you for a few hours. Did you say what time you'd be back?'

Squeezing his hand she answered softly, 'I told Fred I was staying the night with Marie, and I've written to her too.'

'Darling.' His voice was a caress. She let the last of the guilt she'd been harbouring fall from her. This wasn't hurting Fred or any of her family now. She fingered the sapphire Paul had given her. Today she was wearing a low-cut frock, and the blueness sparkled against her skin, but other times she wore it only beneath high-necked blouses and dresses. Although Fred seldom noticed these things she knew she couldn't bear it if he had questioned her about it. Most days, though, she touched the jewel as it lay beneath her handkerchiefs in the little side drawer of her dressing-table.

They spent the afternoon walking. Arms entwined around each other they sauntered through St James's Park, sometimes talking and sometimes content simply to be together, to feel each other's nearness and dearness. Occasionally Paul's lips gently brushed her cheek. 'I do love you, my princess. I always will,' he murmured.

'I love you too,' her voice was light with happiness. 'Oh Paul, why didn't we meet first, before I married Fred, before I had a family?'

'Hush, none of that matters now. We're here together, we have the whole weekend, don't let's even think about what might have been. Let's enjoy what we have.' They got tickets for *Best Bib and Tucker* at the Palladium, and went to Lyons Corner House at Marble Arch for tea before the show. The orchestra leader there came over and asked if she would like a request played. With Paul's leg touching hers beneath the table and his eyes adoring her, she said, 'That Lovely Weekend.'

Of course it made her cry, but she blinked the tears away and smiled at Paul. 'I love you,' she said, 'nothing will change that. Even if we can never be together for long I shall always feel the same.'

'Dearest Queenie ...' The pretty little nippy brought their tea and they both smiled at her. Later, holding hands in the darkness of the theatre, they rocked with laughter as Tommy Trinder had promised they would on the posters that they'd seen around the capital: *If it's laughter you're after, Trinder's the name! You lucky people.* 'We *are* lucky,' she said, more positive about it than ever before, 'to be here together today.' And he kissed her again.

Afterwards they went to Marguerite's Supper Rooms. It was a place for lovers, the padded bench seats with high backs allowing the privacy they craved. Pretty pink tablecloths and a slender vase holding a single pink rose added to the romantic flavour of the restaurant.

'Happy?' Paul asked, reaching across the table and touching her hand.

'More than words can say. I'm almost afraid I'm dreaming and any moment I shall wake and find none of this is happening.'

'It's no dream, my love. It's something to remember all our lives.'

She shivered and reached for his hand again. 'Paul, will you be in danger? No, I don't mean that, I *know* you will, but, oh Paul, come back to me, don't take chances, don't volunteer for crazy jobs ...' Suddenly she was crying, tears gushing from her eyes. He was at her side in a second, his arm comfortingly round her shoulders, his lips kissing her hair.

'Don't cry, my darling, I can't bear it. I won't do crazy things, I promise, but of course there are risks. It would be stupid to deny that, but what about you? Every day you are in danger at home and at the factory. I pray every night that God will keep you safe. Come on now, dry your eyes before that very discreet waiter thinks I've been molesting you.'

She smiled through the haze of her tears and took his proffered handkerchief. 'Sorry, Paul. The whole thing just got to me I suppose. I'm all right now.'

'Attagirl.' Kissing the tip of her nose he said, 'Think I'll stay this side now, where I can feel you close to me. Do you suppose there are others like us in all these alcoves?'

'Mmm, it's a lovely thought, isn't it? Love all around us ...'

Ruth's flat seemed quiet and comforting when they let themselves in. 'This is like an oasis in the middle of the noise and hustle of London,' she said.

'I suppose so. It's certainly a haven for us, sweetheart. Better than a hotel where we'd be with other people some of the time, and subject to questions, signing-in and all the rest.' He carried her through to the bedroom and she shivered with pleasure.

Queenie woke in the early hours of the morning to the sound of planes overhead. For a few seconds she wondered where she was, then Paul stirred and reached for her again. It had been a wonderful night. After the first frenzy of their lovemaking they had lain with their arms round each other until they drifted into sleep. Later they came together again and this time their passion was slower and even more wonderful for her. Afterwards she lay with her head on his chest, listening to his breathing as he slept, and knowing this time she wouldn't let him go. When this ghastly war was over, if he still wanted her, if they were all spared, she would leave Fred and go with her lover to Canada, or anywhere else in the world he fancied.

The noise outside grew louder and involuntarily she snuggled deeper into Paul's arms. 'What is it?' he said, 'God, those planes are low.' As the roar of the engines died away his lips found hers and the vibrations of her body became mixed with the shuddering of the building as the bombs screamed down.

The bomb that blew some of Ruth's windows out, and covered Queenie and Paul with ceiling plaster, actually fell in the next square. Their immediate concern was for each other, but once they knew neither was hurt, they found their clothes, shook the dust from them, hastily dressed and went outside. When Queenie saw a warden heading in their direction she said to Paul, 'He'll want to know who was in the house, all the details ...'

'Leave it to me, darling, and see if you can find something we can board the windows with.'

She turned back to Ruth's flat and started cleaning up. When Paul returned and saw her he burst out laughing.

'What's so funny?' Her voice was sharp with worry.

'You. You've two big smuts of dirt on your cheeks and another like a moustache beneath your nose. You should just see yourself, my love, and you'd laugh too.' He swung her into his arms and kissed her.

The bomb killed everybody in one of the houses and put many others in hospital. Paul and Queenie boarded up Ruth's windows as best they could, then went indoors again. 'I'll see what we can have for breakfast,' she said.

'Good, I'm starving.' His arm circled her waist, and he added quietly, 'Thank God you're safe.'

There was tea and coffee, a half-packet of cornflakes but little else. 'We should have done some shopping yesterday,' Paul said, laughing. 'Never mind, we'll eat out.'

'We wouldn't have been able to buy without ration books, darling. I should have planned better and brought something from home.'

'What? And have your old man go short and question you about it? Never.' Suddenly they were in each other's arms. 'To hell with breakfast,' he said, carrying her to the settee. 'Love me again first, Queenie, then we'll go.'

Later, in Lyons Corner House at Marble Arch they sated their appetite and quenched their thirst. 'This is better,' she said, holding her cup towards him as in a toast, 'I could still taste the dust in that cuppa we had at the flat.'

They went to Hyde Park, each very aware that every minute was taking them nearer to parting time.

'Last evening in that restaurant,' she said, 'it was almost as though there wasn't a war on. It was all so civilized, yet only hours later people in the next street to us were dying, and here,' she looked up at the barrage balloons like huge silver pigs in the sky, 'it's hard to believe we'll ever be a peaceful country again.'

'Of course we will. We shall win through and London will look as it used to. No – it will be better, because we shall build decent houses instead of some of the slums Hitler's knocking down ...'

'You can't replace the people.' Her voice sounded infinitely sad.

They were both silent. After a while he squeezed her hand. 'Reckon we'd better make a move, my princess.'

'Don't come with me,' she said. 'It's better that way. I'll come to the main station with you, then I'll go.' She waited, encircled by his arms until the last minute, then he leapt aboard the Hampshire-bound train. With his 'Take care, my darling,' echoing in her heart, she walked from the platform with tears in her eyes, and automatically made for the tube and home. He said he'd write 'when I can', and she knew it could be months, maybe years before they met again. He talked of returning to London after the war: 'There'll be things to do, rebuilding, replanning, I could sell up in Canada. It's time I came home; when the time comes for me to die I'd like it to be here.'

She knew now that if he did come back it would change her life too. No more deceit: she would leave Fred and go to the only man she had ever truly loved. Outside the tube station she waited for a bus to take her the rest of the way home. She wished with all her heart she had left Fred and made her life with Paul years ago. I should have admitted to myself I'd made a mistake, yet there were the children, and yes, there was my conscience. I'm no better than any of the women who have affairs. Twenty, even ten years ago I couldn't have had such a weekend as this. The guilt, the deceit, the inhibitions simply fell from me once I saw Paul again. It was so right, so perfectly right. I love him so much and I always have. All I've done in the past is hide behind this façade of respectability, because in my heart I've been unfaithful to my husband for years.

So engrossed was she in her thoughts she almost went past her stop. She jumped up when she heard the conductress calling, 'Green Man, Green Man, hold tight and move along the bus there.' Pushing her way to the platform, she just made it before the vehicle moved off. 'Come on, luv,' the cheery little woman said. 'Right, I can take one more now, standing room only, move along the bus please ...'

The first person she saw as she walked down Dason Street was Mrs Wardson.

'Evenin'. Bin gallivanting again?' she said.

'No more than usual,' Queenie retorted, mentally shaking herself back into the environment of the street.

Chapter 8

1941

June Green had been in the children's home at the same time as Anna. She was never a close friend, but always kept in touch. She came to see her after Anna and Joe were married, and sent postcards from various places around the country where she was currently working.

The postcard that arrived one morning towards the end of August said she was back in London and how about meeting? Anna invited her over, and they talked, played with Joanna, talked some more, and reminisced about their years in St Margaret's.

'What work are you doing then?' Anna asked. 'Here, have another piece of cake. Queenie, a woman who lives down the road, gave me the recipe. Doesn't use eggs, see; now there's a shortage you have to be devious, don't you?'

'It's nice, but I won't have any more. Got to watch my figure, Anna. I'm a – a sort of model, see.'

Anna didn't see, but then June had had so many different jobs since she left the home that she wasn't surprised at anything the other girl tried. 'Thought you might be in one of the women's services,' she said. 'I didn't know there'd be a call for models in wartime.'

'Didn't fancy the uniforms, nor the thought of having to do as I'm told all the time, then I met this bloke who runs this …' she

paused for a fraction of a second, 'this agency, and he reckoned
I had what it takes, so Bob's yer uncle.' She grinned, the cheeky,
infectious sort of grin that Anna had often envied when they
lived in the home. It always seemed to put people in authority
on her side.

'Job for the duration if I'm lucky, and I intend to be lucky I can
tell you.'

'You living round this way again then?'

'For a week or two. Tell you what, let's go to the pictures one
afternoon, there's a good film at the Palace next week. Can you
get a baby-sitter for your youngster?'

Anna said no at first, but June was very persuasive. 'Come on,
do you good to get out, and your Joe wouldn't mind, it's not as
if you're going with another bloke, is it? Can be my treat – yes,
'course,' she went on when Anna protested, 'you're not earning
and I am. You'd be doing me a favour too, sometimes it's good
to see friends from the old innocent days.'

'All right. I'll see if Queenie or Rosie will have Joanna for me.
Which day are you off?'

June looked startled, then she smiled. 'Oh, any afternoon. I do
a lot of evening work, see. You drop me a postcard when you've
got it fixed – here, I'll give you my present address.'

By the time Anna had arranged with Queenie to look after
Joanna the following Saturday afternoon when she wasn't at the
factory, she found she was looking forward to a few hours at the
cinema after all.

Since September last year most of the inhabitants of Dason
Street had spent the night either down the Anderson, if they had
one, or in the street shelters built at strategic points along the
way. There had been daylight raids, but the night ones were the
most regular although for the last couple of months they had not
happened every night. Many of the residents of the street now
stayed in their beds until the siren sounded and Anna wouldn't
have dreamt of going out then and leaving Joanna. Saturday

afternoon at the pictures sounded great, June had been most persuasive, and the pull of Clark Gable was hard to resist.

Anna and June left the cinema together, but parted on the corner of Dason Street. Anna offered to wait with her friend until the bus came, but June smiled. "Course not, silly. It's broad daylight, nothing will happen to me. You get back to your baby like you're dying to, and I'll come over again soon. Mind how you go now,' she added.

It was true that Anna was anxious to be home, although she knew Joanna would be fine with Queenie. Suppose every mum feels like this when she leaves her child with someone, she thought, but it was nice to go out and it was a lovely picture.

There was no one about down this end of the street, but hurrying past the entrance to Tailor's Yard she glimpsed a tall figure striding towards her. Seconds later fear engulfed her as she felt a hand clamped over her mouth. 'No noise now, just come with me and you won't get hurt.' The voice was soft, velvety, the accent foreign to her London ears. She tried to pull away, to remove his hand, but it was holding her too strongly. As he turned her into Tailor's Yard his arm which was wound round her neck, twisted it until she thought she would surely choke. A spluttering sound escaped and he said more harshly, 'Be quiet, we're almost there.'

Her high heels caught in the cobbles as he hurried her along; she tried to bite the hand that imprisoned her mouth, but she knew she was making no impression. Then, suddenly he turned her again, into one of the doorways, kicking it open with his black boot, and in the dimness of the passage he released his hand, swooped her into his arms as though she was a mere feather, and even as the scream she was desperately trying to unleash sounded, his mouth crushed down on to hers and she felt the breath oozing from her as she passed out.

*

Queenie took Joanna across the road to Rosie and Jim just after six. 'I'm worried about Anna,' she said. 'She should have come out of the pictures about half past four, quarter to five at the very latest, and how long would it take her to get home? Twenty minutes at the most.'

'Jim'll go and look for her,' Rosie volunteered. 'Go on, mate, have a scout round. Mind,' she swung her ample body round to face Queenie, 'she could have met someone she knew and gone to have a cuppa with them. That café in Church Street, the one near the school, would be open.'

Privately Queenie thought Anna would come straight home from the pictures, and not be tempted to dally, whomever she met, but she said, 'Maybe, but I'm a bit bothered all the same, Rosie. Anna's so – oh, I don't know how to put this, but different from the rest of us, more gentle, less worldly wise, know what I mean?'

Rosie nodded. 'You're right. Hope she's not had an accident, Queenie. There's been no raids this afternoon.' She reached out for Joanna. 'Thinks the world of this little 'un, don't she? And why not? She's a bonny one, right enough.'

Queenie didn't stay long in case Anna arrived while she was out. 'Thanks, Rosie,' she said. Jim had already departed. 'I'll get a bit of tea ready.'

Jim popped into Wentworth's for half an ounce of baccy when he reached Church Street. Sid and Liza were both there behind the counter. Liza walked to the end and bent down, returning a few moments later and scooping some tobacco into the scales.

'There you are Jim, getting scarcer. Soon we won't even have any to hide under the counter the way things are going.'

'Thanks Liza. I appreciate it. Seen anything of young Anna this afternoon?' He was watching the door all the time in case she went by.

'Can't say as I have, no, not today I've not seen her.'

Sid leant across the newspapers in front of him. 'Why, you lost her?' He chuckled.

'Well sort of, Sid. She went to the pictures with a friend. Was due back fivish but she's not turned up and Queenie's a bit bothered.'

The warden looked at his watch. 'Mmm. Where did she go? Down the Palace?'

Jim nodded. 'I'm on me way there now. I haven't passed her yet.'

Sid looked at Liza. 'I'll come with you, Jim. Stretch my legs. OK with you Liza?'

''Course it is. I can cope here. Put your scarf on, though.' Sid grinned and said nothing.

En route they met several neighbours, and to each they put the same question; 'Have you seen Anna Putt?' No one had, but all promised to keep their eyes peeled for her as they went their various ways.

Jim and Sid split at Grey Street, which was where Dason Street began to deteriorate. The houses were smaller and some of the doorsteps obviously weren't scrubbed every day as they were higher up. The children who played in the street were snotty-nosed and many had torn clothes and no shoes. This evening there were no children there and Sid carried on to the end of Dason Street and then to the Palace picture house in the main road. Meanwhile Jim was to check Grey Street, come back through Brown Street, scour Tailor's Yard, and they would meet at the Palace.

Sid found her, staggering up Dason Street in the dark. He spotted Anna before she saw him. She was sort of shuffling along as though in pain, her head and shoulders drooping, hands holding her thin coat around her tiny figure. He went forward at a run. 'Anna, you all right? What happened, gal?'

She raised her head, and the look of sheer terror on her face shook him to the core. Gently he wrapped his arm around her, 'You're shivering. Here, lean on me for a moment, then I'll take you home.'

They met Jim coming out of Brown Street, and together the two men supported her the rest of the way to number 5, where a worried-looking Queenie had switched off the light and was peering through the curtains watching for them.

'Anna dear, come on. I'll make you a nice cup of tea. You been in an accident?' She made to help her off with her coat, but the girl clutched it even more tightly around her. 'No,' she cried hoarsely, 'leave me alone, just leave me alone.' Leaning her head against the door she began to cry, great rasping sobs that spoke of some horror she couldn't bring herself to talk about. As her sobs grew wilder she raised her hands and rhythmically beat them against the hard wood. Her coat fell open and they saw her ripped dress and dishevelled underclothes. Queenie indicated to the men to leave them, mouthing to Sid to 'fetch the doctor'.

Thankful that she had already put Joanna to bed, Queenie said briskly, 'Come and sit down, Anna, you're home and safe now. Come on, there's a good girl,' almost as though she were talking to the child instead of the woman. Anna pulled her coat round her once more as she allowed herself to be led into the front room.

Queenie, who'd had the kettle hot for the last hour and a half, ran into the kitchen to make the tea, 'and plenty of sugar,' she muttered to herself, 'to hell with the rations.' Then she dashed upstairs and took a blanket from the double bed, dragging it down behind her like a bride's train. She wrapped it round Anna. 'There you are, luv, now have a sip of this. Come on, it'll do you good. And when you feel like telling me what happened, well, I'm here to help.'

Anna looked ghastly. There was no vestige of colour in her cheeks, and the wild look she'd had in her eyes when she was in the hall had been replaced by a glazed, unreal stare. It made Queenie feel bad to look at her distress. Although Anna was no longer sobbing as she had been, a shuddering choke escaped from her throat every few seconds. Queenie knew she mustn't rush her, yet every minute counted if they were to catch whoever had done this. She wondered if she should have got Sid to call the police as well as the doctor. 'Anna,' she said in almost a whisper, 'who was it? Who attacked you?'

The sharp rat-tat on the door made Anna draw her legs up into the depths of the big old armchair and bury her face and head in her hands. Almost like a baby returning to the womb position, Queenie thought.

'Don't let anyone in, I don't want to see anyone.' Anna's voice sounded faint and far away, and Queenie murmured soothing noises as she patted the girl's shoulder, then went into the narrow hallway to let the doctor in.

Chapter 9

The rape attack on Anna was the talk of the street the following day, although few people knew whom it had happened to.

'An' this 'uge bloke knocked her out and carried 'er off. Down in Tailor's Yard it was, in one of them sweatshops. Some young girl – got a baby too she 'as. When she come to he had this knife to 'er froat—'

Queenie, who had walked into Wentworth's shop on her way to Anna's, interrupted the woman, who she knew was often the source of malicious street gossip. 'There was no knife, so don't go spreading untrue tales around,' she said angrily.

'Oh I'm sorry, I'm sure. S'pose you know all there is to know about it, then?'

'I know a damn sight more than you do.'

'P'raps she asked for it, eh? They often do—'

Liza said quickly, 'Not this one, she's not the sort. Poor girl, how is she, Queenie?'

'She'll be all right if people don't harass her.' She looked at Mrs Wardson, who stretched her neck high so her pointed chin jutted out in defiance.

'It's the quiet ones you wanter watch,' she said. 'It's all very well you sticking up fer 'er, but how do you know she didn't ask fer it. Going ter the pictures alone and leaving 'er baby at home. If you asks me she was courting trouble.' She marched from the shop, giving Queenie a venomous look as she passed her.

The previous evening Queenie had stayed with Anna while the doctor examined her, or tried to. Anna cringed every time he came near, and at the suggestion of calling the police to find the man she became demented.

'All right, all right,' he said, 'it's your body. I can't make you submit to an examination or a police interrogation. But you could be doing someone else a favour by telling us more. The police can't find someone without a description or something to go on.' He was bad-tempered at being called out to someone who was refusing all help.

'Well that's it,' he spat at Queenie when she went with him to the front door. 'Next time make sure the patient wants the doctor before getting me over on a fool's errand. That'll be three-and-six.' Queenie rummaged in her purse to find the money and pay him.

She checked on Joanna, then went across the road to Rosie and Jim Bateson. She knew Joe couldn't stand Rosie, but then he wasn't here to do much about it, and Queenie didn't want to leave Anna and Joanna alone for the night. Anna had asked about her baby soon after the doctor left, saying only: 'I knew she'd be all right with you,' when Queenie told her she was fast asleep in her cot.

Rosie, whom Jim had stopped from rushing over the road when he returned by saying, 'Leave it fer now, duck, Queenie's with her,' quickly agreed to sleep over at number 5 and keep an eye on Anna and Joanna.

'Just for tonight I should think,' Queenie sighed. 'She's not said much, only that he came at her out of Tailor's Yard and he was tall.'

'Not a lot to go on, is it? I mean, it could be anyone.' Jim took their spare mattress over to Anna's for Rosie to sleep on. He unrolled it in the front room where Rosie said she'd be fine. 'And you'll know I'm here, lovey, if you want anything. OK?'

Anna tried to smile, but it was a weak effort. 'I'll be all right,' she whispered, 'there's no need ...'

Rosie enveloped her in a motherly hug, "Course there is. You've had a terrible shock and it'll be best if someone's here in case you start thinking about it and get the collywobbles in the night.'

The doctor had left a tablet to help her sleep, and it really did knock Anna out. She slept the heavy sleep of the drugged for twelve hours, while Rosie looked after Joanna, and pondered to herself about the tall figure who had abducted and raped the child's pretty young mother.

Two weeks went by, and although Rosie only stayed the one night, she kept a wary eye on Anna. As did Queenie, who popped into number 5 most days. Anna was, if anything, quieter and more subdued than ever. She refused to talk about what had happened, simply saying she was fine now and just wanted to forget the experience.

On the morning she was sick as soon as her feet touched the lino in the bedroom she knew that forgetting was an impossibility. She just made it to the lavatory, and was glad that she was alone apart from her small daughter, still fast asleep in her cot. The thought that she might be pregnant had not been far from her mind ever since she had started to think rationally again. All she could honestly remember of that evening was the terror as this hand clamped itself over her mouth. She knew she had fainted, and when she woke she was aware of this huge figure rising from her – he seemed like a giant, and he was naked from the waist down. Some part of her brain must have registered what had happened, but she had no memory of it, only the knowledge of what had obviously taken place. She tried to shut it from her mind, willing herself to treat it like a bad dream, and had almost succeeded until the morning she was sick.

When Queenie called into number 5 on her way home later that Saturday morning, Anna said without preamble, 'I've put Joanna up for her sleep early because I want to talk – to – to ask you something.'

Queenie sat down. She was worried about Anna, and felt a great relief that at last the girl was prepared to talk about her ordeal. 'I'm ready, luv,' she said in her soft London voice. 'Fire away.'

Anna's lips trembled, and she put her hand to her chin in an effort to stop them. Without looking at Queenie now, she said in a rush, 'I'm two days late and I was sick this morning. Can you do something for me?'

'Oh my God.' Queenie didn't often use such an expression, and Anna slowly lifted her head and looked into the older woman's face. The silence was awful. It lasted seconds in reality, but to Anna it seemed to go on far too long. She was banking on Queenie, had thought she would say immediately: *Of course I can, don't you worry about a thing* ...

It wasn't just the silence, it was the look on Queenie's face and in her eyes. A strange, unbelieving look which frightened Anna, because if Queenie couldn't do something for her she didn't know anyone who could.

At last Queenie spoke. 'We must see about getting Joe home,' she said.

'No.' Swiftly Anna stood up and paced the tiny room. 'Joe mustn't know – he mustn't ever know. I've got to get rid of the baby. Oh Queenie, help me, you know what to do, you must, you must, please ...'

'Joe will have to know, Anna. Oh, why wouldn't you go to the police at the time? It wasn't your fault—'

'I – I couldn't. I can't now. Oh Queenie, it's so awful. You *will* help me, won't you?'

Queenie walked over to the window and gazed through the white nets at the activity in the street outside. There was Rosie coming out of her door opposite, basket over her arm, stopping to have a word with old man Weston next door, who was sitting on his canvas chair on the doorstep. The co-op baker was pulling his cart along Dason Street, and she could hear the United Dairies horse in the distance. It seemed like a normal day, yet what Anna had just told her had turned it into a nightmare.

'No, Anna. There is nothing I can do.'

The words fell between them.

'N-nothing? But there must be, Queenie. I'm not far gone, I can't be. You know when – when it happened. Please, Queenie, help me. I've got to get rid of it—'

'Anna, I bring babies into the world. I've never aborted one in my life. It's ...' she stopped. 'I can't do it, Anna. It's the only thing Mum and me used to disagree on. I'd like to help, but I can't take a life.'

'What am I going to *do*, Queenie?'

Queenie took a deep breath. 'See the doctor, get Joe home, he'd get compassionate leave for this—'

'No, no. Never. I couldn't face that. Joe mustn't ever know what happened. Swear you won't tell him, Queenie.' In her agitation Anna had gripped Queenie's arms and was shaking her. 'He couldn't bear it – I couldn't bear it ...' She was sobbing now, great gulping sobs that filled the room with eerie noise.

'Hush now.' Queenie's arms were round the girl. 'You'll wake Joanna.' What stupid things we say when we're out of our depth, she thought. Aloud she said, 'Leave it a day or two. You may not be ...'

Anna looked at her in amazement, 'I've always thought you so wise, so kind.' She turned away. 'If it wasn't for Joanna I'd do away with myself and Joe need never know what that brute did. He couldn't bear it, I know he couldn't,' she repeated.

'Now look Anna—'

'It's all right, I won't. I love Joe and Joanna too much to do it to them. Forget I said it, and just leave me alone now. I've got to think.'

Queenie thought too; for the rest of that day she struggled with her conscience. Usually so easy-going this was the one area she was passionate about – the only thing she could ever remember quarrelling with her mother over. If she were alive today she'd do it for Anna. Her mind slipped back to the first time she realized how her mother 'helped' people. That was a rape case too, but she learned that 'Woody', as Elizabeth Woodman was affectionately called by her neighbours, always weighed the pros and cons, and made her own decisions as to whether a birth should be allowed to continue.

'You're playing God again,' she'd shouted at her mother one day, when Ada Smith had come round to the neat, clean little house in Ebdon Street where they lived then. For once there was no string of snotty-nosed kids trailing behind her. 'Only He can decide if a child should live or die, not you. You're simply a woman with a bit of knowledge. Maybe God's sending this child for a special reason. Who do you think you are to argue with that?'

'Don't you come all pious with me,' Woody had shouted back, 'God sending the child, indeed. It was that drunken sod Jim Smith who put that baby there in the first place. How d'you think Ada'll manage? She's already got nine, and Jim more out of work than in. When he does have some bees it all goes down the rub-a ...' Yes, the only quarrels she'd ever had with her mother had been over abortion. She knew what her mother's decision would be in this case, could hear her voice echoing down the years; 'Get rid of it for her, gal. Do her a favour.' And her own still voice answered: 'I can't slaughter innocent children. I could kill the man, but not the child.'

She knew what she was going to do by late afternoon. Take the baby and bring it up herself. Fred wouldn't like it, but no matter. There was no joy left in their marriage anyway. Hadn't been any almost since it began, and as long as it didn't interfere with his trips to the pub, his darts and his jaunts with his beery pals, he'd probably hardly notice. He'd had little enough to do with his own kids, she thought. When they were babies the minute they cried he'd given an exaggerated sigh, put his mucky old cap on and disappeared to the King's Head or the Green Man. Now with only the two of them there she had plenty of room, and she owed it to Anna to do something to help her.

She laid the table for tea, hesitating over the small tin of spam – it had cost her precious points, and she had been saving it in case her friend Marie could get over for a visit. Still, Fred liked a bit of cold meat and after all it was a bit of a bombshell she was going to spring on him. She opened it quickly before changing her mind, ran a knife round the edge of the tin, tipped the meat on to a tea plate and placed it in the centre of the table. She covered the lot with a clean teacloth, checked Fluff the cat was out of the room, put her brown coat and shoes on and walked up the road to tell Anna her plan.

Anna was giving her daughter tea. Joanna, at nearly two, was a chubby, lively little girl. Her hair was fair like Anna's, but her eyes were a deeper blue, almost violet, and she had Joe's sudden illuminating smile. Anna let Queenie in, took a cup and saucer from the kitchen cabinet and poured another cup of tea, which she pushed across the table to her.

'Anna, would you let me take the baby,' Queenie said without preamble. 'From the moment it's born you need have nothing further to do with it. What do you think?'

Anna returned her cup to its saucer with a clatter. She had been surprised when she saw who her visitor was, and a faint hope that Queenie had changed her mind surged through her. She dismissed the idea quickly, she'd been too vehement this morning to have done that over something she was so passionate about. Now her suggestion that she would take the baby into her home threw Anna's thoughts into further turmoil.

'Why, Queenie? Why should you do that?'

'It's the *only* way I can help you, Anna. I desperately want to, and it came to me that this was a way out.'

Chapter 10

Anna put Joanna to bed, then sat down to write to Joe. She sat a long time in thought, the pen and pad in front of her. She couldn't tell him of the things that occupied her day as she had when he first went abroad. Not that she'd felt the baby move for the first time yesterday and the strange thoughts it started up in her. Not that she had tried on the smock she'd made when she was expecting Joanna. She couldn't tell him that she was five months pregnant and that when he came home and one day saw a child with Queenie, it was a child his wife had given birth to.

Anna never thought about the day she was raped now. At first she woke in the night, sweating and choking with fear, but she had learned to take a hold of herself and remember it was in the past, it was over. She had been strict with herself as Corny from the home had always taught her to be. 'Self discipline, Anna, is one of the greatest things you can cultivate. It can mean the difference between a happy or an unhappy life,' she used to say, and in her lonely troubles Anna had clung to this philosophy.

'For Joanna and Joe's sake', she murmured to herself when things were extra bad, 'I must go on.' She knew no one but Queenie who was in a position to help her, except of course the doctor and she simply could not bring herself to go to him. If another woman had offered she would have jumped at the chance, in spite of Queenie's warning not to have anything to do with 'back-street abortionists', and as the weeks and months went by even she realized it was too late to do anything but let nature take its course.

Queenie said she would be there when the child was born, that she would take it home with her and, unless she wanted to, she need never see it again. Strangely, since that first movement yesterday Anna felt differently about the baby growing inside her. Not happy, but resigned. It was as though by moving it had established itself as a person, a human entity.

She positioned the pen over the paper. Corny had given it to her for her birthday the first year she was at St Margaret's and she cherished it. Her first fountain pen, indeed her only fountain pen, and it was a good one, everyone said so. She took great care of it and had always felt it helped her to express herself better, but tonight that wasn't true. The words refused to flow. Yet if there was no letter Joe would worry – he might even try to find out whether she was safe, send one of his army mates who was home on leave or get the authorities to check up for bombing in the area. The one thing she was sure about was that he would do something to check whether she and Joanna were all right.

Gripping her pen tightly, and holding it close to the writing pad as though its very proximity would force the words on to the page, she concentrated intently on everything except her condition. She had blocked out the events which led to it months ago.

Dear Joe, she wrote, *How are you? Joanna and me are fine. She's growing so fast now. Every day she does something new. She knows who you are Joe, I make sure and show her your photo every day, and she says daddy to it. I miss you Joe, come home safe,*
love from Anna.

She read it through, and again the baby moved inside her. 'Restless little blighter,' she said. The tears started and ran down her face and dripped on to the letter, and she was powerless to stop them. She just sat there and cried, fishing in her sleeve for a handkerchief that was much too flimsy for the vast mopping-up job needed. How long she stayed there by the table she didn't know, but when she rose she knew she felt better than she had for a long while. Exhausted but renewed at the same time. It was as though the tears had cleansed her.

She hated lying to Joe; well, she reasoned, it was lying by not telling him, but how could he cope with something like this when he was so far away? She knew she would never tell him about it. Perhaps they'd move when he came back in case someone else did; she put her hands together, 'Please God he does come back,' she muttered. She stood up and moved to the kitchen door where there was a roller towel. Pulling it round to a dry bit she dabbed her face, then put the kettle on and made a pot of tea. She tore the page from the writing pad, screwed it up and threw it in the rubbish bin without rereading it. Couldn't send a tear-stained letter like that and she was far too tired to redo it now. Maybe tomorrow I'll find something cheerful to tell him, she thought, after all he won't want to know Joanna talks to his picture and kisses it goodnight. It will only make him sad. It would make me sad if I was miles away and he wrote that to me. I must pull my socks up and do better by him.

Later that week she had a letter from June, to tell her she was joining up.

My job packed up a bit sudden like, she wrote, *and maybe the uniform won't look so bad on me after all. Be nice to get together again before I go, only I'm a bit tied up with a fellow just now. I'll try and get to see you and your little girl on my first leave, though.*

Anna was relieved she wasn't coming over. The fewer people who knew about the baby the better, she thought. It was bad enough half of Dason Street would know, but then, apart from those around this end the rest weren't to know her husband hadn't had leave. It was only a handful of trusted friends who knew he wasn't in England. She had plenty of time to think things out in the evenings when Joanna was in bed. She tried very hard now to write cheerful letters to Joe. She had only had half a dozen from him since he'd been abroad, but the papers and the wireless kept telling people to write to the troops even if they didn't always get an answer quickly. His Christmas letter had been very special, far better than a card, and she had cursed her lack of words with which to write back. She loved him so much, and wouldn't allow herself to think about what he would do if he ever found out about this baby. If only Queenie had agreed to abort it months ago....

Queenie came in most days, either before or after work. 'You're always so busy,' Anna said one Sunday, when she herself had popped into number 52 with some cakes she had made, and Queenie came dashing in as she was knocking on the door. 'Where you been this time?'

'To Amy Cotton's. She had a son early hours this morning. Just popped in on her and made her comfortable. They're both fine. Come on in for a minute.'

Anna bumped the pushchair over the step. 'I don't know what this street would do without you, Queenie. Would you have liked to have been a nurse, really?'

Queenie took off her hat and coat, hanging the coat tidily on a hanger and putting the felt hat on the shelf in the cupboard under the stairs.

'I thought so at one time, but there wasn't any money to spare for that sort of training. I was the eldest, see, and I had to go out to work soon as I left school. I was ten years older than my next brother, Mum had the three boys with not much gap, Anna. She had so many miscarriages between me and them—' Queenie clapped her hand over her mouth. 'That was blooming tactless,' she said, reaching out to touch Anna's hands, 'but they did in them days, of course. Anyway, I got married when I was seventeen and had my own babies to look after.'

'If you ...' Anna made herself look directly into the older woman's eyes, 'what I mean to say is, if you change your mind, you know, about taking on this one,' she tapped her stomach, 'say so, won't you? I'll understand. See, I realize now I was in a bit of a state, and you're, well, you're very kind-hearted, Queenie, but it's a big thing to take on and—'

'Thanks, Anna. But I shan't back down. Now come on, I'll show you what I've made for little Jo.' She glanced down at the child who was still asleep in her pushchair.

Later that night, having decided not to go to the Anderson unless the siren went, and it wasn't sending its fearful warning out as often these days and nights, Anna too looked at her sleeping child and remembered the happiness she and Joe had known when she first realized she was expecting. Now she was five months gone with another baby. A child conceived through a stranger's lust, not love: would it make any difference to the baby? She had to accept what it had done to her – when Jim Bateson put his hand on her shoulder just the other day, in the friendliest of gestures, she had frozen. She knew he was simply being matey and she hated herself afterwards for the hurt she saw in his eyes. She rolled over to the empty space in her bed that night and tried to visualize Joe lying there again. Would she be able to bear him to touch her? The few letters she'd had spoke of his love for her; *it keeps me going Anna darling, knowing I've you and Joanna to come home to. One day we'll be together again, never fear ...*

Fear. There were so many things she feared now. Shadows and silences, sudden noises, even people's innocent questions. Only the other day she'd met someone from Church Street who had a child about the same age as Joanna. They chatted for a few moments, then the woman said, 'Well, I must be off, got to meet her sister from school.' Glancing at Anna's rounding figure, she said, 'What do you want this time, a boy or another girl?'

'I – I don't mind,' she'd answered, letting the brake off Joanna's pushchair.

'Long as it's healthy, eh? Still, nice to have a pigeon pair. I really wanted a boy second time round, but I love this little devil just as much.' She leaned over and adjusted her baby's bonnet, smiling lovingly at the child. 'Tat-ta now, take care of yourself.'

Well, she thought that evening when Joanna was in bed and she picked up the cardigan she was knitting for her, that's something else I must get used to and learn to cope with. In a way it wasn't too difficult, she realized, because it was obvious the woman hadn't known about the rape, or if she had heard a whisper of gossip she certainly hadn't connected it with her. Looking at it sensibly Anna saw that only a handful of people actually knew. She had brought no charges, and although at the time rumours about a rape in Tailor's Yard probably circulated around Dason Street and the surrounding area, there were no names bandied about as far as she knew, and there were plenty of other things going on. A two-day wonder, then people talked about something else.

Anna was surprised that she could work it out like this. Surprised and pleased. She knew she was finding strengths she hadn't been aware of even a few months ago. That night she thought out a plan, a stock answer should anyone ask about Joe or mention her condition. 'Maybe he'll be home again by the time the baby's born,' she'd say, 'who can tell?' The 'again' would do it, give them the idea that she had seen him recently.

Is this me, Anna Putt, who used to be so timid? When she thought about how she had worried about going to the pictures with June, and leaving Joanna with Queenie. But then I was worried about Joanna, and perhaps feeling guilty about enjoying myself away from home for a few hours. These days she never wanted to stir from the house, but with Queenie, and Rosie across the road giving encouragement, she did go out during the day. She did her shopping, took Joanna to the park the other side of the High Street, and had even been to the Saturday market again. She convinced herself she had to do these things for her child's sake, and for Joe's. She drew a great deal on her beloved Mrs Cornfield's teachings, even to sometimes pretending to hold a conversation with her and ask her advice. She always knew what 'Corny' would say, of course, and Anna tried very hard to follow the road she imagined her suggesting.

She had not returned to the Home since the matron died. There was no one else there she had been very close to, and now, with all this trouble on her, she had no desire to be in touch with anyone who had known her in the old days.

At six months pregnant she often felt very tired by midday. Joanna was a lively child, and was beginning not to want a sleep in the afternoons, so Anna seemed to be on the go all the time. Rosie said, not very tactfully one morning when she saw her returning from the shops, 'You look worn out, Anna, why don't you let me have the little 'un for an hour or two this afternoon and you get your head down?'

'I'm all right, Rosie.'

'Well you don't look it, gal.' Then, in a gentler tone, 'You'd be doing me a favour too, a lot of my grandchildren are evacuated to the country, and I don't half miss them. Looking after your little 'un for an hour or two would be lovely.'

The first time she agreed she hadn't known what to do with herself. She had no desire to go out, and indoors without the lively little girl running around seemed strange. She lay on the bed and tried to sleep, but it was impossible. It was difficult enough to sleep at night, let alone during the daytime. Yet she felt tired. She tried to knit, but found she was going too fast and making mistakes in the pattern. She even took out her embroidery, which she hadn't touched for ages, and which she had previously found a relaxing occupation, but this time it didn't work. Finally she settled down to lose herself in the play on the wireless. At least I'm resting this way, she thought, and surely that will do me good. After that first time seldom a week went by without Rosie having Joanna for an afternoon. Sometimes she took the child out, to the park, up the High Street, or down to Brown Street to visit her best pal. But she always told Anna her plans beforehand, 'so you'll know whereabouts we are, luv.' Although appreciating the reasoning behind this thoughtfulness, Anna shivered.

'How's Joe,' Rosie asked one day when she called to collect the little girl.

'Last I heard he was OK, but that was over a fortnight ago. Sometimes it goes weeks an' weeks, Rosie, then I get two or three letters close together.'

'I think I upset your Joe the day she was born,' Rosie said quietly, nodding her head towards Joanna who was playing in a corner of the room. 'I didn't mean to, I was just so thrilled seeing the baby and I sort of blurted it out when he came in.'

'Rosie,' Anna's voice was urgent, 'you won't, won't let on about ...' she couldn't bring herself to say the word rape, 'about this thing that happened to me, will you?'

Rosie shook her head vigorously 'No, your secret's safe with me, luv.'

'See, not many know about it really. That it's not Joe's, I mean, and Queenie's going to have it soon as it's born.'

''Struth, is she?'

'Oh, p'raps I shouldn't have said that.' They stood looking at each other, while in the corner Joanna rocked her dolly to sleep, singing to it in a tuneless little voice.

'Don't worry,' Rosie said, 'it'll go no further than my house. How's Queenie going to explain it though, a young baby appearing when her own are grown up, married and with kids of their own.'

'She said she'd put it about it's an orphan, from friends in another part of London. Look, I don't think I should be telling you this. I mean Queenie mightn't like it.'

'Mum's the word, gal.' Rosie tapped the side of her nose. 'Now don't you worry, a baby's a baby however it got there, it's not the poor little blighter's fault, and I expect that's what Queenie thinks. But it's a handsome thing to do all the same. I can't see my Jim allowing it and he's pretty easy-going.'

After she left, promising to take Joanna to the swings in the park, Anna sank into the armchair. Now what had she done? It was all very well to kid herself that very few people would know, but things got about on the grapevine. She trusted Queenie and Rosie, but what about all the others in the street? Questions were bound to be asked, and folk weren't daft. They'd soon twig. Why oh why did she go to the pictures that afternoon? She wouldn't be in this mess now if she'd stayed home and looked after her daughter instead of gallivanting off to enjoy herself. Whatever made her do it? She tried to remember which film had drawn her so and couldn't. Not a single detail of it came back; only the feel of that huge hand coming across her mouth and almost stopping her from breathing and then, just before she fainted, that heavy dark-brown face bearing down on her … oh no, no, no.

Suddenly it was as though a fog had lifted from her mind and she recalled that terrible evening with clarity. Leaving the Palace picture house, walking to the bus stop with June, even June laughing and telling her to go on and not wait with her for the bus. Then the walk down Dason Street and the man coming out of Tailor's Yard. 'Oh God, why did he do it, why, why?' Her hands were covering her face now, her fingers pressing hard into the softness of her hair. How could she have forgotten that glimpse of her attacker? How?

How long she sat in the armchair, head in hands and rocking rhythmically to and fro, she didn't know. She was completely dry-eyed and what her attacker looked like was totally clear in her mind. She'd only had a glimpse when he turned her into that factory, and then again in those seconds before she lost consciousness, when his face loomed large before her. 'Oh God,' she said again, 'what am I going to do?'

The old Anna, the Anna who existed before Joe went away, before the ... rape – there, she'd allowed the word into her mind at last – before the pregnancy, before these last few awful months, that Anna would have gone to pieces and probably pushed the memories away again. But I mustn't do that, she thought. There's Joanna, and there's Queenie to think of, and Queenie is taking the baby when it's born; I have to tell her the truth.

Painfully she rose from the armchair and slowly, her hands on her stomach, she went upstairs and washed her face. Every movement seemed to her as though someone else was making it. She unscrewed the Ponds vanishing cream and placed three daubs – one on each cheek and one on her nose. As she rubbed it in, then lightly powdered over it, she felt the baby kicking vigorously.

'I blocked him out,' she said to her reflection. 'I thought it wouldn't matter, but now it does. Because if I have a different coloured child everyone will know it isn't Joe's.'

She walked with head down, hoping she wouldn't meet anybody, wouldn't have to talk. Her greatest need now was to get to Queenie's and tell her what she had remembered. Her mind refused to function beyond the point of telling, she dare not imagine any reaction, she only knew she was much too far gone now to do anything about the baby except give it birth.

Queenie had been on early shift at the factory and not long been home. She took one look at Anna's face and bundled her inside. 'What's the matter, love?'

'I've remembered the man, Queenie.'

'You knew him – recognized him?'

She shook her head. 'No, but there's something you've got to know now, Queenie. I – I think you'd better sit down.'

'We both will. Tell me what's on your mind, luv.'

'The man – he was coloured, Queenie. It was a black man who attacked me that night.'

'Oh my poor Anna. You're – you're sure?'

'I'm sure, and – and I've come to say it's all right, I don't expect you to take the baby now.'

Queenie came over and put her arms round the girl. This time there was no hesitation. ''Course I will. I promised, didn't I? Its colour don't make no difference to me, orphans come in all nationalities. Now don't you worry, the arrangements we made stand. Now I'm going to put the kettle on. Where's Joanna?'

'Rosie's got her. She's taken her to the park.'

'Never known a woman love kiddies as much as she does. You'd think seven of her own would have cured her, wouldn't you?'

Anna couldn't manage a laugh, but she smiled. 'She likes them best when they're babies, she tells me. You know, real tiny babies.'

Queenie made a pot of tea and told Anna about her latest trip to Wiltshire to see her grandchildren. 'They've become real country kids since they've been down there,' she said. 'They know the names of all the breeds of animals, they've even ridden a horse. Doris was keen on that, keener than her brother, I think. I said to Jen, I bet Tom only rode one because Doris did – he'd not be outdone by a girl, if I know him.'

Anna gazed at her friend, not really taking in her chatter. She finished her tea and was surprised to discover how her hand shook as she replaced the cup in its saucer. The shaking didn't stop as she reached across to put it on the table, using her other hand to steady it, then suddenly it wasn't just her hands that were shaking, but her face and body were quivering and trembling. Queenie was out of her chair in seconds, her capable arms about the girl, her soft London voice soothing, even as her hands stroked and massaged until the shuddering eased into a series of breathless gasps, before quietening down altogether.

Queenie insisted on walking home with Anna, in spite of the younger woman's protests.

'You've had a bit of a shock,' she said, 'and it'll be company for you. I won't come in, because Fred will be back soon and wanting his tea. That man lives for his food, his pint, his football and darts. I tell you, nothing else matters to him. What he'll do if Jerry drops a bomb on either of those pubs I don't know.'

Five minutes later Rosie brought Joanna home. 'I won't stop,' she said. 'Got a bit of fish when we was out, didn't we, darling?' She kissed the top of Joanna's head. 'Blinking Billy told me he might have some if I looked in today, and Jim do like a nice bit of haddock for his tea.'

Anna was relieved. Rosie's chatter was the last thing she wanted just now. Telling Queenie had taken more out of her than she'd expected, although Queenie's reaction had amazed her. What a marvellous woman, she thought as she prepared tea. Later, when Joanna was tucked up in bed, she recalled Queenie's answer when she asked her about Fred.

'He'll kick up at first in any case; it's a matter of principle with him, but as long as it doesn't interfere with his life style, and it won't, I'll see to that, then there's nothing to worry over.'

For the first time since Joe had been in the Army Anna was glad he wasn't stationed in England now and couldn't suddenly pop home on weekend leave. Her feelings were in turmoil and she needed time to sort them out. She was even contemplating telling Joe the whole story, but not yet, not until he was at least back in England. She went to bed early, feeling absolutely whacked. Gazing at her sleeping child she said quietly, 'If Jerry comes tonight I do believe I'll sleep through it.' Tenderly she tucked a golden wisp of hair out of Joanna's eye, 'Thank heaven you aren't old enough to realize what's going on here,' she whispered. 'God bless, my sweetheart.'

Chapter 11

Anna was lifting Joanna from her highchair when the warning went just before two o'clock that Saturday afternoon. She was tired, feeling awkward and cumbersome, her pregnancy now seven months old. 'Best get down the shelter, lovey. Come along, Mummy'll wash up later.' She thrust a rag doll into her daughter's arms and took a drawstring bag containing some knitting with her, and went through the back door into the garden. Ensconced in the Anderson she sat on a cushion on the too-narrow bench while Joanna played with her doll. Later, if they were here a long while, she would knit, but just now she wanted nothing more than to close her eyes and sleep. She didn't do so, of course; instead she watched her little daughter's engrossed expression as she dressed and undressed her doll, patting the yellow woollen hair into place, and chatting Harry Hemsley's Horace talk to her.

Anna heard the bombs screaming down, and reached for Joanna, hugging her tightly. The baby shifted inside her, and she felt sick with fear. How often did Joe feel like this out there in the thick of it all the time? He had to cope when Jerry was firing at them, she too must be brave now the war had come to Dason Street. Kissing the top of her daughter's fair curls she wondered how everyone else was. Queenie would most likely be in her shelter, and Rosie and Jim opposite would be too, unless they were up town shopping. Rosie did like to go late on a Saturday to get the bargains. Though there were precious few bargains to be had these days unless you possessed money enough to pay for them on the black market.

An extra loud bang made her jump and started Joanna crying. 'It's all right, sweetheart, Mummy's here. Hush now, and soon we'll go back indoors and play for a little while before bedtime.'

When Anna came up from the shelter after the all-clear had sounded it looked as though someone had taken a giant paint-brush, dipped it in luminous red paint and swept it across the sky. It was like that first night of the blitz when the glow from incendiary bombs lit London.

Was there more to come? Could she risk taking Joanna indoors and gathering clothes and food for the night?

All along Dason Street folk were emerging from the shelters and houses. Across the garden fence Anna spoke to the old man who lived next door. 'The world's gorn mad girl, stark staring mad,' he said. Holding tightly to Joanna's hand she went indoors. She could hear voices outside in the street and on opening the front door she saw a number of near neighbours standing in groups.

Rosie came over to her. 'You all right, duck? And the little 'un?'

She nodded. 'We're OK, Rosie.'

Someone said, 'Some poor devils must have copped it. Was just cooking something for tea when the explosions started. Now 'itler's gorn and ruined it.' The woman speaking wiped her hands on her overall and wrapped it more tightly round her skinny waist, as though she found comfort in the movement, then she hobbled down the street, muttering to herself.

'Reckon I'll get back too,' Anna said. 'Come on, Jo.'

'You can come in our shelter tonight if you like,' Rosie offered.

'Thanks, but we'll be OK. I'll make a flask of tea and take some milk for her in case they come back. I've got blankets down there anyway.'

When the siren went again a few hours later Anna was in the bathroom. Hurriedly she gathered their things together and with

Joanna in her arms made for the back door. She came over dizzy in the middle of the kitchen and for a few seconds the room spun crazily. Slithering the little girl to the ground she leant against the table, taking deep breaths. It couldn't be the baby, she mustn't start now with an air-raid on.

When the room tilted as she lifted her head she stumbled to the back door and turned the key. 'Come here, darling,' she said, listening to the planes already overhead, 'we'll go under the stairs.'

It was dark there, but at least they'd be safer than anywhere else in the house, and when it quietened down she would take her daughter to the shelter in the garden. Thank God that the giddiness had passed; although it had left her feeling a slight nausea, she was overwhelmingly relieved that there were no pains. She had already made arrangements with Rosie for looking after Joanna when she did go into labour.

They were under the stairs for hours. Eventually Joanna fell asleep on the blanket Anna had brought down for her. Desperately needing to go to the lavatory again Anna fumbled for the little torch, and eased herself up, then slowly mounted the stairs to the bathroom. The noise was much worse up here, and she cursed herself for not having made it to the Anderson with Joanna. They would withstand anything except a direct hit, or so the government said, but since the siren had sounded this evening there had been no lull in the bombardment. Should she have taken a chance and dashed there with the child anyway? That was a laugh, she thought, she hadn't been able to dash anywhere for the last few weeks in her cumbersome state.

The whistle of falling bombs set her body trembling. She had to get back downstairs to Joanna. Slowly she descended; however much she tried she couldn't seem to move faster, and she was filled with a sense of disgust because of the weight in her stomach that was hampering her. If Joanna was killed, down there, alone ...

Anna was on the bottom stair, her hand on the newel post when the whistling seemed to be filling her head, pushing her forward, and with a huge crack the banister gave way and plaster and beams came crashing down around her.

'Anna, Anna, where are you?' It was Rosie's voice. Somewhere she could hear Joanna crying, but that was muffled and she wasn't sure if she was dreaming. Then Rosie's call again, loud and urgent: 'Anna, ANNA.'

'I'm here' she managed, surprised at how weak her voice was. 'Get Jo, oh please get Joanna, she's under the stairs and she's crying.'

Dust seemed to be everywhere, swirling in circles before her eyes, in her mouth and throat. She tried to rise, but lumps of ceiling were pinning her down. She had to get up and go to Joanna. She hurt all over, and realized she must have passed out. The last thing she recalled was the screaming whistling in her ears.

The crying stopped and Anna caught her breath. 'Jo, Joanna, talk to me; Jo, darling, call out to Mummy.' Her mouth and throat were filling with the acrid taste of wood and plaster dust. Panic overwhelmed her, what had happened to her daughter? Why wasn't she crying any longer? Then came Rosie's voice. 'It's all right, Anna. I've got Joanna and I'll be with you in a moment.' Then, suddenly quite close, the blessed relief of Joanna's babyish tones. 'Jo firsty, Auntie Rosie, Jo firsty, want drink.'

Rosie took the child outside where willing hands looked after her, then she went back with warden Sid Wentworth to help Anna. Carefully they removed some banister rails which were wedged across the lumps of ceiling plaster surrounding her and Sid said, 'We'll soon have you out, love.'

'Joanna...?'

'She's not hurt Anna, don't worry.' Rosie's voice was reassuring and Anna said weakly, 'Should have gone down the shelter.' She started to cough as the dust caught her again.

'Never mind that now, you're both safe.' Rosie's voice was husky with it too as she began to wheeze and cough. Suddenly there was space as the last bits of debris were lifted off, and Rosie and Sid reached out for her. As gently as possible they tried to help her up but it was no use, she couldn't stand. 'It's … it's my foot, I think.' Sid, who was much smaller than Rosie, crouched down beside Anna to see. 'We'll have to carry her, ankle's like a barrage balloon. Are you game, Rosie? We should be able to manage between us.'

Sid took the top half while Rosie supported her legs and between them they got her over to Rosie and Jim's place. She was crying with pain but when she saw Joanna there she summoned a smile. 'All right, sweetheart,' she said.

The bomb had not fallen in Dason Street but in Brown Street, demolishing two houses and killing all the occupants. Half a dozen houses on Anna's side of Dason Street had taken the brunt of the blast, while opposite on Rosie and Jim's side there had not even been a shattered window.

Anna, miraculously, was not badly hurt. A sprained ankle and bruising on her legs where the plaster had fallen, a few scratches on her face were the extent of her injuries. What a blessing Joanna was asleep under the stairs. She felt a tremendous relief that Joanna was untouched, and vowed in future always to use the Anderson, no matter how difficult or inconvenient it was to make it there.

She hadn't wanted to go to hospital but the lady who drove the ambulance was gently insistent.

The hospital bound her foot and checked her over. 'Everything seems in order,' the elderly doctor said. 'Exactly when is the baby due?'

'Two months' time.'

'Well, don't worry, mother, babies are usually tougher than we think and there's a strong heartbeat there.'

They were able to return to number 5 the following night. Sid and Jim boarded up the staircase windows and landing ceiling and Rosie and Queenie cleared up the mess. Even so the smell of dust seemed everywhere, and as fast as she wiped the mantelpiece and furniture so they acquired another layer. She was told to rest her foot, but she discovered that by putting a small amount of pressure on her heel she could slowly hobble round. Queenie and Rosie rolled her mattress up and brought it downstairs with pillows and blankets, and did the same with Joanna's bedding.

'You'll only need to use the stairs to get to the bathroom, Anna. Will you be able to manage?' Rosie asked. 'You're welcome to come across to us until your ankle's walkable, you know. Jim won't mind.'

Queenie solved the problem by giving her a white china chamber pot. 'Used to be Mum's, Anna; she had several, so you can keep this one. Handy thing to have sometimes.'

Jim came over the next evening when the siren went. 'Will you come over to us, Anna? Rosie's worried about you.' She went because of Joanna. What use would she be if anything happened and she couldn't move fast enough. Her ankle was very painful and she wished now that she had rested it more during the day.

Rosie had turned her shelter into a cosy little room. There was a bench all round, two folding canvas chairs, a folding greenbaize card-table, and lots of small cushions with brightly coloured knitted covers scattered around the bench. At one end sat a pile of books and magazines, and at the other a bulging knitting-bag. 'Got to have something to occupy my mind,' Rosie said when she saw Anna looking at it. 'Jim'll tell you I go crazy if I can't be doing something, don't I, Jim?'

They insisted she sit in one of the chairs, with cushions at her back and a small box to rest her foot on, while Joanna slept on a thick blanket on the bench. 'Floor's too damp,' Rosie said. They tied the child in with one of Rosie's ample dress belts, round her waist and slotted into the slats of the bench like reins. 'Now we'll all sleep peacefully knowing she can't fall off,' Rosie said, sounding well pleased with her arrangements. Anna didn't sleep much. The racket going on outside was one thing, the way she felt was another. Everything seemed ultra sore, her stomach, back, her shoulders and legs. There was nothing specific, yet overall she felt really rotten. Rosie read for a while, kissed Jim noisily, murmured goodnight to Anna and was snoring within five minutes. Anna smiled to herself. She wished she was back in her own house, or at least her own shelter, but she felt grateful to her friends for their concern and, if she was to be truthful with herself, this was a better arrangement for a few days while she was so incapacitated with her ankle. Joanna moved slightly on the bench, let out a deep sigh and stayed asleep.

Two days later Anna haemorrhaged and was rushed into hospital.

Anna sat by the window, and watched for Rosie to bring Joanna back from the park. She didn't know how she would have managed these last few weeks without Rosie and Jim Bateson, and Queenie Parkes. It was to Rosie she had staggered when the devastating pains which culminated in her haemorrhage had begun; and it was Rosie and Queenie between them who had looked after Joanna, and still found time in between their other work to visit her in hospital and assure her all was well.

The baby, a dark-skinned boy, died at birth. The doctor could offer no reason except that 'if your dates are right it was a seven-and- half-month baby, but a good weight nevertheless.' Queenie and Rosie could. 'It's a wonder it didn't happen straight away after the bomb, but it was delayed shock, whatever that doctor might say.' And just as well, Rosie privately thought. This was one pregnancy that should have been terminated at the start.

Anna was dumbfounded by the loss she felt. There was relief, and a subdued kind of happiness that Joe would not need to know, but hovering like a grey shadow over it all was this sense of loss.

Grief for a baby she had carried and felt move for seven months. A baby she hadn't wanted, a baby she was going to give away, the result of something so awful she still couldn't think about it without feeling sick and dirty. She felt tremendously mixed up.

Queenie was shocked by her reaction to the news. Her relief was so profound it both frightened and amazed her. Any death, particularly that of a baby, usually devastated her. She sat in her bathroom the evening she and Rosie had brought Anna home from the hospital, and tried to come to terms with herself. Feeling like this now, why had she made such a fuss about aborting the foetus at a few weeks? Was it time she looked into her heart to discover truths she was trying to shut out? It brought another ugly thought into focus. Did she have a colour prejudice? Again she had thought not, and had for many years abhorred the way the Americans went on with the coloured population in their country. She couldn't talk to Fred or to her own children about such matters, nor to Rosie who, she suspected, would straightforwardly say it was a blessing in disguise. There was only one person she might be able to voice her thoughts and unburden her guilt to and that was Paul Tranmer. Something that was not remotely possible, for all that he was so often in her thoughts.

She called round to see Anna early the following morning. The girl looked desperately tired still. 'Did you manage to get some sleep in spite of the raid again last night, Anna?'

Anna shook her head. 'Not really, but I don't think it was entirely the planes going over that kept me awake, Queenie. I keep thinking about ... well, about what has happened. I reckon I could try to move to another district before Joe gets home.'

'But where could you go? Sid and Jim have patched this place up fine, and after the war ...'

'It's not that. If I moved now, Joe could think it was because of the bomb, but it would mean, well, less chance of anyone telling him what happened.'

'Not many people know. Me and Rosie and Jim, and Liza and Sid, and we're not going to say anything. Who else is there? No one, Anna, who really knows the whole story. Oh, folk down the street knew you were having a baby, but they didn't know it wasn't your husband's. They didn't know it was the result of a rape. And by the time Joe's home they'll all have something else to think about.'

'Well, I don't know. I don't want to move really. All the friends I have are down this street ...'

Queenie patted her hand, 'Then don't. Stay here amongst us and get well again. Get well for Joe and Joanna.'

'Did you know they said in the hospital there mustn't be any more babies?' Queenie nodded. 'They said physically I could have another but it would probably kill me.'

Queenie was silent.

'How do I explain that to Joe when – if he comes back from the war?'

'Anna, my old Mum used to say, "Don't meet trouble halfway", and there's a lot of wisdom in that. In any case, doctors have been known to be wrong.'

Joanna came running through from the kitchen, 'Mummy, there's a pussy cat in the garden, come and see, come and see ...'

Anna smiled at her daughter, and as she went through to look she said, over her shoulder, 'Anyway Queenie, you must be pretty relieved by it all. But I'll *never* forget what you were prepared to do for me. Never, as long as I live.'

Except the one thing you wanted seven months ago, Queenie thought, guilt sweeping through her body as once again she felt the pangs of liberation. She was glad Anna was on her way to the garden and couldn't see her face, for surely some of her emotions showed, and she mustn't burden Anna with those too.

Chapter 12

1944

The rough notice pushed into the top of the dugout on the beach at Anzio read, *SEAVIEW BOARDING HOUSE.* Joe grinned to himself as he slid into his hole again. 'What bright spark put that sign out,' he said to his mate Tommy, who was inside reading for the umpteenth time his last letter from home. The paper looked as battle-worn as the soldier, but Tommy folded it again into its now familiar and split creases and, almost reverently, put it in the top pocket of his tunic.

'Think that's a bit of Chalky's work,' he said, rubbing his hands across his eyes. 'Fancies himself as a bit of a signwriter.'

There was a lull in the battle on the narrow beachhead where Joe had recently had nightmares that he would spend the rest of his life. Unlike Tommy, who seemed to gain so much comfort from that precious letter in his pocket, Joe refused to think about Anna and Joanna. He knew that if he reread his latest letter, received over a month ago, he would go to pieces.

'Going to have a kip, Tommy,' he said, sinking down and closing his eyes. As if from a great distance he heard the other soldier's voice. 'Right, I'll wake you when it's time to go.' In spite of his utter weariness Joe was smiling inside at the other man's manner of speaking, *for all the world as if we was waiting for a ruddy train to go on holiday or something,* was how he put it to himself.

He slept on when more men clambered down into 'Seaview', but he was instantly awake when the call came to break out.

It was two days later, although Joe couldn't have put a time or date to it, when, through the drizzling rain and a hail of bullets, Joe fell. Tommy, coming on him a few seconds afterwards, heard the word 'Anna' over and over again. 'Anna, Anna, Anna, Annaaaa ...'

'Oh my God.' Rosie put a hand over her mouth. 'Jim, *Jim*, the telegraph boy's just gone into Anna's place.'

Jim came at a run. Rosie moved from the window and almost fell into his arms. 'Oh, Jim. I'd better go over. Poor little devil.'

'Hold on, gal, Joe might not be dead. He could be taken prisoner like our Ricky ...' He looked at his wife. 'Want me to come too?'

'No, I don't think so. I'll bring her over here if needs be.' She squeezed his hand. 'Not much I can do except be there, make her a cup of tea and look after the youngster. You make yourself one too, duck, I'll see you later.' She took off her overall and slippers, put on her shoes and walked across the road.

Anna had had two letters from Joe that May morning, after not hearing for weeks. Both were dated March. It was a beautiful day and with the loving messages in the letters echoing in her heart, she wanted to run and jump and dance.

I'm fine, Joe had written, *and I've got the snapshot you sent of you and Joanna in my breast pocket, close to my heart. She is like a miniature you, my darling, and if she grows up as beautiful and as kind too I shall be twice blessed.*

She was cleaning the bedroom windows at the back and watching Joanna's antics with her dolls in the garden when the sound from the heavy doorknocker reverberated through the house. She ran down the stairs, still smiling at her daughter's motherly attitudes to her 'babies' as she fussed and cuddled them. The shock when she saw the telegraph boy seemed to paralyse her for a few seconds. Without speaking she took the missive from him. 'No reply,' she said, closing the door. With trembling fingers she opened the orange envelope and drew out the telegram. Her first reaction was relief. He wasn't dead, only wounded. He'd be all right. He'd be able to come home and get well, and … Slowly she uncurled the paper she had screwed up in her hand, and read it again. *Seriously wounded* … 'I must go to him,' she said. 'Joe, oh please be all right, please get well and come home to us …' She was still in the hall when Rosie rapped on the door and called out: 'Anna, it's me, Rosie. May I come in, please?'

The journey across London and then into the furthermost reaches of Surrey seemed endless, the chunting of the train reiterating *nearly there, nearly there, nearly there*, like a cuckoo forever on the same sound. It was now Saturday, and Queenie and Rosie were sharing custody of Joanna for the day. Both had offered to come with her, but she wanted to be alone. Strange how people always seemed to try to protect her, she thought. At one time perhaps she needed it, but not any longer. Not that kind of protection; having someone to smooth the way, iron out the difficulties, cope for you. When you really got down to it no one could do that. In the end you had to cope for yourself in your own way. Nevertheless Anna was grateful to them both. She hadn't wanted to bring her daughter on this cheerless journey, not knowing what she was going to find when she reached her destination. She had tried to discover how badly wounded Joe was when she telephoned the hospital from the call box in the high road, but the line was very crackly, and the sister she spoke to told her hardly anything about his injuries. 'Leg and head mostly,' was all Anna could make out.

The military hospital was grey and forbidding-looking, but

the grounds were cheerful with hospital blue. Young men walking with crutches, being pushed in wheelchairs by laughing nurses, men sprawled beneath trees reading, thinking, dreaming … She went up the steps and into reception where she was directed to Joe's ward.

'Fourth floor,' the young nurse said, and now she was here, and at the end of the corridor through those doors was her husband, her beloved Joe. Injured but alive. She said a silent prayer of thanks to God for Joe's safe return.

Sister came from her office outside the ward just before Anna reached the double doors. 'Joe Putt,' she said, when Anna told her whom she had come to visit. 'Yes, I'll take you to him in a moment, Mrs Putt, but I'd like a word with you first.'

'He's not – he hasn't died, has he, Sister?'

'No, Joe's alive, my dear, but it will be better to know about his condition before you see him. In here, please.'

Coming home, Anna relived the awful afternoon. Joe's physical injuries were bad enough, he had lost one leg and there was doubt about the other, but worse, much worse than this was his mind. It didn't seem to be there. He hadn't recognized her and he had hardly spoken a word all afternoon. 'Yes' and 'No' when one of the nurses asked him whether he would like a cup of tea. A sort of grunt when Anna herself tried to talk to him, and a sharp turning away when she kissed him. She felt devastated. It was as though she had lost him after all – no, no, I mustn't think like that. He's there, beneath the muddle that is his brain now; down far, far below the horror of what happened to him out there, is still my Joe, my kind, wonderful husband.

She tried to talk to him about Joanna but he didn't seem to be taking it in. The blank look on his face most of the time was the worst thing of all, as though nothing and nobody mattered any more. The only time she had seen a glimmer of the real Joe was when she first went in and gently touched his hand. He opened his eyes, smiled at her and very faintly returned the pressure.

Then he slept for half an hour, and she sat contentedly beside the bed, happy just to be there for him. When he woke there was no recognition. The sister had warned her about this, yet that didn't make it easier to bear. Before she left she promised to come again in a few days, but this brought no response, and leaning over the bed she softly kissed his lips. They felt cold, almost lifeless. Sitting in the train that was taking her home Anna shuddered.

Dason Street rejoiced that Joe was alive. 'Well, at least he'll be out of it now, gal, and although he could still cop it here, he's got more chance than in the army,' was Rosie's verdict. Looking skywards she added; 'Please God he has.' Anna told Rosie and Queenie about his amputation, and that there were doubts about his other leg.

'Marvellous what they can do these days,' Rosie said. 'They'll save it if they can, don't you worry. And if worst comes to worst and he does have it off, well just look at that Group Captain Bader and what he does with no legs.'

She had played down his mental state. More because she couldn't bear too much talk about it than for any other reason. She quickly came to terms with the knowledge of the physical disabilities. Together they would overcome them. She told both Queenie and Rosie that mentally he was in a bad way, but she hadn't enlarged on it.

'You mean his mind?' Rosie said bluntly.

'He – he doesn't remember things, Sister said.'

'To be expected, luv. Give him time to heal. The main thing is you've got him back, and when this beastly war's over you'll be able to pick up your lives again.'

With Ricky a prisoner, and some of the others' sons and daughters in the forces, Rosie went through a list of prayers for each one of them every night, kneeling beside the bed, or bunker if they were in the Anderson. Once Jim said, 'Rosie, d'you really think that rigmarole is going to help any of them if their number's called?'

'Jim Bateson, how *dare* you. They're your children too, you know, and if anything I can do or say will keep them safe then I'll do it. Anyway I believe in God, in Jesus, in the church's teachings.'

'What about the losers, Rosie. D'you think they *didn't* believe, then? Is that why—'

They quarrelled that night and didn't make up before going to sleep as they usually did. Not that Rosie could sleep, she lay thinking that if a bomb fell and killed Jim tonight, he'd die with harsh words between them.

In the early hours, she leaned over and softly tickled his chin, her hand running down his chest and on to his stomach.

'Get off, what you doing ... Rosie, Rosie,' he murmured, his arms coming round her ample figure.

'I'm sorry I got all het up, Jim. I don't like us to quarrel like this, luv.'

Aroused fully now, his arm tightened round her, 'Who's quarrelling, darling? Come on, let me love you properly.'

Rosie looked after Joanna a few days later when Anna went again to visit Joe. In the train she dared to hope just a little. Surely each day he would grow stronger in body and mind. Sister had said this was possible: 'Certainly the physical injuries will heal, unfortunately we don't know as much about healing the mind. But try not to over worry my dear. Rest and seeing you could work wonders. Have patience.' When she had pointed out that he didn't seem to know her sister was again reassuring. 'I think he did when you first arrived. There was more response when you touched him than he's shown since being here. Come as often as you can.'

By the time she reached the hospital, however, her buoyant mood had deflated. She had brought with her the latest photographs of Joanna, some on her own and some playing with children in the park. She didn't think she could bear it if he didn't recognize his daughter.

Joe slept for most of her visit. When he did open his eyes he looked down at her hand which was holding his, but he said nothing and his expression remained bland. Anna felt her eyes filling with tears and she turned her head away. The photographs never left her handbag. She stayed an hour and a half, then gently leaned over the bed and kissed his cheek. 'Sleep well darling,' she whispered, 'and come back to us soon.'

'Doctor would like a word, Mrs Putt.'

The doctor was a softly spoken man who looked to be in his early fifties. He looked tired as he gestured her to a chair. He assured her that the amputation was healing well and there was every chance now of saving the other leg. 'It is responding to treatment and we are well pleased with his progress on the physical side.'

'And mentally, Doctor?'

'He is tired: not so much physically tired as mentally exhausted. We can find no brain injury as such, he simply seems to have switched off. Maybe because of some of the horrors he's seen and taken part in, but it will take a long time and a lot of patience on your part to heal him, Mrs Putt.'

Anna felt her lip trembling, but she had to know. 'Will he heal, Doctor? Will he recognize me again, remember …' her voice faltered and she took a deep breath, 'remember how it used to be?'

'I'm sure he will. I would go so far as to say that I think he already does, but his mind is far too fatigued to cope with anything at present. That is how I see the situation. I'm a physician, my dear, I try to mend broken bodies, but these men are returning with broken minds too. I believe your husband will win through, with your help.'

As she rose to go he reached out and touched her arm. 'When

you visit talk to him as much as possible about the everyday things of your life before the war. Just chat about them, don't question him, simply talk about anything you have shared.'

Anna had composed herself by the time she reached home and went to collect Joanna from Rosie.

'Stay and have something to eat with us,' Rosie said, 'it will save you having to bother.'

Anna kept up a façade of brightness throughout the meal. Rosie refused her offer to wash up, or at least help with it. 'Goodness, how long will it take me to rinse a few plates, luv? No, you get off home. And I'll have this little 'un any time; she's been as good as gold, haven't you, my pet?'

After that she visited Joe twice a week, while Queenie and Rosie took turns to look after Joanna, depending on Queenie's factory shifts. As Joe had mentioned in one of his letters, which had arrived on the same day as the telegram, she looked like a miniature Anna. Even more so than he would have been able to tell from the black and white photograph she had sent. The same pale-gold hair, light-blue eyes and daintiness that in her mother gave an air of fragility. In the child, however, it made women say, 'Ah, but she's pretty, she'll break some hearts in a few years' time.'

On her next visit Anna saw the ward sister as she left, and asked her if she thought it would benefit Joe to see his daughter.

'It might. I really couldn't say, but why not bring her and see. Joe's up now and you could sit in the day room with him, or even out in the grounds. How old is she?'

'Four. She was born the day war broke out.'

She took her the following week. Joanna was excited about going on a train, but frightened when the engine roared into the station. She hid her face in her mother's skirt and clung tightly to her hand. Once on board though, she looked about her with interest, and kept the whole carriage amused with her observations and questions.

Anna had told her daughter they were going to a hospital to see Daddy. 'He isn't very well now, but one day he will be, then he will come home to live with us.'

'The man in the photograph?' Joanna said, her eyes wide with wonder. 'Will we see him?'

'Yes, darling, the man in the photograph. Here, shall we read your book for a while now?'

Joanna agreed happily. She loved being read to, and snuggled herself against Anna with a rapturous look on her face.

They ate their sandwiches in the station waiting room, then Anna took the little girl into the toilet. Afterwards she took a small brush from her handbag and brushed the long fair hair until it gleamed. Usually she hurried straight to the hospital, but today she even lingered to fiddle with her own hair and to repowder her nose. Joanna was growing impatient. 'Come on, Mummy, or the host-a-pital will be closed,' she said, and Anna knew she could not keep putting off the moment when she walked through those gates again.

Joe was in a wheelchair in the day room. Some of the other men in there were reading or writing, some were doing jigsaw puzzles, some talking quietly to their relatives or friends. In a corner a group were playing cards, their crutches leaning against the chairs. Joe was just sitting, his eyes closed and his brow creased and furrowed as though his thoughts were not pleasant ones. Holding tightly to Joanna's hand she walked over.

'Hullo Joe,' she said softly. 'It's me, Anna. I've brought your daughter to see you. Open your eyes, darling. Joanna's here with me today.' She spoke quietly but firmly as the doctor had advised some weeks before, and she noticed Joe's eyelids move slightly. It was the merest flutter, but she knew then that he had heard, and she prayed he had also understood her words.

'Is Daddy asleep?' Joanna's voice was strong and confident.

'Yes, Daddy's asleep. We'll sit here for a while until he wakes, Joanna. Come and help me find some chairs,' she said.

'Will my Daddy talk to me when he wakes up?' The child was watching the man in the wheelchair very closely. 'His eyes are moving, Mummy, I fink he's nearly awake now. Is he the man in the photograph? Is he my Daddy?'

Joe's hands relinquished their grip on the sides of the wheelchair and reached forward as though to touch the speaker, then he opened his eyes.

Joanna shrank back against her mother, and Anna reached out for her husband's hand. 'Joe,' she said softly, 'you're awake. I'm so glad because I've brought Joanna with me today.'

'Jo – anna,' he repeated slowly. 'She's only a baby.'

Before she could stop her Joanna unfurled herself from Anna's skirt and said indignantly, 'I'm not a baby. I'm four years old and next year I'll be going to school like the big girls do.'

Joe blinked. Then he moved his head and body forward slightly and looked down at her. 'Jo – anna. Baby Joanna,' he said.

'Daddy, I'm *not* a baby ...'

'Hush darling,' Anna began, but suddenly Joe spoke again, this time in a much stronger voice. 'No, you're not. You must be ...' Turning his head to look at his wife he said clearly, 'How old is she, Anna?'

With tears of happiness streaming down her cheeks Anna told him.

Joe made rapid strides after that. Anna knew he wouldn't be home for some time, possibly not until he had his new leg and had learned to walk with it. 'Or I might not get one for some time, but they'll let me home once I can get along on my other one and some crutches. I'm lucky they saved that one Anna, some of them in here have lost both and that's tragic. But I'll be able to get around all right, you'll see.'

Now he had come back to her mentally she concentrated on the physical injuries, and set about altering the house so it would be easier for him. Rosie helped her. 'Shouldn't overdo it, luv,' she remarked one day. 'I mean Joe'll probably want things as near normal as possible.'

'But he'll need the bed downstairs, Rosie?'

'Might not. I reckon you'd be best leaving things as they are. Time to shift round is when he's home and finds he can't manage. Myself, I don't think that time will come. Joe'll climb the stairs with his wooden leg – or without it, I'd take a bet on that.'

Anna still went to see him twice a week, usually taking Joanna the first time and leaving her with Queenie or Rosie for the second visit. Joe was often out in the grounds waiting for them, and when he saw them come through the gate he'd trundle his wheelchair down the drive to meet them.

The little girl became a great favourite with most of the men on the ward. Unless the weather was inclement they went into the grounds, Anna pushing the wheelchair and Joanna running alongside, usually chattering about the things she had done and seen since her last visit. Joe listened quietly, making the occasional response and, more and more now, smiling at his pretty daughter.

Joanna accepted him as he was. She had never known him any other way and it was easy for her to be natural with the man in the wheelchair. The first time she noticed someone walking in the grounds on crutches, his trouser leg pinned up, she grew very excited and her voice came over loud and clear. 'Daddy, where's that man's ovver leg – what's he jumping for?'

They were sitting beneath a tree, Joe in his chair and Anna on the bench. Anna hushed her but Joe said, 'It's OK, Stalky won't mind, he's got kids of his own.' Then he explained to Joanna that Stalky only had one leg and the crutches meant he could still walk, 'even if it does look like he's jumping, darling. Soon though he'll have two legs again, because the hospital are making him a wooden one.'

'Like my dolly?'

'Yes, something like that, and later on I'll have one too, and we'll be able to have races, you and me.' Turning to Anna he added quietly, 'It's true, I've been talking to the doctors and they say I'll be able to do most things once I'm used to it, even ...' Joanna laughed and went skipping round the tree, but nevertheless he lowered his voice. 'Come here a minute, Anna.'

She bent her head close to him. 'Even that,' he whispered. 'I miss loving you that way, Anna, some nights lately it's been awful.'

'Joe, oh Joe.'

Joanna appeared in front of them. 'We could race round the tree, Daddy, when you get anuvver leg.' Then she was off round the circuit again.

'And who knows, in a year or two she could have a brother or sister,' he said quietly. 'We don't want her to be an only child, do we?'

Anna thought about it all the way home and for most of that night. What was she going to tell him when the time came? That they could love each other but there must be no more children? Or take a chance and if she got pregnant simply go through with it? Maybe she wouldn't die, but if she did it would leave two children motherless, and Joe ... She'd only just got him back – she didn't want either of them to leave the other for a long long time now. At last she fell asleep and dreamt of Joanna and her father chasing each other round one tree after another ... then the dream changed and it became Joe chasing Anna round the trees. There were hundreds of them and she dodged from one to the other. At first she and Joe were laughing as they ran, she slowing up so she didn't get too far ahead of him, then suddenly the trees seemed to close in on her, lean towards her, dark and forbidding, and although she could hear Joe calling her she couldn't see him. She woke up screaming and that woke Joanna.

The picture postcard from June took Anna by surprise. She hadn't thought about her for quite some time. *Will try to come in and see you next week*, it said. She turned it over and saw a London sparkling with lights such as it hadn't been for the last five years.

'Better open that tin of Spam when she comes,' she said to Joanna. 'Here darling, you can have the pretty picture. One day you may see it looking just like that.'

Two days after her card arrived Anna answered the knock on the door to find June standing there and by her side a lanky American soldier.

'Hi Anna,' June said, reaching forward and kissing her on the cheek. 'This is Hank.'

'Hi. Sure is nice to meet you, ma'am.'

Over tea and her precious tin of Spam Hank told her about his home in California, and his mom and pop and kid brother Elmer. While she and June were clearing the dishes from the tea table he was on the floor giving Joanna a piggyback. June closed the kitchen door. 'Well, what do you think of him, Anna? Great, isn't he? And he'd do anything for me.'

Squeals of laughter issued from the other room, and Anna touched June's arm. 'You love him, June?'

'Yea. Silly, isn't it? I mean, me, who's always gone for blokes who can give me a good time, and not wanted too much of the domestic scene really. Totally crazy, but all I want now is for the war to end and for us to be able to get married and start a family.'

'Will you live in America?'

'Yea. It's funny, y'know, I'd live anywhere with Hank, go anywhere with him. He's the only one I've truly cared about. All the others I could take or leave, know what I mean? But Hank, he's special. I don't even care if we're poor – I just want him to come back from the war OK.'

Anna nodded, too moved to speak.

'Don't mention other men when we're talking, will you, Anna, because Hank's a bit – well a bit old-fashioned I guess. I've not,' her voice was almost a whisper now, 'not always led a blameless life. I've enjoyed myself and I've enjoyed the money and being able to buy nice things, but none of that matters with Hank. That's all in the past, but I don't think he'd understand. His family are very religious, I think.'

Anna turned from the sink to look at her friend. 'Of course I won't say anything. Didn't know much about your other boyfriends anyway, but you've really got it bad this time, haven't you? Don't rush into anything, though, I mean, he's a long way from home and—'

'Oh, he's not married or anything,' June interrupted. 'Yeah, I guess I have got it bad, but there's still me underneath it all, you know, the practical, look-after-number-one girl I've always been.'

When they returned to the other room Hank was sitting in the armchair, with Joanna on his lap. He was telling her a story, and the little girl was gazing rapturously into his face.

Anna told them about Joe's injuries later in the evening, when her daughter was tucked up in bed, having been read to and kissed goodnight by both Anna and Hank.

'Gee, but that's tough, honey,' the American said, 'but he's still a lucky guy; he's got you and the little cutie upstairs.'

'And he's out of it now,' June added. 'I mean, it's not something you'd wish on anyone, to be without a leg, but he's alive, and he's coming home, and that's the important thing.' She slid her arm through Hank's as they sat together on the settee, and very gently he stroked her fingers.

A few days later the postman delivered a parcel addressed to Miss Joanna Putt. Inside was an oblong box, and when Joanna lifted the lid they both gasped with admiration at the doll lying there. Carefully Anna lifted her out. 'Isn't she beautiful, Joanna?' she said, fingering the doll's silky, golden curls and enjoying the feel of the lovely blue taffeta frock she was wearing.

There was a note inside, *For the cute little Joanna – keep your happy smile, sweetheart, love from Auntie June and Uncle Hank.*

'And I can't write and thank them,' Anna wailed. 'I've no idea where they are.'

The following day a bouquet of flowers was delivered, and the note on these said, *Thanks for making a homesick Yank so welcome. One day I hope June and I will have a sweet kid like your Joanna. See you.*

'Well, these Yanks have plenty of "bees 'n' honey",' Rosie said when she saw the gifts, 'but it's generous of him, I'll give you that.'

Chapter 13

1944

'Sid, the invasion's started. Our troops landed in France this morning.' Liza's voice was high with excitement as she ran downstairs and burst into the shop. There were no customers. 'All listening to the news I reckon,' she said later.

'Thank God.' Sid went halfway upstairs so he could hear the wireless and keep an eye on the shop at the same time. 'Where?'

'Northern coast of France was all John Snagge said. There'll be more later, I expect, and it'll be in the evening papers.'

'We must make sure the regulars have one.' Sid was suddenly all shopkeeper again. 'There'll be a rush for them.'

Everyone who came in during that Tuesday afternoon was full of the news. It had been expected, of course, but no one knew when or where. For the last few months they had seen more and more activity in the skies as the Flying Fortresses roared overhead, on their way to bomb Germany, and long before that in many of the factories, which suddenly changed their production lines. No one really knew what the finished article would be, but it didn't take much intelligence to know it was to do with the coming invasion. Rosie had returned from a visit to a friend in Barking and told Jim about the dry dock in the creek that had been dug out and opened up, 'for hush hush work.'

Tension mounted even more when masses of armoured vehicles clogged roads going south. And these last few weeks there had been a sort of quiet frenzy of underlying anticipation, a buoyancy of knowing, unofficial though it was, that the victory Winnie promised could be in sight. Even more posters went up on hoardings and any reasonable surface left near bomb sites, *Careless Talk Costs Lives – Be Like Dad, Keep Mum.*

'It's the beginning of the end,' Ada Smith said to Liza later that afternoon, 'though Gawd knows 'ow many of our lads'll be killed before that comes.'

The evening papers came out triumphantly with headlines like LANDINGS SUCCEED – SECOND FRONT UNDER WAY.

'Berlin here we come,' old Mr Mags was heard to mutter in Wentworth's shop, 'and not before bloody time, either.'

Queenie listened to the news, read the *Daily Mirror* and went around with a prayer permanently in her heart. *Please God, keep Paul safe.* She had no idea where he was now. That he had been in France before D-Day she felt certain, but beyond that she had no idea. Would they keep undercover men there or would they move them on to take soundings and prepare for the push forward. She didn't even know what he really did, she had only the sure knowledge in her heart that he would rather be part of a challenge than not.

Anna visited Joe, but they didn't talk about the news. Although he was so much more his old self now, she didn't know how talk of battles and bloodshed would affect him. He'd had a few minor setbacks with his leg that wasn't there, but on D-Day plus six one of the doctors saw her when she brought Joanna in from the grounds so she could use the toilet. 'Ah, Mrs Putt,' he said, 'a pity your husband couldn't come home yet after all, but we think we're on the way to solving the problem.'

'W-what problem, Doctor?'

'Well, the – ah, he hasn't told you. There is trouble in his leg. Although we avoided it before, it was always on the cards of course that we might have to amputate both, but we hoped it wouldn't be necessary to do so. Then this new problem flared.

We are trying something else now, a pretty new treatment, and it will be some weeks before we'll see any results, but of course if there is any sign of gangrene ...'

Joanna was holding herself and fairly dancing up and down now in her anxiety to go to the lavatory, and the doctor patted her on the head, saying. 'Better let this little one relieve herself. Don't worry, we shall save his other leg if it's humanly possible.' Then he was gone, walking briskly down the corridor, and she had no alternative but to see to her daughter's needs.

Joe was as cross as she'd ever seen him, and pretty close to tears too, when she gently asked why he hadn't confided in her.

'Because I'm ashamed,' he said after the outburst. 'They need beds for men coming back from France and if it wasn't for this,' he struck his leg almost viciously, 'some other poor blighter could be here.'

'But Joe, it isn't your fault—'

'I don't want to talk about it,' he said fiercely, 'so shut up and leave me to deal with this my own way.'

She snapped at Joanna in the train going home, and saw an elderly woman sitting in the corner glance sharply at her, a definite look of disapproval on her face. When a bunch of GIs crowded into the carriage, laughing and talking, their mouths stretching and chewing, Joanna said excitedly, 'That's like Uncle Hank, Mummy, isn't it?' and the woman in the corner rose from her seat, glared across at Anna, and said icily, 'Disgusting.'

Less than a week later the Home Secretary and Minister for Home Security, Herbert Morrison, announced a new danger that had hit London. Pilotless planes, he called them, but in Dason Street and all over the country the people called them flying bombs, buzz bombs, and doodlebugs. The first time Rosie actually saw one was within days of the official announcement of this new weapon. She had returned from shopping and was wondering whether to pop into Anna with a Weldon pattern she had bought for a child's pretty cardigan she thought she might knit for Joanna. She heard this strange noise above, and looked skywards. The plane she saw was flying very low and trailing a flame from its tail. She rushed indoors. 'Jim, quick,' she shouted, 'it's one of those flying bombs Morrison was talking about.' By the time Jim came outside it was gone from sight, but they both heard the engine suddenly cut out, and a few seconds later the explosion.

'Oh, God,' she said, turning into his arms, 'some poor devils have copped it.'

When Anna next visited Joe she went alone, leaving Joanna with Rosie and Jim. The early-morning sunshine had disappeared and the sky was cloudy, the atmosphere grey and heavy. It was almost a week since she had known about the problem with his leg and, bearing in mind the doctor's words that it would probably be quite some time before they knew if the treatment was working, she hadn't worried them. She had written her usual weekly letter to Joe, a short enough one this time, she thought now, but a difficult one.

She was rapidly discovering how the war and his injuries had changed him. From the gentle, easy-going man he had been, he was now so tense and moody. I can understand it, she thought, as the train steamed its way through the countryside, but I wish he would let me in again. Somehow he's shutting me out from his suffering, from his thoughts and dreams. Since that day when he had talked about lovemaking and adding to their family he hadn't mentioned intimate matters again.

Did he think I wouldn't want to because of his injuries? she wondered now, her heart leaping with fear. Is that the message my silence conveyed to him that day? The more she thought about it the more she realized that he had become reticent and closed up from that time. Oh, dear God, what have I done? That's it, when I didn't respond at all he thought ... she closed her eyes tightly to shut away her tears. To come home wounded in body and mind, and to believe your wife no longer wanted you to touch her because you only had one leg – how she must have hurt him.

Yet hadn't she changed too, and wasn't she hiding things from him? More than ever now she knew she couldn't tell him the one thing she most wanted to – that it was something quite different that had kept her silent when he most needed her love.

The train stopped with such a jerk that she fell forward. As people pushed past her she opened her bag and took her compact out. Next stop would be hers. Just what she would say or do she didn't know, but somehow she had to let Joe know that she wanted his arms around her and his body probing hers again. That she needed it as much as he did. Somehow she had to convince him of this and wipe out the hurt and damage she had done.

Joe wasn't at the gate to greet her, and although there were a few in wheelchairs and on crutches roaming the front grounds, it wasn't, after all, a particularly good afternoon to be outside. She hurried up the steps and into the hospital. He wasn't in the day room either. She didn't go in, she could see well enough from the door who was there. One of the men she and Joanna often spoke to smiled and waved, and she waved back before turning into the corridor and making for the ward. Perhaps he was asleep.

But Joe's bed was empty. Empty and made – not empty as though he had just got out of it to go along to the lavatory or anything. Fear held her in a vice so tight that for a few moments she couldn't move. She stood there, gripping the round knob on the iron bedrail, gazing at the pristine bed with its freshly laundered sheets ...

A voice said quietly, 'Find sister, she'll know, find sister,' and she realized it was her own voice. She was thinking aloud. Someone in the next bed moaned, and she hurried away, head down, and bumped into Sister Jones as she came through the ward doors.

'Mrs Putt, Joe's in theatre,' she said quickly. 'If you'd like to wait he should be back soon, they took him down this morning. Mind, he'll probably not be round properly, but you've had a long journey and I expect you'd like to see him anyway. Mrs Putt, are you all – nurse, fetch a chair quickly.' The sister caught Anna in her professional arms before she slid completely to the floor.

She recovered fairly quickly. 'I'm so sorry,' she said, feeling foolish and a fraud when everyone here was so busy. 'Seeing the bed, made up like that for a moment I thought – I thought Joe had died. I really am so sorry to have been a nuisance,' she repeated.

'It's all right, my dear. We couldn't stop you coming today because the decision to operate was only made this morning. If it has worked, it will save his leg. We shall know within twenty-four hours.'

Joe returned from theatre twenty minutes or so later, and she stayed on by his bedside for another hour. There was nothing she could do, and he didn't wake or know she was there, but the nurse who sat by him too, assured her he was 'doing fine' and would probably sleep on for quite a time. 'Telephone tomorrow,' she said, as Anna reluctantly left for home. 'Joe should be sitting up and taking notice again by then.'

'You poor kid,' Rosie said, when Anna collected Joanna, and told her about Joe's op. 'What a shame they couldn't have let you know, but I suppose something flared up. One thing, he's in the best place; they're performing miracles, some of these doctors and nurses. And they've got some new wonder drug, haven't they? Pencil something or other—'

'Penicillin,' Jim said, as he handed Anna a cup of tea, 'I was reading about it only the other day. It's saving thousands of lives on the battlefield.'

Anna took Joanna with her when she went to telephone from the box near the Green Man the following morning. She was still a bit nervous of the telephone, and what with that, trying to cope with Joanna's childish chatter, and to black out the picture of a white-faced, unconscious Joe as he'd been yesterday, her voice came out in a husky whisper and the operator had to ask her twice to repeat the number she required.

Eventually she was through to the ward, and a brisk voice said, 'He had a good night and is as well as can be expected.' The line went dead before she could find out when would be best to visit again, but he was still alive, she told herself as she pushed the door of the kiosk and came out into the air again.

Queenie popped in on her way home from the factory that evening, and Anna took the opportunity to slip up to the telephone box while she stayed with Joanna. This time she was told he was doing well, had eaten, and was looking forward to seeing her the following day. Her feet scarcely touched the ground as she went back down Dason Street. When she and Joanna reached the hospital the following day almost the first words Joe said were, 'It's worked, Anna. They reckon I'll be able to hang on to this leg at least, and I must say I'm glad. It's going to make all the difference to getting a job once I'm out of here, having a leg to stand on.' And for the first time since his invalidism, Anna heard him laugh.

'I've promised to stay with my Margery's youngest kids on Sunday, Liza,' Rosie said when she went into the shop one Wednesday in July. 'Fancy coming with me? It's ages since you've seen them.'

'We don't close 'til one, Rosie.'

'That's all right, she's not going out 'til three. It's some outing that's arranged with the school, and she can't very well take the two smallest. They'll be back by half six to seven, she said.'

'Well I'd like to. I'll have a word with Sid first and let you know.'

'OK, luv.'

'Now what can I get you, Rosie?'

'Some dolly mixtures I think. They'll go a long way.' She pushed her ration book across the counter. 'That's all the coupons I've got left, so use them all. Give the kids a treat.'

Rosie's daughter Margery lived in Walthamstow. She had six children ranging in age from twelve to three. The three-year-olds were twin boys, conceived on one of her husband's leaves. 'Could 'ave done without them,' she confided to her mother more than once, 'with Jack away for the duration and the others just getting off me hands like. Still, they're lovely kids even though they're little devils at times. What mischief one doesn't think of, the other does. You've always got to be one step ahead with them two, I tell you.'

Liza mentioned the plan to Sid that evening. 'Why not?' he said. 'Do you good to get away from the shop for a couple of hours, and I can cope with Pam and Audrey.'

Pam and Audrey were the latest in the long line of bombed children the Wentworths had given a temporary home to. They weren't related, and in fact had come from different districts, although both on the same day. Pam's mother was killed when the shelter at the factory where she worked got a direct hit. Her father was abroad and the thirteen-and-a-half-year-old had come to Liza and Sid two months previously. Audrey arrived at the same time. Her mother had been injured in a different attack and looked like being in hospital for a long while. Her father was in the Air Force; he had been home on compassionate leave and was very relieved to be able to leave his only daughter where he could see she was well looked after. Devastated by his wife's injuries, he really hadn't the heart at that time to help his child. Liza and Sid took her to see her mother every week, although there were times when the poor woman didn't know who the girl was. On these occasions they hustled her out pretty quickly. She was eighteen months younger than Pam but the two girls became good friends, their aloneness in the world creating a strong bond between them.

Liza had her dinner before the shop closed, leaving Sid to deal with the few last-minute customers. They had discussed closing earlier on a Sunday now there was so little they could sell. 'After all folks can't come in for a big box of chocolates to keep the wife sweet if they've been down the boozer too long, not without using up about three months' coupons, and we've not got too many ciggies anyway.' The creases in Sid's craggy face doubled when he grinned.

'No, once they've had their papers we could shut up shop and have it easy, Sid. Let's do it. Give us a bit more time to ourselves, and with the kids,' she added.

'We'd have to put a notice up, let them all know we're closing earlier, of course, but there's no problem in that.'

'We'll do it next month, shall we? I'll write something out over the weekend and stick it on the door. That'll give them plenty of warning.'

She was ready to go when he came up the stairs. 'Your dinner's in the oven, you can leave the plate soaking and I'll do it when I get in tonight. Should be back between six and seven.'

He kissed her, 'Mind how you go, luv. Enjoy yourself.'

She was up at Rosie's place five minutes before the appointed time. 'I've bought the twins a colouring book each and some crayons,' she said, tapping her bag.

'That's real nice of you, Liza, keep 'em quiet while we have a cuppa "rosy", won't it? That and the sweets. They're not bad kids really, specially when they're on their own. The older ones tease them of course, and fights break out. Still, as I've told Margy what can you expect when you've got so many? She's the only one of mine who wouldn't let her kids be evacuated.'

'She's lucky to have them,' Liza said wistfully, 'Sid and I couldn't have any.'

'Luck of the draw, duck, I mean, look at me, I had seven. Lovely when they're babies, mind you, but not without problems as they grow up, as I know well enough.'

She gave Jim a noisy kiss. 'Won't be late, luv. Don't do anything I wouldn't do while I'm gone, now.'

'Chance 'ud be a fine thing, Rosie. Here, slip the kids these to spend on the outing.' Four shiny half-crowns changed hands, 'and give Margy my love.' He stood at the door to watch the two women as they hurried to the top of Dason Street to catch the bus.

'He's a good 'un is Jim,' Rosie confided. 'Good husband and a good father to his kids.'

They were walking down Edgley Street forty minutes later. The houses were terraced, built in Queen Victoria's reign; most of them looked neat, with white stone steps, red Cardinal-polished tiles, and tidily clipped hedges enclosing the tiny space between the gate and front doors. The few that didn't stood out sharply against the spruceness of the others. On this sunny Sunday afternoon there were not many children outside playing, most of the schoolchildren from the area were going on the outing, and in many cases their younger brothers and sisters too. They passed a grandma pushing a pram, and an old man sedately riding a bike, otherwise all was still.

'The Sunday hush,' Rosie said, laughing, 'that's what Jim and me call it.' She unlatched the gate of number 12. Suddenly the front door burst open and a rush of children tumbled out. 'Hey, Gran, we're going on the outing to Soufend.'

'Me too, I'm going to …'

'All the kids in the class'll be there. There's 'musements and things …'

Rosie put her hands over her ears. 'One at a time, one at a time. I can't hear any of you if you shout and all talk at once. Listen, you remember Mrs Wentworth, don't you? From the shop near where I live. Well then, say hullo to her properly now.'

'Hullo, Mrs Wentworth,' the eldest girl said. 'Are you coming with us, or staying to help Gran look after the horrors?'

Margery appeared and shooed them all in to finish getting ready.

'And you shouldn't talk about your little brothers like that, Shirley,' she called after the girl's back, 'I remember when you were just as naughty as them, y'know.'

Liza loved Rosie's family. She had met most of them over the years, and she envied her friend her grandmotherhood.

'Mum, I've heard from Jack,' Margery said. 'Got two letters in two days. Only short ones, but he's OK.'

'Thank God. Send him our love when you write. Tell him to keep his head down and the concertina squeezing, and we'll have a whale of a party when it's over.'

Margery tied a flashy red bow on her six-year-old's long hair, 'A right old knees-up, eh, Mum?' Raising her voice she called through the open door, 'Doreen, are you ready? It's nearly time to leave.'

After much coming and going, running up and down stairs, the children lined up for inspection. There was a lot of excited chatter, four half-crowns found their way into four eager hands, 'Cor, thanks, Gran, say thank you to Grandad when you get back, won't you?'

'I'll do that. Off you go, then. Enjoy yourselves. And behave yourselves too,' she added.

The twins seemed quite happy not to be going on the outing. 'Wot we going to do, Gran?' David asked as soon as the door had closed behind the others.

'Thought we could go to the park. I've brought some bread for the ducks.'

'Whoopee! Can we go on a boat too? There's lots of them on the pond.'

'Oh, I'm not making any promises in that direction, Sunny Jim. Go to the lavvy now, both of you, then we'll get off.' Together they pushed through the narrow back door which led to the yard, and Rosie grinned as they raced to see who would be first into the lavatory.

'Margy could do with one of them double seaters with her

brood,' she said, turning to Liza. 'Just hark at the noise those two generate.'

'I suppose they're all right. I mean they won't hurt each other, will they?'

'They might. But you can't wrap them in cotton wool, can you? 'Tisn't as though they were babies. They'll both give as good as they get, you'll see. But they're loveable little devils. Angelic they were when they were little, like two cherubs. Used to love to see them when they'd just had a bath. Margy did them in the sink when they were very tiny, then in that old galvanized bath hanging on the hook outside the back door once they could sit up. Gorgeous they were. Did all my kids in that bath too, so it's seen some service.'

The noise from the twins grew louder and suddenly they erupted into the room, 'He punched me, look, Gran.' Peter thrust a skinny arm in front of her face.

'And what did you do to him?'

'Nuffin—'

'Yes 'e did, 'e 'it me, see—'

Rosie put an arm round both of them, 'It's six of one and half a dozen of the other I reckon, don't you, Liza? Come on now, straighten your trousers and tuck your shirt in, David. Here, there's two bags of bread crusts for the ducks.' She handed them one each, and ushered them out of the house. Liza smiled at her, 'You're a good grandma Rosie,' she said.

The flowers in the park were bright and cheerful and as the twins skipped ahead of them making for the swings, the two women settled to a steady comfortable pace. 'They can't come to much harm in this part of the park,' Rosie said, 'but we'll have to hang on to them when we get further up by the lake.'

'Still, there's the two of us. Are you going to take them on a boat, Rosie?'

'Don't be daft. They'd have us all in the water and I can't swim. Neither can they.'

They reached the recreation section. David and Peter were already on the swings, and Rosie and Liza sat on the seat nearby and watched them.

'Hardly think there was a war on when it's like this, would you, Liza?'

Her friend nodded. 'Except that there's not many men about.'

'Only the too ancient and too modern. None of the right vintage, eh?' Rosie's laugh rang out, causing others to turn and smile at her.

'David, stop that,' she suddenly yelled, 'you'll tip him off.' When the boys had exhausted the possibilities of the swings and seesaw, and frightened all the other children on the roundabout by running with it and pushing so fast they were all giddy, the quartet left the area and went on over a little bridge to what was known locally as 'the second park'. It was all part of Holbrook Park, but had a completely different flavour from the first part, which had trees, flowers, seats, the children's playground, areas of grass for ball games and dog-walking.

Holbrook Park was named after Francis Holbrook, a nine-teenth-century philanthropist who gave the land 'for the pleasure and delight of the people', and in this second section were alleys with descriptive names like Honeysuckle Walk, Rose Path, Lupin Lane, Wallflower Way and Bluebell Bay. All were a riot of colour, scent and beauty in their various seasons. Seats beneath the trees abounded, and decorative rustic bridges crossing and recrossing a trickling brook added to the romance of this 'second park'. Before the war flower-beds had been another attraction, but now these were small allotments, doing their bit by growing radishes instead of roses, carrots rather than cornflowers, lettuces in place of lilies, while the once-magnificent begonia bed now housed beetroot. At the far end of the park was the boating lake and tea-hut. This hadn't changed much, the same old man was in charge of the hiring of boats, but he was alone. In the old days he had always had a young lad to help him.

'Gran, can we 'ave a boat out? Go on, let's, it 'ud be fun.'

United now in their efforts to persuade her to take them on the lake, the boys joined forces, tugging at her hands and pleading with their eyes.

At first Rosie laughed, then she grew irritated with their keeping on about it. 'I said *no* and that's what I meant. Now stop worrying. We're all going in for a slap-up tea, ice cream an' all, and afterwards you can feed the ducks on the little pond. Come on.' She pushed them both in front of her and into the wooden teashop.

'Pity we had to come past the boating lake to get here,' she murmured to Liza, 'I reckon it's time we had a sit down. My feet are killing me, how about yours?'

Liza, who was a third of Rosie's weight said she was OK, 'But a cuppa would really go down well.'

'It certainly will. I thought it would be a treat for the kids too, you know, with the others on the outing, the little 'uns won't feel they've missed out on it all.'

'Better than the outing for them, really. I mean the seaside isn't much just now if what you read is true. Barbed wire and everything.'

'Think they've still got the amusements down at Southend though, Liza, and the older ones love that.'

They bought some Tizer for the twins, followed by an ice cream each, and both women settled down to enjoy the tea.

'That feels better,' Rosie said, licking her lips to savour the last drop of taste. 'Right kids, let's go feed the ducks. And stay close to us,' she added. 'We don't want either of you falling in; the ducks will come close enough, you'll see.'

Rosie had been saving her crusts for several days so there would be enough. 'And the water'll soften the stale bits, won't it?' she'd said to Jim. 'Gives me a good excuse not to eat the crusts too,' she'd added laughing. 'I'm afraid they'll break my plate one of these fine days, but we shouldn't waste them.'

When the bread was gone Rosie and Liza took a firm hold of the children's hands and began the trek back through the park. 'Oh, Gran, let's go on a boat....'

'Me too,' Peter shouted. 'Peter wants go on boat ...'

'No boat, but you can have another turn on the swings and roundabout. Go on.' She released his hand. Liza let David off too, and the boys raced towards the playground. The women smiled at each other, 'Full of it, aren't they, Liza? Margy says it's more of a relief to get these two in bed at night than it was with any of the others.'

'I suppose being a pair they set each other off. They're gorgeous kids though, Rosie.'

They reached the recreation ground and made for the seat, Rosie looking round for the twins as she walked. Suddenly she gripped Liza's arm. 'I can't see them, they're not here.' Her eyes scanned the area, darting from the group of swings to the roundabout, the seesaw and the pretend motorbikes and rocking-horse.

'Liza, where are they? Oh my God, *no* ...' But they both knew, and together they ran back towards the boating lake.

'Little devils,' Rosie panted. 'Must have sneaked up through the trees. I'll give them both the hiding of their lives ...' They were in sight of the lake now and with fear in their hearts they saw a crowd gathered at the edge.

Liza was there slightly ahead of Rosie, and she elbowed her way through. 'Please, it's our kids there, let me in ...' The boys were sitting on the ground. The water was running from the tops of their heads right down into their boots, but all Rosie's mind registered was the fact that they were alive. They were even shivering, which proved it to her beyond all doubt. She dashed up to them, yanked them to their feet, one with each hand. 'You little buggers,' she said, hugging them to her chubby bosoms.

It wasn't quite clear what had happened. Someone said they saw the boys suddenly appear from among the trees opposite the boating lake. 'They were holding hands and racing down the grassy bank, and I think they simply couldn't stop quickly enough. I was too far away to do anything but shout, but two women walking close to the water reached down and pulled them out.'

Rosie tried to find the women to thank them, but they had gone. 'Everyone was helping by then and they just walked away,' their informant told them.

'Well, God will bless them, that's for sure,' Rosie proclaimed to the crowd, and to her grandsons she said roughly, 'Come on, home and out of those wet clothes, then I'll deal with you.'

But once indoors and the boys dried and changed she hadn't the heart to grumble at them beyond saying, 'Let this be a lesson to you to *always* do as you're told in future.'

To Liza she said: 'They've had a fright, and that's no bad thing, more effective than anything I could say or do.'

'We'll have a cup of tea, Liza I've brought some with me, never like to eat into Margy's rations, then we'll have a game of something with the kids, shall we, before the others get back?'

They had just started on the magnetic fishing game which the twins loved, when the siren went. As its wailing ended they heard the unmistakable sound of doodlebugs in the distance. 'Under the Morrison, quick,' Rosie said, but even while they were scrambling to do her bidding there was an uncanny silence around them. 'God, the engine's cut out ...' She managed to hold one of them close to her as the noise of falling masonry drowned all their screams and the house shattered around them.

The people of Dason Street were stunned by the tragedy. 'To come home from an outing to find your babies, your mother and her friend dead, simply doesn't bear thinking about,' Anna said to Queenie when the news reached them. 'Whatever will Sid and Jim do?'

Queenie moved her head slowly from side to side. 'I don't know, luv, I can't quite believe it myself. This bloody war.'

Anna had never heard Queenie swear before and she glanced at her sharply. She looked far from well, and it wasn't entirely the news about Rosie and Liza that was responsible. Anna realized her friend had looked peaky for a few weeks.

'I'm afraid to go to either of them, Anna, but I must. Specially to Sid because there's those girls to think of. Poor kids, they've already experienced more destruction in their young lives than they should have. Liza was, well, she told me only last week that she and Sid were going to – to try to adopt them two ...' Turning away she suddenly covered her face with her hands and wept.

'Queenie, oh Queenie, don't.' Awkwardly she put her arms round the older woman.

'I'm sorry. It all seems too awful for words.' Queenie looked up. 'It's so senseless. Two women and two children and how many others that we didn't know gone in that bombing. They weren't in the forces, they weren't on the battlefield, they were innocent people trying to cope with war. The world's gone mad, Anna, stark staring mad.'

Jim stayed home after Rosie died. Several of his children, daughters and daughters-in-law, asked him to go and live with them, but he refused. 'I've got to be here, in case she comes back,' he told them.

'But Dad, she won't, she can't, the bomb killed her, Dad. You have to accept that.'

'No, I must be in when she gets home,' he said to them all, as though he hadn't heard what they were asking.

He poddled about in the house, vacuuming and dusting, and when Queenie called he said, 'I'm glad to see you, luv. Could you get my rations when you go to the shops? I'll give you me ration book.'

When she returned he paid her and began putting the food

away. 'Jim ...' she stopped and he turned from the larder, his face grey.

'Yes?'

'Jim, why not go to one of your girls for a holiday, just for a few days. It would be a break, see your grandchildren ...' Her voice petered out as a vision of the twins who had died came into her mind. But he had others, lots of others and they all wanted to help.

His fingers worked their way round the tiny piece of cheese he had in his hand. 'I know you mean well, Queenie luv, and I do appreciate it, honest, but it ain't no use. If I went to any of the kids I'd have to believe Rosie's not coming back, and ... and I can't do that.' His voice broke and abruptly he turned away. After a moment he said gruffly, 'Thanks for getting the grub in. I paid you, didn't I?' Then he walked past her and up the stairs. Queenie let herself out quietly and walked home with tears in her eyes.

Her heart was aching for Jim and Sid. If only the twins had gone on the outing with the rest of the family, but because two children were deemed too young to go, four people died. Queenie's mind wouldn't stop thinking about them all. She woke at night picturing Rosie's daughter Margery, and the older children, arriving home from a happy afternoon by the sea....

She couldn't talk to Fred about it, nor could she bear to listen to comments from the street's residents. Anna's wide, sensitive eyes filled with tears whenever she spoke of any of them, and Queenie didn't want to burden the young girl with her own depression. Added to her grief for the bereaved was worry about Paul. There had been no letter for several weeks.

Never one to parade her emotions, she would have welcomed being able to talk openly about him now. Just to voice her concern somehow would have helped. One evening when Fred had gone to the pub and she was alone in the house she knew she had to tell someone how she was feeling, and not someone who would say 'snap out of it, you can't help anyone by being miserable.' She already knew that, and she sensed that what she was experiencing now was different from misery. At times it seemed a grey curtain came down over everything in her life and she could neither lift it up nor see through it.

She wrote to Marie.

I think I'm on the verge of a breakdown. I cry a lot when I'm alone, and just lately it's happened at work too. So far it has been during the dinner/lunch break and I've managed to escape from the canteen and howl silently in the lavatory. I don't think I can keep it up much longer and some of the girls are asking if I'm all right. I tell them I've had an eye infection and that's the reason for the redness and puffiness.

Marie, help me please. Tell me what I can do. It all started when two of my friends here died …

The letter ran on to both sides of eight pages. In it she talked about Rosie, Liza, and the twins, about tensions among the factory girls and her growing fears at being caged inside the building all day, and finally about Paul – her love and worry over him. Queenie's writing became more erratic as she progressed, but once started she poured it all out on paper to Marie.

Apart from the evening his wife was killed Sid Wentworth carried on with his duties as street warden. Pam and Audrey were marvellous, drawing on their own experiences to help him. At first he closed his mind to the events of that day and evening. He rose at the usual time each morning, sorted his newspapers and opened the shop. In one way the normality of routine helped, and when, as happened more than once, he called through to the back room to ask or tell Liza something, he was glad there was no one to witness his distress.

The evening he opened the wardrobe with the intention of throwing all his wife's clothes into a box and giving them to the WVS or the Salvation Army, was the one Pam and Audrey came in earlier than expected, and found him crying. They looked at the half-filled cardboard box, at the man kneeling on the floor clasping a yellow blouse to his chest, and Pam said quietly, 'Come on, Aud, let's get him downstairs with a cup of tea and you and me'll finish this, eh?'

The other girl nodded her head in agreement. 'Uncle Sid, time you took a break,' she said gently. 'Leave this job to us.'

When Queenie went into the shop the following morning Sid began to talk about Liza for the first time since her death. 'It's the kind of day Liza enjoyed,' he said. 'She never liked the heat; this temperature suited her best.' Seeing the astonished look on Queenie's face he attempted a smile. 'Sorted her clothes last night, see. The girls helped me. Matter of fact I couldn't have done it without them. Now I've got to pick up the threads. Life has to go on and there's them to think about too.'

'You'll let them stay?'

'Oh yes. I couldn't do anything else. They've already had too much abandonment in their young lives. We all had a talk last night and we shall help each other.'

Another customer entered the shop and Sid was almost his usual self as he bandied words with them. Queenie left with very mixed-up feelings: a great sadness for the loss of Liza and relief that Sid and the two girls seemed to be coping.

Since her own outpourings in her letter to Marie she had felt better. The grey blanket hadn't lifted, but she could see chinks in it like tiny peepholes, and she knew her cure lay within herself. There were so many people who needed her help that she really hadn't time to be ill. She called on Anna one Sunday morning nearly a month after Rosie's and Liza's deaths.

'How's Joe?'

'Doing well. He thinks they'll let him come home soon.'

'That's the best news this street's had for some time, Anna. And you – and Joanna?' Anna handed her friend a cup of tea, 'OK, both of us. I keep telling myself how lucky I am that Joe's come out of it so well.' Her glance went towards the window. 'There's poor Jim over there without Rosie, I feel so sorry for him, Queenie. He loved her so much and he refuses to believe she's gone. When you see him he says things like; "Must go, Rosie'll be back soon, and I'll have the kettle on for tea."' Anna's voice and eyes were full of tears, 'Yet you feel he does know, really – I mean he doesn't go looking for her or anything like that, so he must know, deep inside himself that she's never coming home.'

Queenie reached out her hand to the younger woman. 'We all have to find our own way of dealing with death, my dear. Maybe he can handle it that way, and it doesn't hurt anyone. And maybe he's not so far from the truth if he can think of her as simply being out somewhere for a while and coming home eventually.'

Anna sighed and turned her gaze from the window and the house opposite. 'I suppose so, but it's not healthy really, is it? Even if he realizes the truth but can't admit it to himself now, the longer he indulges in make-believe the more difficult it will be for him.'

'Anna, I don't know the answer. All we can do is watch out for him. See, when she went off that afternoon with Liza, he expected her back a few hours later. They had no time to say goodbye, no inkling that she wouldn't be back. Even in these times, that must be one of the hardest things of all to happen.'

Through the other window they could see Joanna playing in the garden and Queenie stood up. 'I can't stop too long, Fred will be home from the pub and wanting his dinner. I'll just pop out and see my favourite little girl.'

'You're one of her favourite people too, you and Ros—' she stopped abruptly and turned pale. 'Yes,' she said quietly, 'I can see how Jim thinks she might be coming home any time now.'

Joanna ran into Queenie's arms., 'Auntie Queenie, come and play,' she said. Queenie picked her up and kissed her.

'Not now, sweetheart, but soon you can come down to my house and play.'

As she left number 5 she saw the curtains move in the house opposite, and caught a glimpse of Jim's anxious face as he looked out.

Chapter 14

Joanna started school in September when she was five. She was a bit wary that first day, and clung to Anna's hand very tightly when they reached the school, but there were no tears. She was a sociable little girl and used to being with others when her mother visited the hospital without her. It was Anna who was lonely during those early autumn days.

Joe came home in October. Anna had decorated the hall and front room with balloons on which she had written; *WELCOME HOME JOE*, and Joanna did some drawings of people with huge heads and thin stick like arms, which she said were 'Mummy, Daddy and me.'

Anna was going to put a banner across the front door, but she couldn't bear the thought of Jim looking across and seeing WELCOME HOME, so she hung it across the back door instead. 'He'll see it when he goes into the garden,' she told Queenie, 'and then there's no harm nor hurt done.'

Queenie thought how mature Anna had become during these last few years. She was no longer the innocent young bride Joe had left when he went to war.

Anna didn't know exactly when he would be home. 'Monday or Tuesday,' was the nearest time she had, 'After the doctor has checked him out again.' She spent the weekend cleaning and polishing the furniture; she washed the net curtains all round the house, put clean sheets on their bed, and hugged Joanna so many time, saying, 'Soon Daddy will be home with us, Jo-Jo my darling,' that the child was looking quite bewildered. 'Is it a party, Mummy?' she said. 'We had balloons at school when it was Mary's birthday.'

'A sort of party because we're so pleased Daddy will be home with us, darling.'

Anna wanted to go to the hospital and fetch him, but because they didn't know which day it would be Joe said best to leave him to come by himself. 'Don't worry, Anna, I'm used to it now and I manage very well with my leg.'

'But getting on the train and the bus—'

'The bus stops right outside the station. No distance at all to walk. I've been on one several times from here and there's no problem, so don't go making any, there's a good girl. We're taught to be as independent as possible here, luv, and that's how I want it,' he added in a gentler tone. So she polished and scrubbed until everything gleamed in the late afternoon sunlight, and she hoarded her cheese ration for three weeks so she could give him a decent wedge of one of his favourite foods when he came home.

The train was no problem, and the bus conductress cheerily indicated the front seat and put his crutches in the luggage cubbyhole where he could still reach them. She helped a woman with a pushchair which, folded down, also went into the space in front of him, and she ruffled the toddler's hair. I must learn to accept help cheerfully, Joe thought, like the mother there, like all the others who will come home and need assistance, at least for a while. And he took a deep breath and determined not to get uptight when anyone looked at him with pity, or tried to help.

Sitting on the bus he watched the familiar landmarks go by. Home. He was actually going home. Minus a leg, but otherwise in good health. It had been dodgy when he was first wounded, he realized that now. Those early days in the hospital were a blur of confusion when he tried to think about them. He was a bit nervous. All very well to boast to Anna that he could manage perfectly, but so far his bus travel had been within a restricted area, and the drivers knew the men in their hospital blue and were patient and cheerful. Now he was back in the real world, without the shield of doctors and nurses. He had wanted to do this journey on his own – to be able to walk down Dason Street to his house, to Anna and Joanna. Already he had missed her babyhood, but because she had visited the hospital frequently with Anna, he did at least know his daughter. They were friends. He was looking forward to being able to take her out. Maybe later there would be two of them to take to the park, or even three. He and Anna were still young, and the doctors had told him, when he asked them, that nothing was damaged in that area, he could still father children. Still, mustn't rush things, he thought; there would be time for that later. Right now the most important thoughts in his head were about getting home to his wife and daughter. Later he would sort out what he could do for work, because they would undoubtedly need more than his army pension to live on.

His excitement grew as the bus neared the Green Man. He knew he was a lucky man because he was out of the fray now, honourably so. Yes, he could be killed here in London, but that had always been on the cards. Goodness, you could get run over crossing the street … no doubt about it he had been fortunate. He'd had plenty of time to think in the hospital, and he knew he was glad that if he had to lose a limb it was a leg rather than an arm. You needed your arms and hands for so much. Just look at him: he'd done carpentry and metalwork, to say nothing of the painting and embroidery they all did for a while as occupational therapy. It hadn't seemed so bad in there doing embroidery, in fact he had quite enjoyed it after the first few times, but he doubted he'd try his hand at it outside the hospital. Get some funny looks. He smiled to himself and gazed out of the window. Nearly there. The old Green Man. Never thought he'd be so thrilled to see it again.

Joe reached for his crutches, and fought the 'I can manage' that bubbled inside him, saying, 'Thank you,' instead, when the conductress got there first and handed them to him. He eased himself off the platform, feeling suddenly very cumbersome.

He stood for a few minutes after the bus had gone, simply looking and breathing the air of his particular patch of happy hunting-ground. He saw the grimy buildings, the boarded-up windows, the cheerful cockney graffiti, and it had never looked more enticing. Then he joined several others waiting to cross the road, and was glad there was no one he knew among them. Safely on to the pavement the other side he began the walk down Dason Street to his wife and daughter.

Sid had a visit from a Mrs Goldysmith that autumn. He was so angry when she left that he couldn't remember what ministry she said she was from but, as he told Queenie, 'They won't take Pam and Audrey from me, I'll fight it tooth and nail. The only way those two girls will leave is to get married eventually, or because they *want* to go. I'm not having some bossy little woman coming here and telling me who I have in my own home.'

'I'm right behind you, Sid,' said Queenie, 'and so will half the street be if it comes to that. Why did she want to take them away, and where would they go? Audrey's mother's not in a fit state to have her back, is she? And last time she was talking to me she said she didn't know where her dad was, that she hadn't heard for ages.'

'That's right. Her mum will never be fit. You see, it wasn't only physical injuries, Queenie. It's all affected her mind too. She's in an asylum now, poor soul. And Pam's mum was killed in the raid at the factory where she worked. Her dad's abroad, she hears from him only very occasionally. Don't suppose the bloke knows what to write, really. I mean, after all this time he hardly knows her, does he?'

'So why, Sid? Is it because, because they're girls...?'

He nodded. 'I suppose it could be difficult, now they're growing up, but it isn't, Queenie. I can talk to them all right; like my own daughters they are now. *We can't leave them here without a woman in the house*, Mrs La-di-da says, and we understand you are now a widower.'

Queenie smiled at his mimicry. It gave her a clear enough picture of the woman.

'Blooming cheek. How did she know, anyway?'

Sid shrugged his shoulders. 'I don't know. They check up, I suppose. Or some busybody could have told them.'

'It's a pity some people don't mind their own business,' Queenie said, sharply. 'What are you going to do – or rather, what is she going to do next. This woman from the ministry?'

'I don't know, but the kids and I have discussed it, and they both say they just won't go. I tell you, Queenie, I could have cried when they rallied round so firm and, well, family like. "They can't split us up now," Pam said. "I wouldn't know what to do without you and Aud." And Audrey backed her up too. "They'll have us to deal with if anyone comes round to try to take us away," she told me, "and we're not little kids any more. We'd run away from wherever they put us and come back here. However long it takes and no matter how many times they take us back."'

'Good for them. They're a couple of nice girls, Sid. Well, listen, if you need any help, references, or anything, well you know where to come, don't you?'

'Thanks, Queenie, you're a real pal. Are you feeling all right? You look a bit under the weather yourself.'

'I'm OK. Guess we're all a bit jaded, but it looks as if the end's in sight, in spite of everything.'

'We're still getting bombed,' Sid pointed out. 'Adolph's secret weapons.'

'Mmm. Whatever this recent one is it doesn't half make a loud bang. I suppose the government will tell us eventually. Seems daft to me keeping it all hush-hush when everyone knows he's still chucking something our way.'

Sid, as street warden, had actually had a memo about the V2s which had been hitting London for over a month, but he said nothing further on the subject.

Mrs Goldysmith did visit Sid Wentworth again one afternoon while the girls were at school. They arrived home to find her sitting in the back room while Sid was serving a customer.

'OK, Uncle Sid, we'll deal with it,' they chorused.

'Now girls, don't antagonize her; remember she represents authority, and,' his voice dropped to a whisper, 'she could probably enforce it. Let's try every other method first.'

Pam touched her finger to her lips, then rested it against his cheek as a kiss. 'Leave it to us, we'll be diplomacy itself,' she whispered back.

'Unless she gets too tough,' she added softly to Audrey, as they took their school coats off in the tiny hall that separated the shop from the back room.

When Sid went through half an hour later during a lull in business he found Mrs Goldysmith sipping tea from one of Liza's best cups, and on the table by her side was a plate with a doily and several biscuits on it. The lady herself was chatting amicably with Pam and Audrey.

'Ah, Mr Wentworth. You have two powerful allies here,' she said, 'they have shown me their room, and,' she glanced at them almost mischievously, 'almost threatened me with anarchy should I be so foolish as to remove them from your care. It does seem foolish to place them somewhere else if they are going to keep coming back, and I do not doubt this for one moment, having talked to them. Therefore we shall let the matter rest, and I will call and see you every so often in case you have any problems you wish to discuss. Now I really must go. Thank you for your hospitality.' She stood up, and Pam and Audrey rose from their chairs also.

'I'll see you out,' Sid said, as behind Mrs Goldysmith's back two happy girls gave him a broad wink each.

Jim Bateson lifted the corner of the net curtain one Sunday a few weeks later and saw Queenie come out of number 5 with Joanna dancing by her side. It was a warm enough day, and the child's coat was flying open to reveal the lemon-coloured cardigan Rosie had knitted for her. Queenie paused at the gate to turn and wave to Anna, then they set off down the street. Suddenly, as he watched them, Queenie turned into his Rosie, or so it seemed. Jim blinked hard, lifted the curtain higher and continued to watch as the two figures moved on into the distance. 'Ah, Rosie loves that child,' he said, letting the curtain fall back into place. He wandered through the house, putting a cushion straight here, emptying an ashtray there. In the kitchen he began to set the table for tea. 'Wonder what we're going to have,' he muttered. 'Well, I'll get the bread out and the kettle on anyway.'

When they hadn't returned half an hour later he went to his gate and gazed down the road. Pam and Audrey from the corner shop came by. 'Hullo, Mr Bateson.'

'Oh, hullo,' he said. 'Must go in and make the tea.' He turned quickly and shuffled back indoors.

The girls giggled as they hurried on. 'Poor old boy,' Pam said. 'He's going a bit funny, I heard.'

'Don't often see him, do we? I mean, Uncle Sid lost his wife at the same time, but he's not become a recluse. It's time he pulled his socks up, he'll go daft else, I reckon.'

Pam glanced back, but there was no sign of Jim Bateson at his gate now. 'Well it must get lonely. He's there all by himself, not like all of us. I mean we've got Uncle Sid and he's got us. I know it's not the same Aud, and no one could replace Aunt Liza for him, but, well, you know ...'

'He has to make an effort, you mean, and it keeps him right?'

'Yes, sort of. I feel sorry for old Jim Bateson.'

Meanwhile Jim had gone to the kitchen and turned the kettle down low on the gas. He looked in the cupboard to see what else he could put on the table.

'Not much of anything there. 'Spect Rosie'll go shopping tomorrow.' He walked back to the front door and then to the gate to see if she was coming.

Queenie had been going to cross to the uneven number side of Dason Street, then she saw Jim Bateson at his gate and stayed on the even side to have a word with him.

'You've been a long time,' he said, smiling at her. 'Tea's all ready, only got to turn the kettle up. You going to bring the little 'un in for tea?'

'No, her mum will be waiting for her. You all right, Jim?'

'Yep. Glad you're home though. I miss you, you know. Come on.' He took Queenie's arm and tried to propel her up the path.

'Jim,' she said softly, 'it's me, Queenie. I'll just take Joanna home then I'll come and have a cuppa with you. OK?'

'Don't be long then,' he replied, 'don't stay nattering now. You've been gone ages this afternoon.'

Queenie went across the road, but declined Anna's invitation to come in and see Joe for a few minutes. 'I'm worried about Jim Bateson, luv,' she said. 'He's behaving most strangely. I believe he thinks I'm Rosie. I must go and see he's all right.'

'Want me to come too? Joanna'll be all right with her father.'

'No, luv. I'll come over if I need you. He perhaps just wants to talk.'

But Jim was still confused when she returned. 'Oh it's you, Queenie,' he said. 'How long will Rosie be?'

'Rosie wasn't with me. Only Joanna, and I've just taken her home.'

He peered into her face as though he couldn't see clearly. 'That cardigan you knitted her looks nice. You said the colour would suit her, didn't you?' Rubbing his eyes he turned away. Queenie followed him into the kitchen and noticed the table set with places for two.

'Let's have a cup of tea,' she said, going towards the gas stove. 'Then I must get back home, but I'll come in and see you tomorrow, Jim.'

She was at the stove, had turned the gas up and warmed the teapot, when she felt his hands round her waist. 'What's the matter, Rosie luv? you never seem to be in these days.'

Slowly she turned to face him. 'Jim, I'm not Rosie, I'm Queenie from number 52. Listen, luv, why don't you go and see the doctor tomorrow? Have a chat with him, and ask him if you can have a tonic.'

He was shaking his head but not in a manner of understanding or agreeing, more in a bewildered way.

'Another thing, you could go and stay with one of your girls for a few days, Jim. Be a bit of company for you.' She eased him into one of the chairs, made the tea and poured him a cup.

When she left half an hour later, he was washing up, meticulously cleaning the cups and the plates which they hadn't used. 'I'll pop in after work tomorrow, Jim,' she said, but he didn't answer, simply continued agitating the mop up and down the inside of the cup.

Queenie called into Sid's shop after she left Jim the following evening. She needed some of the Bateson clans' addresses, and Jim wasn't coherent enough to tell her. 'I'm sorry to ask you this, Sid, but you're the only one who might know.'

'That's all right, luv. We'll look in Liza's book. She knew them all and often went with Rosie to see them. She loved the kids,' he said sadly.

'Thanks, Sid.'

'I'll look when I've closed and pop round to your place later this evening, or send one of the girls with it. That be OK?'

He came himself, bringing three London addresses. 'No, I won't stop, Queenie. I thought of going to see Jim myself, but I chickened out. If you think it'd do any good, though, I'll go, but I can't see that it will, can you?'

She shook her head. 'Best we get on to his family Sid. They've been over I know, but they only see him for an hour and within the family group. It's a bit different, I reckon. I'm sure they don't know how he really is. He desperately needs help, but I don't think the likes of you and me can get near him.'

'Is he eating, looking after himself?'

'Yes.' She omitted to say he not only prepared meals for himself, but for his dead wife too. When she had called in on her way back from the factory there was a tin of dried-egg powder on the side and he was dishing up two omelettes.

She wrote to one of the addresses, stressing that Jim didn't know what she was doing, but setting out, as much as she could, his mental state. *I've tried to persuade him to see a doctor, but he refuses,* she wrote. *He has many friends in Dason Street, but we don't know how to help him now.*

Several members of the Bateson family descended on the street the following Sunday, including Margery. She called on both Queenie and Jim, and told them he was going to one of her sisters for a week or two, 'until we've sorted things out a bit. Will you keep an eye on the place for him?' Her eyes misted a little. 'They mightn't have much of value to a thief, but the house is full of their own treasures and mementoes.'

Queenie put her hand on the woman's arm. ''Course we will. And maybe with a bit of company like, your dad will be well enough to come back in a while.'

'It knocked us all sideways,' Margery said, 'but you have to get on with life again. Well I had to because of the other children, but between you and me, Queenie, I don't think Dad realizes the twins went that day, as well as me Mum.'

Joe was sitting by the window when Jim Bateson left with his family. 'There's a lot of activity over the road, Anna,' he called to his wife who was in the kitchen. 'I think they're taking Jim away.'

She hurried in, wiping her hands on a tea towel. 'Poor Jim, he was lost without Rosie, yet he always seemed so strong. Wouldn't have thought he'd go to pieces like this.'

'I'm sorry I was so nasty with Rosie,' Joe said quietly. 'You always stood up for her. Now it's too late I wish with all my heart I'd been friendlier.'

Anna said nothing. She was thinking of the night Rosie and Jim had saved their lives, and pulled her from the wreckage. Joe didn't know about that, only the fact that the windows were blown out and bits of the ceiling came down. Jim and Sid had been the ones who'd come along and boarded up the window and made good where necessary. She realized Joe had presumed that she and Joanna were in the shelter that night. She looked at her husband and thought again how lucky they had all been after all.

'Come on, luv, there's not much we can do for him now. Tea will be ready soon. Will you call Jo-Jo?'

In November the government officially acknowledged that V2s, faster-than-sound long-range rockets, had taken over from the VIs. There was no warning for these. 'At least you're spared the nerve-racking; is it going to cut out or go on?' Jenny said to Queenie, 'and you probably wouldn't know too much about it if one hit the house. I saw where one fell last week. Left a huge crater; doubt if anyone was left alive.'

She had seriously thought about having her children home until the doodlebugs started, and there'd been another exodus of children from London. Now with this new danger, and mostly not even time to sound the warning, she was glad they were still in the country. 'Although what's to stop something falling on them down there, too?' she said more than once to Queenie. 'After all, no place is immune in this war.'

'These pilotless things are timed and distanced Jen. They're aimed at London, and apart from those our planes are intercepting over the coast, and managing to tip and turn back towards Germany, they aren't likely to fall anywhere else.'

'Anyway,' Jenny pursed her lips in a sort of rueful grin at her mother, 'Tom would be very disappointed if I made him come home. Funny, isn't it, to think if it hadn't been for the war he'd probably never have got such a taste for country life?'

Towards the end of the month a van collected Rosie and Jim's furniture, and a few days later their house had new occupants. Joe, who was going to have to wait some time for what Joanna called his 'new leg', wasn't yet fit enough for work, and he spent a lot of time sitting by the window making furniture for the second-hand doll's house they had bought and hidden for Joanna for Christmas.

'New people moving in over the road, Anna,' he called. 'Got a posh settee, they have.' Anna dried her hands and joined him by the net curtains. 'Mmm. Well, with so many homeless it wouldn't do to leave the place empty, would it?' she said, seeing in her mind's eye Rosie coming out of the front door, basket on her arm, ready to go to market, or bustling happily across the road with some little thing she'd bought or made for Joanna. She turned away intending to return to the kitchen where she had been washing up, when a sudden shout from Joe made her turn back. 'Well, what d'you know? Look who's moving in, Anna.'

She saw the man first. He turned at the gate and waited for the woman and little girl, who let go of her mother's hand and ran towards him, then all three fairly danced up the tiny path to the front door.

'Well, well, you don't see many black people round here, do you? Wonder where they've come from? There was a black chap in my mob, and he came from Camberwell ...' but Anna wasn't listening. She was staring at the little family who were even now disappearing through the doorway of Rosie and Jim's old house, and in spite of the warm jumper she was wearing, she was shivering. Slowly she walked back to the kitchen.

Although the man now living opposite them wasn't anything like her attacker to look at, the fact that he was black evoked the similarity in her mind, and panic struck at her every time she went out.

A few days later Joanna burst in from school, saying: 'We've got a new girl in my class and she only lives across the road, Mummy. She's asked me to go and play on Saturday.'

Anna bit her lip hard, and smiled at her daughter. 'All right,' she said. 'Mind you behave yourself.'

'Yes, I will. Her name's Chloe – isn't that pretty? And she's got ever such pretty hair too.'

The second time Joanna went to play with Chloe, Joe suggested they might ask Chloe back. 'And her parents,' he said. 'Be a friendly thing to do. I met them when I was out the front the other day. Charlotte and Benno they're called, they were bombed out. Come from Walthamstow.'

When Anna didn't answer Joe said, 'Well, are you going to?'

'Maybe. I'm – I'm busy now.'

'I'll go then,' he said, reaching for his crutches.

'There's no hurry. I'll do it later.'

'Anna, what is it? You've been offhand every time I've mentioned the new folk over the road. It's not because they're black, is it?'

''Course not. Don't be silly, Joe.'

'All right then. I'll go and ask them if they'd like to pop in for half an hour on Sunday morning. And the kids can play together.'

'Joanna goes to Sunday School.'

'After Sunday School then.'

Anna's lip quivered. If she refused to have them in the house what good would it do. She didn't really know why she felt threatened, because the situation was so different. But she couldn't disassociate herself from the trauma of Tailor's Yard and the fact it was a black man who had raped her.

'The rations won't run to much—'

'For heaven's sake, Anna, stop making excuses and let's have the truth. I can't believe you're behaving like this. You've acted strange ever since they moved in, come to think about it. Why?' Suddenly he lowered his voice and said more gently, 'Come on, luv, if something's bothering you about them you can tell me, can't you?'

But of course that was the one thing she couldn't do. They quarrelled that night, and lay in bed together but each very much in their own space. Monday morning, after Joanna had left for school, Joe rose from his chair and stumped to the door. Anna watched in fear and trembling. What would he tell them? 'I want to be friends with you but my wife doesn't.' Of course not, she chided herself. Joe paused at the door, 'Do you want to come with me,' he said.

It was a truce, and she badly wanted to use it. 'Would look silly both of us going,' she said. 'People don't stand on ceremony like that round here, now do they? But tell them they'll be welcome.'

She missed Rosie and Jim more than ever at Christmastime. She recalled the great gatherings they used to have, the wonderful warm welcome always. Remembering the last few years when she and Joanna had spent most of the time with them and their vast family she shut herself in the toilet and wept silently and alone.

Joe had become very friendly with Charlotte and Benno, as indeed Joanna had with Chloe. Anna admitted they were good people, she liked them, but she didn't encourage them. Benno, so Joe told her, had been invalided out of the army last year, and was now a driver for the London Passenger Transport Board.

'I reckon I'll get my old job back once I've got two legs again,' he said to her one day. 'But I had high hopes that after the war was over I'd be able to go for something bigger and better.'

'So you might luv, given time. But your old job'll suit you 'til then, won't it? And it's not too far to go, either.'

'It'll do. It will have to, and maybe I'll try setting up a little carpentry shop somewhere later. I've enjoyed making these things for our kid's doll's house, you know. Be a bit of a sideline to put some jam on our bread after the war, wouldn't it, luv?'

Chapter 15

Paul's intuition, more than anything more specific, warned him he wasn't alone. Yet he knew he hadn't been followed. Whoever was there, lurking in the shadows, had come because of a tip off. Someone had betrayed him. A huge wave of thankfulness that he had at least finished the job, another troop train wouldn't go anywhere tonight, and every hour's delay counted. Already in France when the Allies landed on 6 June, he had steadily worked his way into the hinterland, disrupting important rail communications. Keeping perfectly still, he felt goose-pimples starting at his wrists, and increasing in pace as they ran up his arms, across his shoulders, down his back and legs, before racing upwards over his stomach and seeming to dance on his chest and restrict his breathing. Just like when he was a child at the Saturday-morning film show at the Odeon, when the baddy crept up on the good guy.

But this was no film, and if there was someone out there his time would be up. It was possible that it was his imagination playing tricks; there came a time, even when you had been involved as long as he had, when you metaphorically looked over your shoulder for no reason other than that you were jumpy.

If he made a run for it his chances were almost nil. If he stayed where he was they weren't a lot better. Whoever was there probably knew his exact position by now. Sweat formed over the goose-pimples, and he stayed, still as a statue, knowing it was his best bet. If he was prepared, he might, God willing, dodge the bullet.

How long should he give it before deciding it was his imagination run riot? If it wasn't, his stalker would have the patience to wait for him to make a move. He would be an easy target.

As his intuition had told him earlier that someone else was there, so it also gave him a one-second alarm warning, and he fell flat on his stomach as the shots rang out. Three, in quick succession, but as he went down there had been that split second before the bullets whizzed through to him, so he shifted to one side so that his head was beneath the immobilized train. Even so, he realized he had been hit in the back. He wriggled further under the train. They would come to make sure he was dead. Mustn't leave his feet sticking out in case they moved. Too numb now to feel any pain, he heard the crunch of boots, was aware of heavy breath as someone bent down; then the noise of the boots growing fainter coincided with him passing out.

The next conscious thought Paul had was that someone was pulling on his legs. He groaned.

'Sshh.' Silently his rescuers, for there were two of them, pulled him out. Gritting his teeth and with tears of pain now coursing down his face, he had the illogical thought, *I could see Queenie again.*

They took him to a flat, carrying him as gently as possible up many stairs, then laid him, face down, on a wonderfully soft mattress. He felt a woman's hands tending his wounds.

How long he slept he never knew. But it was daylight when he woke, and the woman was there with a bowl of soup. 'The doctor – say rest,' she said in hesitant English.

'*Merci, Madame.*' It was painful to talk, even more so to drink the soup, but he managed most of it, and her eyes acknowledged the fact as she removed the bowl and settled him as comfortably as she could. Then, a finger to her lips, she glided away from the bed and silently through the door. Once again he closed his eyes and slept.

Two days later the men were there again. They moved him to another place. The journey took half an hour, he checked it with his watch, knowing they wouldn't tell him where he was even if he had the strength to ask. The pain in his back and stomach seemed a little easier, *unless I'm getting used to it*, he thought.

Three times he was moved in just over a week, and each move involved stairs which caused excruciating pain as he was carried up or down. Twice he was taken to an attic room, once deep in a cellar, with hidden, dusty bottles of French wine and the occasional scurry of mice for company.

One evening, just as he was dozing and forming pictures of Queenie in his mind, a young lad and an older man entered his hiding-place. Hastily they threw a blanket over him and, with one at each end, made their way up the stairs and into a courtyard. Van doors clanged shut and he pushed the blanket from his face and tried to sit. The van started up and, rolling over, he found the most comfortable position he could, and tried not to wonder if he would ever walk again. At least I put more transport out of action before they caught me, he thought, and now it's in the lap of the gods whether I live or die. Obviously no one was going to keep him too long, but how many 'safe' houses were there in the area? Because he wasn't capable of finding his own way yet. He felt great admiration for these men and women who were putting their heads on the block for him and others like him.

The van slid to a stop, the back doors opened and two uniformed men were there with a stretcher. He could hardly believe his eyes when the next set of stairs he felt himself being carried up were the steps on to an aeroplane. There was no time to thank his rescuers; within seconds of the doors closing the plane was away, and as he felt nausea rising in him with a pain he didn't think he could contain, he felt the prick of a needle, and knew no more.

Paul Tranmer opened his eyes slowly. They felt heavy and strained. The quietness startled him. Where was this place? Had he died and was this Heaven, or was there some other place you went to? He hadn't been to church for a long while, and he wasn't sure he believed in either Heaven or Hell. Perhaps there was somewhere in between where those who were not good enough for Heaven, and not bad enough for Hell, rested. He hoped it wouldn't be as quiet as this all the time. Slowly he moved his head. A soft voice with an Irish accent said, 'Hullo there. How are you feeling now?'

'Fine.' He was surprised at the weakness of his vocal cords. It came out like a whisper. He tried again. 'Just fine.' He wanted to ask where he was but seemed to lack the strength, so he closed his eyes again and drifted into a dreamy sleep.

It felt as though he were floating, and then he became aware of someone close to him, and knew it was Queenie. The fragrance of her body was warm against his, the softness of her lovely hair like a downy pillow, and he nuzzled his face into it, all the while feeling the excitement in her dear breasts as they moved against him. His own breathing quickened, their lips came together in a passionate kiss and their bodies melted into each other until they became one glorious burst of colour and love. A great peacefulness enveloped him and the strangest lightness of weight. They really were floating, and all around them now was a great cushion of palest blue. They landed with a slight bump, and as he turned to make sure Queenie was safe the gentle Irish voice he'd heard before said, 'That must have been some dream – try to sleep now,' and a cool hand rested for a few seconds against his forehead.

Queenie had felt tired all day. When she left the factory at six o'clock it was as much as she could do to drag herself home.

There had been no word from Paul for nearly six weeks and she was worried. He had said he would write as often as possible, and for the first few months she had received a card or a letter every ten days or so. Of course it wasn't easy for him to do this, and although she didn't know exactly where he was or what he was doing, she realized he wasn't stationed in a civilized place with a pillar box on the corner. Even so, he would write something and get it to her if it was humanly possible.

She took a deep, calming breath as she walked down Dason Street. If he was dead how would she be able to find out? There would be no reason for the authorities to tell her. His sister though, she might, she would, yes, surely she would contact her if anything happened to Paul?

She saw Jim's curtains move sufficiently for him to see out and a wave of sadness for him overcame her. Why did it have to be Rosie? Or Liza, come to that. What fate decreed they should go to Margery's on that day, be in the house at that particular time? The same hand of fate would decide whether Paul would come through the war, whether any of them would. Queenie shivered, in spite of the warm sun on this balmy August evening.

She felt edgy and her weariness persisted. 'We need a thunderstorm to clear the air,' she said when Fred wandered into the kitchen as she was finishing the washing up.

'Mmm. I'm off then. Going down the King's tonight. Darts match on. Be finished 'bout nine if you want to come down then.'

She felt the surprise stirring in her bones. It was seldom enough they went for a drink together, and he had never before suggested that she might meet him at the pub later. She turned from the kitchen sink and smiled at him. 'It's tempting,' she said, 'but to be truthful I'm so tired I could drop, so I think I'll have an early night.'

'Suit yourself.' He said it cheerily and went out whistling.

Queenie straightened the cushions on the three-piece in the other room, emptied the ashtray, and stood by the mantelpiece for a moment looking at the photograph of Doris and Tom which Jenny had given her the other day. It was taken on the farm, 'With Gert and Daisy, two of our cows', it read on the back. She couldn't see Tom ever wanting to come back to the smoke, he'd really taken to country life. Doris was another matter, Queenie thought the little girl would soon settle in once she was home. She blew the photograph a kiss, then walked out of the room and up the stairs to bed.

In the bathroom a dreadful thought occurred to her. Suppose the pub was bombed tonight? It was so unusual for Fred to bother about her movements. Normally he called to her on his way out. 'Just going,' or 'I'm off, then.' Or maybe this house was going to cop it?

Now Queenie, she told herself sternly, be sensible. You are simply over-imaginative tonight because of this weather and your weariness. A good night's sleep is what you need, my girl.

In the bedroom she folded her clean clothes neatly on and over the back of the chair and climbed into the iron-railed double bed she still shared with Fred, although they hadn't been intimate for years. Even as she wondered if she was too tired to fall asleep quickly, she felt her senses leaving her, and a delicious lightness taking over. Within five minutes she was fast asleep.

Queenie did not know how long she had been flying – it seemed such a natural state to be in. Maybe not exactly flying, she thought, but floating, I seem to be floating in some enchanted place. She also didn't know how long Paul had been by her side, but suddenly she realized that he was there. She turned her head, and he was smiling at her and drawing closer. She reached out her arms and he came into them, rubbing his face against her hair in the way she loved. Excitement tingled throughout her body, she felt his heartbeats against her own, his lips sought and met hers with passion and a sweet tenderness combined, then their bodies closed in together, and a rainbow of colour burst around her. Afterwards she felt curiously light, resting on a featherbed of gentle blue. She felt the bump as they landed, and turning to him with love in her eyes she murmured, 'Paul, Paul ...'

Fred, who had just heaved himself into bed, looked down at her, but she seemed to be fast asleep.

Ruth Pearson, née Tranmer, alighted from the bus at the Green Man. She thought about taking a taxi, but there weren't any about and the walk would probably do her good. Paul had said it was about halfway down Dason Street. She wasn't sure what she would say if Queenie's husband was there, but decided to tackle that when the need arose. Paul had begged her to let Queenie know he was in hospital. 'But do it carefully, Ruth, please.'

She had laughed softly, although she felt more like crying to see this once strong and handsome young brother of hers in such a pitiable state.

'Of course. I'll be the soul of discretion. Now stop worrying. I won't risk writing, I'll go myself and I'll see no one but Queenie. That's a promise,' she added softly.

'She's very, very special.' Paul's voice was faint.

Now Ruth was here, walking down the street where this woman, who had held her brother's affections for so many years, lived. She saw the curtains twitch in one of the houses near the top, and met a woman pushing a pram a little further down. For the most part the houses were neat and clean, she thought. It reminded her of their childhood home where, until she was twelve years old, she had lived with her mother and father, and brother Paul. That was the year her father left, one day before her twelfth birthday. It had taken her a long time to get over that. Of course their mother's bitterness hadn't helped; Paul was just a toddler, not quite two, and he remembered nothing of their father, and believed for years, until she enlightened him, that his father had died when he was a baby.

Although Ruth never saw their father again, she could conjure his image to mind even now. His black bushy beard which used to tickle when he hugged and kissed her, his dark, smouldering eyes which always seemed to be laughing, and that huge bellow of a voice which teased and joked, told incredible stories with an actor's flair, yet could be so soft and gentle when she wasn't well or had fallen over and needed comfort.

Paul had told her it was a long street and she was watching the numbers now. She planned to walk past at first to see if anyone was about. Ruth had met Queenie just once, but she knew 'the young lovers' as she called them to herself, had made use of her flat on several occasions and she had been happy to help them. Her own marriage had been short but happy, and since Harry had died she had never met anyone else she wanted to spend the rest of her life with. He had left her comfortably off and after his death, she resumed the career she had given up to marry.

Number 52, that was it. Ruth walked by as planned. There was no sign of life, so she walked on a little, before turning and coming back. Without hesitation this time she unlatched the gate and went up to the door.

Queenie was cooking the fish she had been fortunate enough to buy from 'Blinking Billy' this morning on her way to work. She turned the gas down and went to answer the door, knowing Fred wouldn't stir from the other room to see who it was. Although Ruth's face was familiar she had seen her only once, and now she didn't recognize her.

'Is it all right to talk?' Ruth whispered. 'I've come about Paul.'

Queenie's stomach and legs shook inside and suddenly didn't seem to belong to her any more. 'It's Ruth, isn't it? Sorry, I didn't quite—'

'That's all right, my dear. Why should you? We've met only once, I believe, and that was a good few years ago.'

Queenie motioned for her to come inside. She seemed to have no voice left, her mind was already trying to receive the news she was sure Ruth had come to impart.

Smelling the fish Ruth said, 'You're cooking your meal, I can come back later.'

'No, that's all right. I – I couldn't put you to all that trouble.' Queenie ushered her into the kitchen. 'if you don't mind coming in here, it's ...' she looked straight into Ruth's eyes, 'more private, you see.'

'Of course. Look, if that meal is as ready as it looks, why not dish up before we talk. I'm really sorry to have called at such an inconvenient time.'

Queenie, who was trying not to think, nodded and frantically dished up Fred's meal. Her own she put on to a plate and placed it in the oven without switching on. She seemed to be working on automatic pilot.

'We can go in the other room while he's eating,' she said. 'I'll just call him.' She hurried away. The scrubbed wooden table was already laid with a check tablecloth and two sets of cutlery, and Ruth looked round the clean and homely kitchen with interest.

When Fred was settled with his meal Queenie took Ruth into the sitting room. 'Please sit down. I can guess why you've come and I'm – I'm grateful.' Her lips trembled, but remembering this woman was a guest in her home she said as steadily as she could manage, 'I haven't even offered you a cup of tea. Would you like one? It won't take two ticks.'

Ruth reached out and touched her arm. 'No, really my dear, I'm fine. You want to know about Paul.'

Queenie sat down very quickly, afraid her legs really would give out when Ruth told her the news she had dreaded ever since he joined up.

'Paul is in hospital,' Ruth said quietly, 'and is in—'

'He's ... he's alive?' Queenie's voice was tinged with amazement. She had been so sure this woman had come with news of Paul's death.

'Yes. But he is very weak.'

The two women gazed at each other for a few seconds without speaking. Queenie broke the silence first. 'Thank you, Ruth, for coming to tell me. I'll go to him.'

As she left Ruth said quietly, her voice thick with emotion, 'Don't leave it too long, Queenie, will you?'

She walked back to the bus stop head down so no one would see the tears in her eyes. She had done everything she could for Paul now, and she was desperately sorry for the woman she had just left. Poor soul, to be tied to that moron who had barged into the kitchen for his meal without so much as wishing their visitor good evening; who sat down heavily and started eating so noisily. Paul must have seemed like a god to someone having that to contend with every day. But more than all this was the love in her eyes when they spoke of Paul. What a pity, what a tragic pity these two people who had loved so long and so deeply, had been apart all these years. Ruth brushed the tears from her eyes and turned out of Dason Street into the High Road without looking back.

Queenie went to work the following morning. The idea of going to see Paul instead was strong in her, but old disciplines die hard, and she clocked in as usual.

'There's a shepherd's pie in the oven, only needs heating up, Fred. I'll be late tonight.' He grunted. There was no other word for it, she thought dismally, as she rushed about, trying to do all the necessary jobs before she left.

Somehow she got through the day, clocked out and went to the hospital in central London.

Ruth was sitting by the side of Paul's bed, and she stood up and greeted Queenie warmly with a kiss on her cheek. 'He's not really asleep,' she said softly, 'just resting his eyes, as he used to tell our Mum many years ago.' Her own eyes were glittering with unshed tears. 'I'll be away, then.' She leaned over the bed. 'See you tomorrow, Paul. You've another visitor here now.'

'Please don't let me drive you away,' Queenie said.

Ruth smiled suddenly and for the first time Queenie saw the likeness between brother and sister. 'I've been here long enough. Anyway it's you he wants to see.' Her hand rested briefly on Queenie's shoulder, then she walked slowly from the bed and out of the ward.

Queenie moved closer. 'Paul, it's me, Queenie.' His hands were lying outside the counterpane, and she laid her own on them and felt him move. Bending over the figure lying so flat in the bed, she touched his cheek with her lips. 'Paul.'

His eyes opened and for a moment there was wonder in them, then they dulled with pain. 'Queenie, my princess.' His voice was low, a whisper of its usual volume.

'Paul, I'm here, darling.'

'In – the – flesh. I'm – not dreaming.' His speech was weak and halting, but his eyes, now open wide, gazed steadfastly into hers.

'It's no dream. Oh Paul ...'

She stayed until he fell asleep, kissing him sometimes, very gently in case she disturbed the pain, holding his hand, whispering endearments, loving him with every thought in her head, with every beat of her heart.

It was late when she reached home. Fred had just come in from the pub.

'Where the hell 'ave you been,' he shouted.

'Visiting a friend. I told you I'd be late.'

'Late, late,' he thrust his face close to hers, 'you didn't say you'd be out all bloody night. Where've you been, eh?'

She pushed him from her. 'I've already told you. I'm no later than you, and what's more I'll be late again tomorrow. I'll leave something in the oven for you; it'll be cooked, all you'll need do is switch on and warm it up. I'm going to bed, I'm tired.'

'Tired, are you? Wot you been doing then? Been with a lover? Coming home this time of night. You should be ashamed of yourself'.'

Ruth was in the sister's tiny office when Queenie visited the following evening. They called her in, and Ruth said, 'This is Queenie, Sister. She is a very special friend.'

'Sit down, my dear.' The sister's voice was brisk, firm, her tone a no-nonsense one. 'To put you in the picture – there is nothing further we can do for Paul Tranmer. We are keeping him as free of pain as is humanly possible. All his family should know.' She stood up and walked to the door. 'You may come in at any time and stay as long as you wish.' Her hand rested briefly on Queenie's shoulder then she walked to the door, and her voice took on a mantle of gentleness. 'I am sorry.'

When she had left Ruth said quietly, 'I've been in, he was asking for you.'

Paul was awake when she reached his bedside. He was obviously drugged, but the recognition for her was there. 'Princess, you came.' If anything his voice was weaker than yesterday, yet he had stayed awake.

'Of course I came.' Trying to sound light-hearted nearly choked her, yet if she hadn't she would have burst into tears and she wanted to spare him that.

'Didn't know – if – you'd get – away again.' Wincing he turned from her and she saw the clenched hands and felt as though she was grappling with him at the pain. A few moments later his fingers relaxed, and slowly he moved his head back within her vision. 'I'm sorry, my darling.'

This time she couldn't stop the tears. 'No need to be. Tell me what I can do to help.'

'Be here. Near me.' He was silent for so long she thought he had gone back to sleep. Her hand was in his, lying against his chest, and she was comforted by the rhythmic feel of his breathing, even though she realized it was too shallow. He wasn't asleep.

'Didn't take tablets.' He managed a grin that was almost like normal. 'Wanted to be awake, to look at you ...' Another pain gripped him and she made as though to call the nurse but his eyes told her not to and when the spasm had passed she said, 'Don't talk sweetheart, just rest and—'

'Time for – rest later. Come close.' She leant over him, cupping his face in her hands. 'I love you,' he said, 'always.'

'I know, I love you too ...' He missed seeing the tears suddenly pouring down her cheeks because another pain hit him and he rolled away from her. By the time he looked again she had composed herself. 'This is ridiculous,' she said. 'I'll ask Sister for your tablet—'

His grip was surprisingly strong for a dying man. 'I need you, not a – bloody tablet. Shouldn't have – told you. Yours – is the – last face I want to see.'

'For God's sake, Paul. How can you say such things to me.' She was almost in the bed with him, burying her face in his hair, holding him so gently, loving him and willing him to live.

'Because we know, you and me. Just – stay a little while.'

'As long as you want me, Paul.'

He closed his eyes then, and when the sister came along some ten minutes or so later she felt his pulse, looked at Queenie and said, 'I'm glad you were here in time.'

Startled she said, 'He's not...?'

Sister shook her head. 'No, but it's a miracle he's held on this long. Would you like a cup of tea, my dear?'

She refused because she didn't think she could swallow anything. She stayed a few more minutes, watching him, loving him, praying silently that it would be quick and peaceful for him. Sister wasn't in her office and Queenie hurried along the clinical corridor, and out into the busy street to catch the bus for home.

Fred was still out when she arrived. He hadn't washed up, of course, and she set about the task quickly, then made a small pot of tea and forced herself to eat a couple of jam sandwiches. She switched the wireless on, anything to stop her thoughts gravitating to that hospital bed until she had prepared tomorrow's food. She caught the last bit of the nine o'clock news. *Our troops are pushing forward....*

When Fred returned from the pub, and came noisily upstairs to bed, she was already there, lying on her side, eyes closed, and pretending to be asleep. Fred was snorting and snoring long before that blissful state occurred, and it seemed hardly any time at all before the alarm bell jangled into her tortured dreams the following morning.

She made her mind up suddenly to return to the hospital instead of going in to work. She slipped out of the house early while Fred was still asleep and walked down the road. She posted a note through a fellow worker's letterbox. *Have migraine – please tell Alf I won't be in today*, she had written. She was home, and had breakfast on the go by the time Fred was up and dressed.

She left the house just before her usual time, as though she was off to the factory, and cut through Grey Street and into the High Road that way. There was less chance of meeting anyone she knew. The buses were crowded with workers, so she began to walk. In any case it was far too early to go to the hospital.

She went into a café after a while and assuaged the sick feeling inside her with toast and tea. Queenie wasn't sure whether it was entirely hunger that was causing the gnawing in her stomach, or her feelings of grief over Paul. Why, oh why hadn't he stayed in Canada? Why had he come home and joined up – and with such an organization?

'I'm in no more danger than you are every day, here in London.' She seemed to hear his voice telling her that again and again. With her fingers round the warming mug of tea, she gave her thoughts free rein. Of course Paul wouldn't sit the war out in a safe place. It wasn't in his nature to do that, and it was typical of him to join something daring and challenging; that element of excitement had always been bubbling away inside him.

Sometimes she had wondered if that was what kept him loving her, the knowledge that their long-term union was unattainable. No, she thought now, lifting the drink to her lips, he could find that kind of out-of-bounds excitement in many activities and in other relationships. She knew with a certainty deep in her being that Paul's love for her was not sparked from an unachievable dream.

If she had been willing to leave Fred all those years ago, when the children were small, they could have been together. Even later, when the family was off her hands, they could have had time with each other; except that she was still married to Fred, and he needed her, he had *always* needed her. Poor husband that he was as provider and father, she didn't think he had looked at another woman since their wedding day. Not in that way.

Queenie pushed her chair back and stood up so suddenly that several other diners in the café looked across at her. Outside she walked on, jostling with the human mass going to work. You could think properly when you walked. I'm the coward, she thought, I'm the one who always backed out. I made the children my excuse, Fred my excuse, even the distance from London ...

Suddenly she felt whacked, absolutely played out. At the next stop she waited for a bus, and joined the throng of humanity going about its business. Watching the faces on the long seat opposite her she wondered about their lives. That woman with the Veronica Lake hairstyle, for instance, where was she going and why? Was she happy? Glancing at the woman's hands, which were beautifully manicured and holding an elegant black handbag, Queenie saw that she wore a wedding ring. Was she in love with her husband? Was he away in the forces and did she worry about him, or was she off for a secret meeting with a lover?

Aware that she was staring she shifted her gaze further along the row to someone round about her own age: a small, chubby person clutching a brown paper carrier bag and continually wetting her lips then swallowing. Queenie wondered about them both, the one exuding confidence and poise and the other ill at ease, shabby and with tired pale-blue eyes. Yet who but them knew about their lives and their loves, their happinesses and sadnesses? We all have to get on with what life sends us, she thought, but oh, how I wish I had gone to Paul when I had the chance.

Aware of the rush of tears suddenly clouding her eyes at the same time as she realized it was her stop, Queenie stumbled and almost fell down the step. Only the conductress's steadying arm prevented an accident. 'Whoa there,' she said cheerily, 'where's the fire, I ain't heard the sirens go.' As Queenie stepped on to the pavement, the little woman swung round to the edge of the platform, holding on to the supporting pole with one hand and surveying the queue on the pavement, 'room for six inside,' she called, then, winking at Queenie, 'That's more like it love, he'll wait, don't you fret.'

The curtains round Paul's bed were closed. Queenie wasn't sure what to do and had started back down the ward to wait in the corridor when the sister she had seen before came by. 'I'm glad you're here,' she said quietly, 'he has been asking for you.' She held the dark-grey curtain open a fraction for Queenie to go through, before following her. A doctor was bending over the bed. He straightened up as they entered. 'Nothing more I can do.' His voice was gruff. 'Keep him as comfortable as you can, Sister.' He walked past Queenie without looking at her and the sister indicated the space he had vacated. 'Tell him it's you. Hearing is always the last thing to go,' she said simply. 'I'll be in my office.' Then she too left, and Queenie was alone with Paul.

Gently she held his hand which was resting outside the cover. 'It's me, Paul. Queenie. Can you hear me, darling?'

'Princess.'

'I love you,' she said.

'Queenie ...'

She bent closer, his voice was so faint. 'Yes, my love?'

'Sit – where – I can – look – at you.'

For a few seconds his eyes were as blue as she could ever recall. They closed and opened several times, then he smiled. 'Wish – I – could – kiss – you.'

Softly she touched his lips with hers. She felt the pressure of his fingers, then with a gentle sigh he was gone.

Queenie sat on by the bed for several minutes, then she crossed his hands and closed his eyes. Afterwards she didn't remember walking through the ward and into the sister's little cubby-hole of an office, but she must have done so because suddenly she was there, sipping a cup of strong sweet tea.

She wandered around London afterwards, stopping during the middle of the afternoon because she was simply too weary to go any further. She was near Marble Arch and she went into the Corner House for refreshment. Tidying her hair in the ladies, she was surprised to discover she looked the same as ever, yet she felt so different. She hadn't cried all day, she had just walked and walked, not once boarding a bus or going on the underground, yet she couldn't have said where she had been during the past hours.

There was a very elderly commissionaire by the door. 'Just for one?' he said. 'This way please.' The small orchestra was playing and she realized too late that she had meant to go into the self-service part. Wearily she sat on the chair and let the music surround her. The pert nippy in her apron and headband took her order. 'Cup of tea and a bun please,' and the band went into their next tune. *I haven't said thanks for that lovely weekend, Those few days of heaven you helped me to spend* ... Halfway through the words and music reached her heart and she stood up and rushed through the restaurant, almost knocking the tray containing her tea and bun from the waitress's hand.

Head down and tears streaming, she hurried through the now darkening streets. When the torrent had eased she knew she had to get home before she collapsed from fatigue. She caught a bus to Victoria then one to the Green Man, relieved there was no one near her whom she recognized. All she wanted now was to get home and blot out everything else.

Chapter 16

After Paul's death Queenie never seemed to stop working. After all day at the factory she came home, prepared meals and sometimes almost spring-cleaned the house through. She knitted until she fell asleep over her work, woollies for Joanna, pretty sleeveless tops for Audrey and Pam, a pullover for Tom, jumper for Doris, and countless blanket squares for refugees. She unpicked some of her own cardigans so she could re-use the wool for all this activity. Sometimes the click, click, click of her needles made her want to scream, yet without them in her hands it was as though she had St Vitus's Dance. At least her knitting made her sit down and co-ordinate her movements. In the past she had found it a relaxing occupation, but now she felt she would never again be relaxed or restful. She had to be on the go no matter how tired she was.

On the surface she seemed the same, although Anna sensed some great unhappiness in her friend, and wondered to herself whether it could be delayed reaction over Liza and Rosie's deaths. She did not voice her thoughts, but she was very, very gentle with Queenie when she called in to see them.

Queenie never stayed anywhere, even at Anna and Joe's place, long enough to have more than a 'pass the time of day conversation' with them now. She was terrified she might break down if talk went deeper.

She did not know how Paul had been injured and sometimes while the knitting needles clacked on, her mind conjured images of what might have happened. Most of her thoughts after her initial grieving were of regret, however. What had it all been for? She had stayed with her husband mainly because of the children; now those children were adults leading their own lives, and her grandchildren were seeming to grow more distant as the years went by. If it hadn't been for the war Doris and Tom would not have been living in Wiltshire which still seemed like a foreign land to her. The other grandchildren would be able to come for visits, but as it was now, she was at the factory all week, and they all had so much to do at weekends.

Fred carried on as he had for years, going to the pub every night, grunting and groaning over the slightest ache or pain or change to his routine that involved him having to do anything differently. True, he was out working more now, but that was during the day and she wasn't home then anyway. The loneliness in her heart became a physical ache as the weeks went by and she tried to pretend to everyone she knew that she was fine, 'just a little tired perhaps, but when the war's over we can all have a good rest.'

Her rest came before that, when she collapsed at work one morning. She reached for the next bit to put on the machine when suddenly she seemed caught in a whirlpool with the water eddying round her faster and faster and faster ... When she came to she was in the rest room. Struggling to sit up, she asked what had happened.

'You fainted, Queenie,' said the nurse. 'Did you have any breakfast this morning?' She couldn't remember. 'I think so,' she said, 'I usually do.'

'Well, you had better have the rest of the day off, probably more. I should go and see your doctor. Anyway, rest here for a while longer, and when you feel better cut off home. I've already told Alf not to expect you in for a day or two. Need a proper check you do. You'll go to the surgery, won't you now?'

She agreed because it was the easiest thing to do, but really she had no intention of bothering the doctor when she knew what was ailing her. Still, perhaps a couple of days' rest would do her good. Paul certainly wouldn't be pleased to see her buckling under the strain like this. Oh Paul, Paul ... tears rained down her cheeks and, rolling over on the couch, she hid her face in the pillow and sobbed.

Queenie's couple of days off developed into over a week, but she admitted to Anna that the rest was doing her good. Secretly she thought the crying bout she hadn't been able to control that day in the factory had been her salvation. How often in the past had she advised a woman to 'have a good cry and you'll feel better.' She didn't 'feel better' about events, of course, but she was coping now, just about. She had popped into the doctor's surgery one evening, but there were so many there that she didn't wait. After all, she thought, with a touch of her old humour, I know what he'll say anyway; 'Stress, the war, rationing, shortages, working too hard, your age ...'

Luxuriating in the bath when all was quiet one afternoon, and feeling a bit guilty at doing so in the middle of the day, although she had only used the regulation amount of water, she stirred herself sufficiently to decide not to waste precious hours off work, but to do some turning out of cupboards and drawers. She had meant to do so weeks ago, leave everything in order in case she died suddenly, and now was a perfect opportunity. Spurred on by the thought of putting this time to good use, she dried and dressed herself and set to. The kitchen cupboard didn't take long; it contained mostly things she used every day, but the drawers in the built-in cupboard in the sitting room housed stuff from years back. She stacked everything in piles around her, letters here, receipts here, the children's school reports here – really it was pointless to keep these now, and she doubted they would want them anyway.

Tucked away in the left-hand corner of the bottom drawer was a small envelope-type handbag. It contained a bundle of letters from Paul. Knowing what they were she was prepared, and took them out carefully. Not to be read, she knew she couldn't do that yet, but equally she wanted to keep them. Fingering the sapphire on the slender chain, which she always wore beneath her high-necked blouses she took a deep, deep breath and laid the handbag on the floor. Perhaps the sensible course would be to burn them.... A knock on the door panicked her and she quickly thrust the letters back inside the bag and tucked it behind the cushion of her chair.

A child was hopping on and off the step. One of the Johnson tribe. 'Me Mum says can yer come, Mrs Parkes? It's the baby – it's started.'

Queenie gasped. The woman's child wasn't due for another two months. 'I'll just get a few things,' she said. 'You go home and stay close by now, I might need you to fetch the doctor. Tell your Mum I'm on the way,' she called after the still hopping figure.

It took minutes only to write a note for Fred to say where she was, and to collect the Gladstone-type bag she always kept ready, then she hurried down Dason Street to the already over-crowded house where the children ranged in age from fourteen to three. There was speculation about most of the fathers, and certainly this latest baby wasn't sired by Riva's husband, for almost everyone around knew he had been taken prisoner two years ago.

The front door was ajar and Queenie went in and rushed upstairs. She could hear a terrible groaning, which culminated in a harsh scream as she reached the landing. Riva was kneeling on the end of the bed, hands gripping the iron rail, long, dark hair tossing about wildly, pain-filled eyes almost black with intensity. Sweat poured in rivulets down her cheeks and neck, and Queenie knew there was no time to fetch the doctor, seven months or not, this baby was definitely on its way.

The child who had fetched her appeared at her side. 'Is me Mum going ter die, then?'

'No, of course not. Can you boil a kettle of water and fetch it up without scalding yourself, Angie?'

''Course I can,' Angie's voice was scornful. 'Do it most of the time; she's always ill or 'aving another kid, ain't she?'

Riva's screams were continuous now, and Queenie said sharply, 'Stop that, Riva, it isn't necessary.'

Angie sauntered off as though next week would do, and Queenie got the woman into a better position on the bed. She had stopped screaming and, as though she was reading Queenie's thoughts, said, 'She's seen it all before, it won't frighten her.'

Another contraction had her almost strangling Queenie, and emitting screams that Queenie thought owed as much to her Mediterranean temperament as to her labour pains.

'You're nearly there. Work with me now, Riva, come on ...'

'Aaahh ...'

Angie appeared with a kettle of boiling water at the same moment the baby's head emerged. Within minutes the rest of the olive-skinned body slithered through the birth canal. Riva gave a shuddering sigh and vowed aloud, 'Never again, not for *anyone*,' and Queenie held the tiny boy safely in her hands.

'It's a son, Riva, and he's yelling his head off. Hark.'

Queenie walked home with the wonderful feeling she always had when another child had been safely delivered into the world. Although Riva had said 'another mouth to feed, I'll never manage,' when she was tidied and comfortable again and had her new son in her arms, she gazed at him with love. Pity he was too young to realize, Queenie thought, smiling to herself, because it will probably be the only time when she *will* look at him in that way. Before she left some of the other children had come home, and they burst into the bedroom to have a peep at the latest arrival. When Queenie suggested she give them their tea Riva chortled merrily. 'They'll manage, they always do. Thanks for your help, luv, I'll send you something up later.'

It was cold and dank outside. 'One of the dark days before Christmas', Queenie remembered her mum used to say, but handling the tiny scrap of humanity and helping him into the world, gave Queenie the first glimpse of joy she'd had for many months. No matter that the war wasn't over yet, that people were still being killed all over the world, this little boy was a promise of new life, a hope perhaps for the future.

Common sense prevailed as she walked on, hugging her coat closely round her against the damp and cold air. Born into that family the child would probably have to fight for everything, from his first mouthful of food to his bed space, but briefly, the sight, smell and feel of the infant had released a warmth of feeling she hadn't known since Paul's death.

Queenie called into the doctor's surgery on her way home. 'Just to let him know that Riva Johnson had her baby just over an hour ago,' she told his wife. 'I think she got her dates wrong though; this looks like a full-term baby to me.' She stopped at Sid's shop for the *Evening News* and Pam and Audrey dashed in as she reached the door, 'Hullo, Mrs Parkes, saw you going into the *señora*'s place a while back . What she have?'

'A boy.'

'How many does that make? One, two, there's Juanita who's in my class, and Angela, and Bobby, and ...'

'About ten I should think.' Audrey interrupted her friend. 'Nita said only the other day she wasn't looking forward to it because every time her mum has another one *she* gets landed with looking after it, because Angie does a disappearing act.'

Queenie was smiling to herself as she walked on home. Those two girls had settled in so well, you would have thought they'd been born right here in Dason Street. And she loved their name for Riva Johnson – the *señora*. Prima donna too, she thought. She was still smiling as she entered her house.

Fred was standing in the hall, hands behind his back, his face angrily scarlet. 'So, you came back.'

Puzzled, she said, 'Didn't you see my note? Mrs Johnson started with her baby and—'

'Called away in a hurry, were you?'

'Yes, I left a note—'

'You left a lot of notes, or rather your boyfriend did.' He whipped his hands from behind his back and she saw he was clutching Paul's letters.

Queenie's first instinct was to grab the letters, yet even in her shocked state she knew he wouldn't let them go.

'Fred, please give those to me.'

'Oh no. These are evidence, these are. "*My princess* ... Humph."' There was a world of scorn in his voice. '"*My love, Paul.*"' He was shaking now, waving the letters wildly in front of her face and pulling them away each time she moved by so much as a blink.

'Look I can explain—'

'Explain? *Explain*? No need, these do it for you, *my princess* ...' She shuddered at his words, at the venom in his voice. Suddenly she was angry. 'You had no right to read those. In any case, they are perfectly normal letters from a friend—'

'Huh.' He stuffed the letters back into the handbag which she now saw was lying on the first stair. He threw it up the stairs out of her reach and advanced, fist at the ready.

'I've been faithful to you all these years, and no woman is going to make a laughing stock of Fred Parkes ...'

Queenie didn't try to duck – it was all true, and maybe he was entitled to hit her ...

His reaction when he did came through in spite of the jagged silver stars that were flashing all around her. 'Queenie, Queenie, oh God, I've not killed you, 'ave I? Queen, speak to me, say something, for Gawd's sake. Queen I love you, that's why I'm jealous as hell, Queenie, Queenie ...' and she realized that this great hulk of a man was crying like a baby, as he bent over and cradled her in his arms.

Struggling free she said shakily, 'I'm all right. Let me get up.'

'I'm sorry,' he said, 'I wouldn't hurt you for the world. What you going to do? Are you going off with – with this bloke?'

'Paul's dead.'

They were both silent for a few seconds, then he said, 'I often thought there was someone else, yet you stayed. Was he married?'

Queenie shook her head.

'Then ...' Fred was staring at her. 'What d'you leave that bag there for? You must 'ave known I'd need some money. I tell you the shock I had you wouldn't believe. I'd rather not have known about it.'

'Then you shouldn't go rifling through my handbag.' Her voice sounded harsh even to her, 'but now you do know I'll go if you want, just say the word and I'll leave. Nothing matters any more ...'

"Course I don't want you to go. I – I couldn't manage without you, Queen, you've always been the only woman for me.'

'Oh, God.' Queenie turned away and, burying her face in her hands, she sank to the ground and sobbed.

Queenie returned to work two days after the showdown with Fred. Physically she was feeling better, and she knew that mentally it would be the best thing for her. Less time to think, to go over and over in her mind and heart the events of the last few weeks. She found it embarrassing that Fred asked if she wanted to go to the pub in the evenings, even suggesting not going himself if she needed company. This new image after all the years of selfishness threw her.

'It's too late, Queenie, isn't it? Too late for me to make amends for the years of neglect,' he said in a rare moment of insight.

There was no suitable answer, but she tried to meet him halfway as he seemed to be doing with her. 'You go, Fred. I'm fine really. Only a bit tired.'

'Sure?'

She didn't like this new mood of solicitousness on his part, and hoped it was a passing phase. 'I need you, Queenie,' he said. 'I need to know you're there for me all the time.' That was more like the old Fred – she could cope with that!

'I'll be here,' she said.

'And – I do – love you, Queenie.'

She knew it wasn't easy for him to say such things. It was only the second time he'd talked about love in all the years of their marriage. She patted his arm gently. 'I know, love,' she said as though he was a child. She wanted to reassure him there would be no one else, but she didn't know how to, so she smiled and patted him again, and he went off to the King's Head secure in the knowledge that she would be there when he returned. She wished she could say, 'I love you too,' but at present she couldn't. In this new seeing mood of his he would know it wasn't true anyway.

The day before she returned to the factory she went to see Riva Johnson and make sure she, the new baby and the rest of the children were coping. Riva was directing operations from the kitchen, the new baby was asleep in a drawer from the chest of drawers. 'Makes a good cot,' Riva said when Queenie bent down to examine him. 'They've all used it 'til they got too big and started climbing out.'

'How do you feel?'

'Like you always do after you've 'ad a baby. Bloody glad to be flat again. Angie,' her voice was strident as she yelled after her daughter who had slipped through while she was talking, 'where you going?'

'Out.'

'No you're not, you can help me, that lot'll be starving when they come in.' She pushed past Queenie to grip the girl's arm and pull her back into the kitchen. 'You can go out when the meal's prepared and not before. Understand?'

Queenie left them to it. She felt sorry for Angela Johnson and the rest of the Johnson tribe, but they'd survive. Probably get out as soon as they left school. Angie had once confided to her that when she was old enough she was going to get a live-in job with one of the firms up West. 'Nice clean hostels they have,' she said. 'My friend's sister works for one of them big shops and she gets bed and board and a wage every week. That's what I'll do the minute I can leave school.'

Queenie hoped the dream would come true for her; the child deserved a decent break. She was the eldest and must be about thirteen now, so she wouldn't have too much longer to wait.

Two weeks later there was a letter from Paul's sister Ruth, asking her to meet her 'at a time and place convenient to yourself. I will come to your house if you can't manage anything else, but as this is of a rather private nature I think it best if we meet elsewhere. It can be my flat if you wish.'

Knowing she couldn't face Ruth's flat, she wrote back suggesting Lyons Corner House at Marble Arch. It had to be a weekend now she was back at work. She showed Fred Ruth's card confirming the time and day, because she wanted him to know she was not meeting a man, and the card backed this theory up nicely. *Lyons Corner House, Marble Arch fine with me. I'll be there around 3 on Saturday afternoon. Looking forward to seeing you again, Ruth.*

The fact that he had never heard of Ruth didn't seem odd, because he knew very little about her friends, except for Marie whom she had known for so long.

'Enjoy your outing,' he said when she left after lunch that Saturday, 'and don't worry about tea if you want to go to a show or anything. I'll get meself something.'

Amazed and a bit disconcerted at the change of habits after all these years, she said quickly, 'Well, thanks, but I don't suppose I'll be late.'

Ruth was waiting when Queenie arrived at the venue at five

minutes to three. 'I'll tell you what it's about over a cup of tea,' she said as they made their way inside.

They talked about the weather and the war while they waited for their refreshment. Ruth ordered two sticky buns as well. 'Paul loved sticky buns when he was a child,' she said, giving Queenie a glimpse of the little boy he once was.

After they had eaten Ruth opened her handbag. 'When he joined up Paul asked me to make sure you received this should anything happen to him,' she said quickly, handing Queenie a sealed manila envelope, 'and I thought you might like a few snaps I've sorted out. They're in here.' Another, smaller envelope changed hands.

'Thank you, Ruth. You've been so good to me.'

'Nonsense. You'd have done the same for me if positions had been reversed, I'm sure.' She picked up the bill. 'Guess we'd better go, there's usually a queue of people waiting to come in about this time. I know I always do when I'm up here. Saves the tea ration.'

Queenie laughed nervously, and the two women had a good–natured fight over who would pay, then they emerged once more into Oxford Street. Ruth held out her hand. 'Good luck, Queenie.'

'Thank you. You too. And thank you for all the trouble you've taken.' She glanced at the two envelopes in her hand.

'That's all right. He was adamant I give it to you personally, "so I know she receives it," he said, "otherwise I shall return and haunt you."'

Leaning forward she kissed Queenie on the cheek, 'We would have got on well as sisters-in-law, don't you think so?'

Queenie nodded, too full of emotion to trust her words. She liked this woman, and would always feel grateful to her for her understanding.

Fred was out when she reached home. She had the two envelopes in her handbag and she hurried upstairs to put the bag beneath her pillow. It should be safe there until she could look at the contents in private. Her hand strayed to her neck where the beautiful sapphire nestled, hanging low into her cleavage. What was in the envelope from Paul? Some photographs, a letter, something for her to keep, a lock of hair maybe...? She would open it later, when they had eaten and Fred had gone to the pub.

After Fred left Queenie forced herself to do the washing up before she escaped to the bathroom. Her stomach was playing strange tricks as she handled the businesslike buff-coloured envelope. It was nearly three months since Paul's death, almost a quarter of a year without him in her world. She had told herself repeatedly that before he had often been gone from her for years at a time, and there had been no guarantee that he would return; yet she always knew she *would* see him again, there would be another time. Now ...

Perched on the edge of the bath she took a deep breath and gently prised the envelope open. Inside was a slender book. She took it out and examined it. It was a post office savings book made out in her name. Wonderingly she opened it and nearly fell backwards into the empty bath when she saw the amount deposited in her name: £700.

Her first instinct was that she couldn't possibly take this, it was a small fortune. She looked again in the envelope to discover a sheet of cream writing paper, folded in half. She slithered down and sat on the floor to read the short letter.

Dearest Queenie, my lovely princess, please, please don't be cross. You will only have this in your hands if I am dead. You and I have never minced words with each other and I'm not going to do so now. This money is for you. It comes with all my love. Enjoy it. I've entrusted it to Ruth so it can be given to you without any fuss or knowledge to anyone else. If there is a heaven, and if I qualify and get in, then I know we shall be

together again one day. Look after your dear self, think of me
sometimes, my darling, but not with sadness because my days
with you are among the best moments of my life....

She could see no more for the tears blurring her vision and,
slowly, she stood up, the letter and bank book still in her hand.

'Queenie, will you help me organize the street party for the kids
when peace is declared?' Sid said one evening when she called
in for her paper.

''Course I will. Tell you what, come round after you close one
night and we'll work it out.'

'Thanks, luv. This evening be OK?'

They sat at her kitchen table with pencils and paper, and Sid's
notebook which contained details of the last street party in 1937.

'Let's see, we got the piano from Ma Duckton, I reckon she'll
let us have it again. And there's that old boy who plays the
accordion, used to be on the halls, Vera whats-er-name's father,
he's still going strong. That should cover us for singing and
dancing. How about food, Queenie?'

'Well, if we let everyone know I'm sure most of them will
contribute something. Bread's not on ration and if we all bring a
tin of something if we've got one tucked away for an emergency,
we can make sandwiches. There's sausages, such as they are,
and jellies for the kids, oh, we'll find plenty, don't worry.'

Sid was ticking items off from the list. 'Trestle-tables', he said.
'Vicar at Holy Trinity'll let us use those from the church hall if we
have a collection for his funds, and if everyone brings a chair like
they did for the coronation—'

'And some double sheets for cloths,' she interrupted. 'Shall I
start a fund for buying drinks, d'you think?'

'Be a good idea. Last time the kids got through gallons of
lemonade and Tizer, and the tea that was drunk would have
kept a Chinaman in luxury all his life.'

'Wasn't on ration then, Sid. Reckon the adults will have to have lemonade too. Can get the powder though, that's not on coupons, is it, and we can make it up ourselves. Be cheaper too.'

Sid bit his lip suddenly. 'It'll be a great day. I promised all the kids the biggest street party ever when the war was over, and that's what they'll have – in spite of everything, that's what they'll have.'

Queenie reached across and touched his hand, her own thoughts of Paul as strong as she knew his of Liza must be.

After a moment or two Sid said shakily, 'I thought we could appoint an agent for each of the side streets, and their tables would be like branches of ours, you know, Dason Street will be the trunk of the tree and Grey Street, Brown Street, King Street, Church Street, Ebdon Street, and even Tailor's Yard can be the branches.'

Mention of Tailor's Yard reminded Queenie of Anna's ordeal there. She wondered how the girl was feeling now that a black family had moved into Rosie and Jim's old place. Must revive the memory every time she sees him, she thought, but she kept silent, because although Sid was one of the few who knew about the rape, even he hadn't known the nationality of the man. Only she and Anna herself knew that.

'What a marvellous idea, Sid. Let's sort out a few good organizing names in each of the "branches".'

The street party, held on Saturday 12 May, 'so everyone can come, and those who want to can lie in on Sunday morning, eh, Queenie?' was one of the largest anyone in the district had experienced. Enlisting the help of the police, Dason Street and all the 'branches' were closed to traffic from midday. Willing hands erected trestle-tables, covered them with white sheets. 'Everyone will be sleeping sheetless tonight – hope they all know which belongs to which,' one wag said. The array of food was nothing short of amazing. Jellies and blancmanges, sandwiches, cakes and biscuits. 'Whole ones too, not broken ones,' Anna commented, thinking of the coupons they must have cost.

'Black market, some of them,' Sid said quietly.

'Fell orf the back of a lorry more like,' said one toothless great-grandfather, grinning, and patting young Joanna's fair head. 'You'll remember this party all yer life, my gal'

The party was due to begin at two and was to be heralded with the pealing of the church bells. As the joyous sound echoed across Dason Street, people came from their houses, walking, running, skipping, most carrying with them a kitchen chair or stool. Queenie and Anna, with Pam and Audrey helping them, directed everyone to a place. 'Come on, luv, there's room by here.' Queenie lifted a solemn faced child on to the stool she was dragging with her. 'Poor little devil's not seen so much food altogether since she's been born, I reckon,' she said to whoever might be listening.

Joe walked from number 5 with Joanna. He met Benno, Charlotte, and young Chloe, and together they went to where they could see Anna busy getting everyone into place.

'Mummy, where shall Chloe and me sit?'

Anna looked across, her heart seemed to give one tremendous leap, so much that she thought she might be having a heart attack, then suddenly the hammering eased, and as Joe smiled at her and blew a kiss, she realized the answer to her problem lay within herself. She *must* put the past behind her completely, a new era was dawning for them all. Joanna was today experiencing a peaceful world for the first time in her six years. They had come through, and were here together, the three of them … *that* was what mattered now.

Queenie was too busy to think of anything except making the party a success, checking that everyone had something to eat and drink, all the children had paper hats and no one was feeling left out. Even Fred was here, this very moment passing a plate of goodies over the heads of one group to reach another.

An aeroplane flew overhead and dozens of tiny heads looked up to watch its progress. 'It's all right,' a small boy said, 'it's one of ours.'

When the food had been consumed and children's mouths wiped the tables were cleared and folded, and Ma Duckton's piano was pushed into roughly the centre of the long street. Someone brought her a beer and a chair that forced her hindquarters to overflow on each side, and the old lady sat down and began thumping out the music. Starting with 'Roll Out The Barrel', Dason Street and all its 'branches' sang and danced, and those who couldn't or wouldn't dance sat on their doorsteps and watched and talked.

Union Jacks fluttered from almost every window, flags that had been carefully put away after Queen Mary and King George's silver jubilee in 1935, brought out again for the coronation of King George and his lovely Queen Elizabeth in 1937, then packed away for the duration. If anyone had doubted during the last six years that they would be needed, in the wonderful euphoria of victory they would have denied those doubts.

When the younger children were growing sleepy and Ma Duckton's arthritic fingers were faltering, they changed musicians and seventy-three-year-old Bill Perks took over with his piano accordion. Queenie asked him to start with the conga so the little ones could have a last fling before going to bed. In a short while there was a long line snaking down the street, turning into each of the side ones as it reached them, then back into Dason Street. *Aye, aye, aye, I conga, aye, aye, aye, I conga, la, la, la, la, la, la, la, la* … they sang as the line reached Tailor's Yard and turned back for the return trip. Bill walked alongside, accordion at full blast, and as they reached their homes some of the women dropped out with the smallest children to settle them in their beds.

Later, Bill's accordion, in dance tempo, had even those who weren't waltzing tapping their feet and humming along with 'Ramona', 'Russian Rose', etc.

Queenie saw Anna and Joe sitting on kitchen chairs outside their house. 'Joanna in bed?' she asked, joining them.

'Mmm, she was played out. Fell asleep insisting she wasn't tired and could dance some more.' Anna laughed, and Joe covered her hand with his.

Sid came up to them. 'Well, it's all but over,' he said. 'Now we've got to get used to the peace. Saw your Fred a while back, Queenie, he was looking for you. Said to tell you he was going down the King's Head.'

Pam and Audrey sauntered by with a couple of boys. 'Wouldn't think they were all still at school, would you?' Sid said. 'I can see I'll have my work cut out keeping those two in order. Do you know what Pam came out with the other night, then?'

'What?' Queenie's voice was encouraging.

'She said I needed a holiday now the end of the war was imminent, and she and Audrey had worked it out that they could run the shop during the school holidays while I went off for a few days' break. Told me not to worry, they'd keep things ticking over *and* they'd behave themselves. "We know the score," she said, "so you don't need to have fears where boys are concerned. We can both handle them."

'I'm lucky to have those two, you know. I think they've been my salvation.' He looked across to Rosie and Jim's old place and the others followed his gaze but said nothing.

An hour later most of the revellers had gone indoors. Sid took a last walk round his patch to check that everything was all right, 'although the worst I'll expect to find now is the odd drunk, thank God.'

They watched until he was out of sight, then Queenie rose. 'I'd best be going,' she said. 'Good-night.' She hugged them both and walked down the now deserted street.

The terraced houses huddled together in comradeship; as she passed the top of Church Street she glimpsed the spire of the church silhouetted against the night sky. And an idea was born – she would start a fund to send all the kids from Dason Street on a seaside or country day out once a year. With the money Paul had given her. Yes, that was what she would do. She would invest it so it gained interest more than a post office account, run jumble sales during the year to add to it, but that would be the nucleus of the fund. The Tranmer Fund she would call it, and there would be no restriction on which children could go; it wouldn't depend on their financial circumstances: the only qualification would be that they must live in Dason Street or one of its 'branches'. She gazed into the night sky as she drew level with number 52, and remembered the words of the child this afternoon when the plane went over: 'It's all right, it's one of ours.' Please God they would never need to think this way again, and Rosie, Liza, Paul, and all the thousands of other men, women and children who died before their natural time, had done so for a lasting peace.